OF INK, WIT & INTRIGUE

To, Charlotte,

With best wishes,

Sue C-B

SUSAN COOPER-BRIDGEWATER

of INK, WIT and ROGUE of BONE

LORD ROCHESTER,
IN CHAINS OF QUICKSILVER

Matador
9 Priory Business Park
Kibworth Beauchamp
Leicestershire LE8 0RX, UK
Tel: (+44) 116 279 2299
Fax: (+44) 116 279 2277
Email: books@troubador.co.uk
Web: www.troubador.co.uk/matador

ISBN 978-1783063-079

British Library Cataloguing in Publication Data.
A catalogue record for this book is available from the British Library.

Typeset in Aldine by Troubador Publishing Ltd
Printed and bound in the UK by TJ International, Padstow, Cornwall

Matador is an imprint of Troubador Publishing Ltd

To Davey, with love

The buckram puppet never stirred its eyes,
But grave as owl it looked, as woodcock wise.
He scorned the empty talking of this mad age
And spoke all proverbs, sentences, and adage,

from 'Tunbridge Wells'
by John Wilmot,
2nd Earl of Rochester

ॐॐ
Contents
ॐॐ

Prologue

Thirty-three years seems ephemeral for this individual's life but, according to my century's capricious mortality, a greater number of years than many a wretched soul has been granted.

This intimate episodic account has been deliberately wrought for the sceptical, and there will be many such who, curious of its contents, will mull it over if they have a mind.

The script lays bare the sequence of my remorseful life and those who doggedly read on will, I trust, charitably agree that the theatricalities to which I resorted were excusably acted out. Frankly, I am far more sincere than my reputation gives credit. I have sustained intense love, both physical and emotional, for females and males alike, although on occasion I appeared ruthless, insensitive yet sometimes cowardly to several who dared cross my path. With heartfelt gratitude, I salute them all.

I surrender this testimony of my life and have laid bare some obscure events, the truth of which is for you to ponder upon.

Your not so obedient servant,

Rochester

ঌ∘ଔ

CHAPTER ONE

Infant to Young Scholar

All Fools' Day, Ditchley Manor, Oxfordshire 1647. I cried out, freed from the confines of my mother's womb. Exhausted, she lay upon her bed over blooded linen sheets. Two women had attended her during this perilous ordeal and I was straightway taken and swaddled by Midwife Sarah.

> *'Sarah! Sarah! How, towards the end, I came to loath your very being, your vigilant dexterity having ensured my survival and continued existence. How I now wished you had faltered and secured John Wilmot's infant mortality.'*

The courageous lady lying-in was Anne Wilmot, Countess of Rochester, a staunch Protestant and a woman of immeasurable strength and fortitude. She was pretty of face but strong willed and with a gritty determination to succeed throughout her long years.

Anne St. John, for that was my mother's maiden name, was the eldest daughter born to Sir John St. John of Lydiard Tregoze in the county of Wiltshire. Her first betrothal in 1632, her eighteenth year, was to Sir Francis Henry Lee of Ditchley, known as Harry. This happy and fruitful union, during its seven years, celebrated the birth of a daughter and a son. After Harry's tragic death from the virulent smallpox in 1639, his widow, who was pregnant with his child, gave birth to a second son. She remained a widow for five years until in April 1644 she married Henry Wilmot, First Earl of Rochester, who was to be my father. He was handsome, brave and alluring to the female sex and soon won my mother's love and affection. She unhappily saw little of him, he being a prominent royalist officer, and as our King's faithful ally he was all too frequently engaged in aiding the cause.

In September 1651, four years after my birth, my heroic father accompanied Charles, the eldest son of our executed King, in his flight from Worcester and England after Cromwell's victorious army trounced the royalists. Father's enforced exile abroad left my mother overseeing alone her three sons, her darling daughter, Eleanor, having died in infancy. During these troubled times, as a young child, I listened intently to tales of Cavaliers' courage and their daring in the bloody conflicts at Edgehill and Naseby and so learned that their defeat in the latter of these had sealed this country's fate.

As a boy, in the gardens and orchards at Ditchley, I enacted fantastical battles riding on the swiftest black horse, dressed in the grandest clothes and wearing a handsome, large brimmed hat adorned with golden feathers. My silver spurs flashed in the sunlight against my horse's heaving, sweating flanks. I gloried in many a victory won by this fearless royalist. In truth, my only real fears were of the long and arduous sermons preaching religious horrors from the pulpit of our nearby church.

The Countess employed Francis Giffard, a local rector and fervent man of God, to take charge of my early education at home. Giffard's potent Protestant preachings of damnation, hell's fires and the evils of sinful thoughts and deeds so terrified me that when darkness fell they fuelled my imagination beyond my control, their damnable legacy holding terrors until I came to embrace death itself.

დენდ

When I was nine years old I too was exiled, accompanied by Reverend Giffard, to commence my further education at Burford. This pretty, small town is built on the long slope of a hill where at the bottom stands the Grammar School with the River Windrush running close by and the parish church of St. John the Baptist within a stone's throw. In this house of God, in May 1649, after his defeating of the Levellers nearby, Cromwell imprisoned three hundred or more of those brave mutineers after murdering three of their company pitilessly; Corporal Perkins, Cornet Thompson and Private Church.

A few brutal older boys at the school mercilessly taunted my young fellow pupils and me, as fresh boys to the school, and treated us roughly. Although I had my share of harsh punishment during the day, at times when the tutors were not in attendance, I was fortunate indeed having lodgings in the town so was mercifully excused the evil night terrors perpetrated on the resident younger boys. The bruising and battering of their bodies was all too evident as they sat looking pale and in pain on the hard wooden benches of the classroom. Alas, they were too terrified to speak of their agony and courageously endured their lot. Mr. John Martin, our headmaster, turned a blind eye to the oppressive régime meted out by these few, he believing such treatment would make sober and God-fearing men of the younger boys. His conviction was evidently ill founded, it having nurtured such malicious souls.

Mr. Martin was fair but strict. He was of average height and thin featured. His eyes were of the palest blue, which I believed was due to the incessant gloom of the classroom that over time had faded out the true blue. The school's windows were small and set so high in the walls as to allow little light to penetrate, and the illumination in the room benefited but little from a few meagre candles placed in the drearier parts. It was cold and damp in the winter months, as chilling moist air blew in through those tiny portals from the flowing Windrush. It was a little better in the summer, but still cool and dismally dark compared with the cheerful warm sunlit world beyond its confines.

I was an agreeable and studious pupil, proving to be gifted and mastering most subjects with ease. The most absorbing lessons were those for Latin, and I have held a love of that language all my days. Our time at learning was so very long and arduous, beginning at six of the clock in the morning and finishing at six of the clock in the evening but with a welcome dinner and respite at eleven of the clock for two hours. We ended the day as we began, with prayers and readings. The long and tiring days left my sleep undisturbed, so throughout the dark nights I slumbered soundly, in the company of Giffard in our lodgings, until morning bells awakened us.

In February 1658, aged eleven years and still at Burford, I succeeded to my dear father's title as Second Earl of Rochester after his needless death at Ghent in the Spanish Netherlands. Father had been cruelly exiled in the Low Countries, valiantly pursuing the royalist cause, where the harsh winters and living a poor and virtually penniless existence took their toll on royalist morale and expelled the life breath from him.

In this same year, after relentless tyranny, Cromwell, the people's most hated and seditious Protector, died. Rumours flourished that witchcraft, sorcery and the devil's hand were to blame for his death, though the truth of the matter was that a broken heart and ague closed his damned eyes forever. Either way, if the devil had taken his revenge, I saluted Satan and drank his health.

At twelve years old, having concluded my education at Burford, I returned home to Ditchley, soon to enter Wadham College at Oxford.

❧

"John!" shouted my mother, "Look sharp boy. Stop daydreaming and get aboard the coach."

"Yes mother. I'm coming."

Feelings of excitement and anxiety combined to overwhelm me as my diligent mother organized my trunk and baggage onto the waiting coach. Therein were my personal belongings; an assortment

of books, the largest a Bible given to me at the age of five, together
with clothes and other effects.

"John, see to it that you uphold the good name of Wilmot,"
mother implored, as I gave her a farewell kiss on the cheek.

The coach pulled away on that bitter-cold winter's morning and
I peered through the open window with a solemn waving of my
hand as mother, servants and the security of Ditchley receded into
the distance. After travelling nervously and uncomfortably for many
a mile, my long, lonely journey came at last to an end. The bursar
of Wadham, a man of tall stature, unwashed in appearance and
decidedly the worse for drink, grudgingly escorted me to my
lodging. Wadham was to be my home and seat of learning for near
on two years. The lengthy hours of study were in truth more
arduous than those at Burford, but in the heady atmosphere of the
Oxford streets there was ample time for illicit diversions when
moments of leisure permitted.

During this time, with Parliament in complete disarray and
Cromwell's heir having failed miserably through his short rule, the
exiled Prince was, by political and public demand, restored to the
throne of England. In Oxford, as in all towns and cities, the populace
celebrated the arrival of the Stuart Monarch. The people
congregated in the streets indulging in music, singing and Morris
dancing; all spectacles not observed for far too long. Great bonfires
were lit. Banners blew in the breeze. Fountains flowed with wine
and drunkenness was rife. During the earlier part of this time, with
chaos growing, I took opportunity to ramble through the town of
an evening with my fellow students, many older than myself. With
their guiding hand, I visited the inns and taverns and observed the
true nature of the brothels and other places of immorality, and so
began my apprenticeship in all things madly pleasurable. It was
during this time that I became effortlessly accustomed to the
drinking of wine. This claret wine, with its warm, purple-red hue
became my muse. It enlightened my mind and fuelled my body's

sensual awareness. I was entirely without fear of reproach for I was young, virile and abundantly healthy.

Through the long evenings in the quietness of my room, when at times compelled to study and refrain from amusement, thoughts of my late father troubled my mind. I now longed for his company at this joyous time. His allegiance had not been in vain, yet how I wished for him to have witnessed the King's return with his own eyes. Life can cast bittersweet, but my father's untimely passing was one of the cruellest blows. I longed to be brave and spirited like him. I hoped one day to prove my birth and to serve the King unconditionally. At my desk, I penned a poem to His Sacred Majesty to make him aware of my devoted loyalty. The poem nearing its end, I concluded with the lines...

∾

> *In whom a cold respect were treason to*
> *A father's ashes, greater than to you;*
> *Whose one ambition 'tis for to be known*
> *By daring loyalty your Wilmot's son.*

∾

I wrote this from the heart to Charles and hoped His Majesty would remember Henry's sacrifice through me. It had the desired effect and evoked such emotion in the King that he graciously awarded me a tidy sum.

The time arrived to leave Wadham and the beautiful city of Oxford, this Earl now fourteen, a Gentleman and learned Oxford graduate.

CHAPTER TWO

Touring Beyond the Sea

On leaving Oxford, I travelled back to Ditchley. There I sought eagerly the King's reply to the Countess's request for my legal passage to Europe and his preference of a suitable travelling companion. In due course, the King's sealed consent was delivered, detailing my escort as one Dr. Andrew Balfour M.D., a thirty-one year old Scot. Charles confirmed that Balfour was an educated man of impeccable manners and much travelled abroad.

On a cold and dull November morning, with very few belongings, for travelling light was a necessity, I bade my mother farewell. With two of Ditchley's servants, away we rattled, the coach speeding on its way to London. On arriving there, I was greatly fatigued from journeying the inhospitable roads and from disturbed sleep in the lodging rooms of busy inns. Feeling a little apprehensive, I was at last introduced to my touring companion.

"My Lord Rochester! We meet at last," said Balfour, in his broad Scot's brogue.

This affable young man, smiling, offered a hand of friendship and any fear I held was soon dispelled.

"This way, my Lord. I have lodgings nearby where you can rest after your obviously tiring journey. My servant will take care of your belongings."

"That will be most welcome," I said.

Balfour and I were most content in each other's company for the King had been shrewd in his choice of companion. Over the next three days, the two of us were busy making arrangements for our journey.

On the allotted day, we hired horses and rode post from London to the Sussex coast, resting over several nights. At Rye, we then took ship and crossed the choppy waters of the Channel en-route to Dieppe. Dr. Balfour was much amused by me on the short sea journey; it was my first time aboard a ship in windy, turbulent waters and seasickness overcame me. My naturally fair complexion served to enhance the green hue upon my face and, staring into the deep, dark waters, I retched over the rails of the ship. Balfour opened a leather bag that contained a variety of medicinal remedies and handed me a small bottle.

"Here, my Lord! Drink from this. It will ease the turbulent humours in your stomach," he said.

Drinking a little of this potion, the overwhelming feeling of nausea subsided and my ill condition gradually eased.

Disembarking at Dieppe, we boarded a coach and travelled on to Paris. In this fine city, Balfour and I visited notable ancient buildings of great architectural interest, among them the impressive Cathedral of Nôtre Dame. We strolled the banks of the Seine and traversed its many bridges. Of particular interest was the Pont Neuf with its grotesques carved upon the cornices. We frequented bookshops where were purchased a variety of expensive books, Dr. Balfour having a fancy for those of a medical nature.

Before we had commenced our tour, His Majesty expressed a fervent wish. He had arranged that we would be welcomed at the Court of Louis XIV and there to be received by our King's beloved sister, the beautiful and charming Henriette Anne, Duchesse d'Orléans, to whom King Charles always referred fondly as Minette. He declared that his absolute trust in me was equal to that he had held for my father and so, on my return to England, I was to bring back safely a miniature portrait of her; one which he had longed for since her removal to France as a young girl. Minette was sister by marriage to the Sun King, Louis. The Stuart Princess had married Louis' brother Philippe, Duc d'Orléans on that most ill-fated of days, the First of April.

On a clear, bright and sunny day, we arrived at Louis' Court to be welcomed and offered lodgings that, although modestly furnished, were sufficient for our stay. The château of Saint-Germain-en-Laye, Louis' principal residence, is some eleven miles west of Paris. It is magnificent and suited the French King's opulent style, one to which he had been accustomed since his birth there in 1638. With its lavish interiors and landscaped beauty this building is indeed fit for a king.

Anon, I was introduced to Minette. She was more beautiful than I had imagined, and her conversation and wit were very pleasing. Her fluent use of the French language had one believing she was a native of France. All too soon however, I became aware that her marriage to Philippe was unfortunate in the extreme. If Louis was the sun, then Philippe surely was a dark and mysterious moon casting a winter's shadow upon his wife.

Philippe, by nature, held himself in high esteem. A beautiful prince, renowned for his courage and bravery, he would attire himself to perfection. The wearing of a hat never marred his long, flowing, curled periwig. He went to great lengths in applying his exaggerated facial cosmetics and made certain they were to his liking, even before riding into battle.

Sadly for Minette, only the Duc's amorous affections and sexual desires for men rivalled his love of combat. He had an overwhelming fondness for extravagant clothes and jewellery, and his all-consuming passion was his princely Château de Saint-Cloud, where he entertained guests to excess in spectacular style.

Our stay at Saint-Germain came all too soon to an end, but before we returned to the Capital, Minette showed to me the precious miniature. It was beautifully set in silver embellished with blue enamel. She begged that I guard it with my life and deliver it to her brother safely. I assured the Duchesse that on our return journey I would visit her once more to take possession of this most cherished thing and gave her my word that I would deliver it securely to His Majesty.

Back in Paris, we visited the theatre to watch a play by Molière. At the end of the performance, I was introduced to him and I congratulated the man on a wonderfully entertaining play. This was the beginning of my great love of the theatre and I now longed to write a play myself, being so utterly fascinated by the lure of the stage, its sights, sounds and trappings. I knew I would accomplish it.

In spring, we left Paris and hiring horses travelled south, riding through miles of uninhabited country. For much of the time we skirted along rivers, this being an easier terrain for our horses. The villages were few, but the hospitality of the peasants was most generous to we two weary English travellers. After many weeks' trek, we finally arrived at the town of Avignon with its riverside houses and ancient bridge.

We took lodgings in the east of the town and rested for two days, hardly venturing outside. Our strength regained, we walked abroad in and around this ancient place. In the evenings, we would convene in the eating-houses feasting on such delicacies as wild duck, cured hams and the most palatable of breads baked fresh daily, I delighting in many glasses of French wine. Although imbibing wine in my early days at Oxford, I had never before drunk such quantity and Andrew, a prudent and sober man, refraining from over-indulgence tried intensely to discourage my want, but to no avail.

As the hot summer months relented to a cool autumn breeze, we travelled back to Paris for the winter. There we planned our tour of Italy, to commence in the coming spring. We arranged for the books, prints and artefacts purchased during our travels in France to be carefully shipped back to England, sending word for them to be collected and safely stored there to await our return.

જ•૬

As spring awakened Paris again, we began our journey to Italy. This most Latin of countries, abundant with music, theatre, carnival and the most worthy of architecture, consumed me from the first. Often our accommodation was of the poorest quality, but the country at large, with its sturdy ancient Roman structures and fine Italianate style, is by contrast rich in the arts. Its natives, with their fiery and passionate nature, are a far cry from the many subdued and cheerless Londoners so often encountered back in England's capital.

In Rome, we were indeed fortunate to be invited by Balfour's friends, with whom he was acquainted from prior visits, to tour the Vatican and to survey the countless paintings hanging therein. And so we were also privileged to read at will the rare books and cherished early manuscripts in its libraries.

Although indoctrinated in the Protestant faith by my mother and at Burford, I now had serious thoughts as to my true devotion. I found myself being drawn towards the Catholic faith, which runs so very fervent in that realm, but my predisposition towards atheism nevertheless prevailed.

Our stay in Rome at an end, we travelled on to Venice to be greeted by a cityscape set upon the sea with its unique maze of canals populated by the legendary Venetian gondolas, plying their trade or else moored bobbing on the waters. These boats are the only mode of transport through the city apart from one's own legs or the stifling interior of a sedan. We usually chose the gondolas propelled by strong, attractive young men. They steered the boats with long poles, navigating the murky waters so skilfully.

Venice by day is beyond doubt a charming city, but in the evenings, its grandeur is a delight. Enhanced by the warm candlelight glowing from its windows and open doorways, the Venice of night was irresistible. Balfour and I attended several concerts and dramas there. The Italian Commedia were the most popular of entertainments, where were staged bizarre acrobatic feats of equilibrium and daring. Clownish actors, so outrageously comic, pranced and strutted so that we felt weak with the laughter of it. It was here that I was first acquainted with the marionette shows; these tiny wooden characters dressed in the most elaborate of costumes were so unlike anything I had yet seen on a stage. My favourite was *Scaramuchio*, a bragging yet cowardly Grandee.

ॐॐ

"Balfour! Balfour! Help me! For God's sake, help me," I cried.

I had woken sweating profusely with such a griping in my guts and such dizziness in my head.

"Balfour! What is it?" I pleaded.

"Stay calm, my Lord, and let me examine you."

He examined my stomach and bowels and pronounced that my discomfort was merely due to an over-indulgence at dinner. He offered another of his remedies, which, despite its evil taste, I drank eagerly. He then ordered me to rest and declared he would return within the hour, when my poor state of health would be vastly improved. Even though I felt tired and somewhat drowsy, the unceasing, troublesome pain would not allow me sleep's pleasure and a state of delirium ensued.

An hour passed and my dis-ease had still not abated. In fact, my condition had worsened so much that I became unaware of my surroundings. Balfour returned, examined me again and grew concerned. The pestilence had visited the province several months before our arrival, and fear of it now hung heavy on his mind. We had arrived in Italy free of it, as our certificates obtained in Cannes bore witness, but Balfour became greatly alarmed at the possibility of contagion. Masking his face with a muslin cloth, he inspected my armpits and groin for any signs of the deathly buboes. He announced that all seemed clear, but as a precaution kept the windows and door to my room securely shut and sent for a local physician.

Arriving, the physician stood some distance from my bed and

declared I was to be bled. Ordering his anxious assistant to proceed he left hurriedly, causing Balfour to feel most uneasy. The assistant, with shaking hands, tightly bound my upper arm and quickly, with a sharp knife, made the incision. I felt the trickling of warm blood, but was not alarmed for I had been bled before; at an early age, I had often suffered ill ease in my bowels, not able to pass a stool for several days and on rare occasions for two weeks, and bleeding and the giving of clysters had greatly alleviated my condition, the satisfaction in shitting freely having been most welcome.

The blood extracted and the bleeding stopped, my arm was bandaged and laid across my chest. Balfour then paid a fee to the nervous assistant who swiftly abandoned the room. I was administered supplementary medicine prepared meticulously by Balfour and I relapsed into a sweating, fitful sleep.

"I will die. I know I will die," I murmured, turning towards Balfour.

"Nonsense, my Lord. You will overcome this illness. Be patient and all will be well," he said quietly. But I perceived a modicum of doubt in his voice.

Balfour, holding a smouldering pipe of tobacco, was enveloped in a haze of smoke, which drifted silently across the airless room. He had lit the pipe reluctantly as a safeguard against possible contagion, for he abhorred the unwholesome habit of tobacco. Courageously he sat masked close by, nursing me at every hour. I had not eaten for days and only water and medicine had passed my parched mouth. Presently I roused and to Balfour's great relief, and my own, the suffering and delirium had subsided. He yet again inspected my armpits and groin where thankfully no signs were evident, and so concluded all was now fine.

Balfour's elation on my recovery prompted him to remark wryly that, although in greater agony, I did not appear as deathly as at the time of my seasickness. I found his comment reassuringly amusing.

After two days' convalescence, I was able to sit up and enter into discourse with him regarding our journeys. Following a further period of rest at our lodgings, I felt vastly improved and ready to acquaint myself once again with the streets of Venice and its teaming life.

I was introduced to the radiant Latino women. Their seductive dark eyes, lustrous locks and unforgettable white teeth sparked passions in me not manifest since my heady days in Oxford. My mind and body fully recovered, I was keen to bed these beauties and found them more than willing to oblige. They were not common whores, but women of breeding and quality whose conversations, wit and gaiety made their company all the more pleasurable. They spoke of the theatre and its plays and would recount great performances. I accompanied them to many of these, and so became acquainted with the charm of Italian plays, their intriguing plots and the array of characters portrayed by the most discerning of actors.

With the afternoons bathed in warm sunlight, I walked alone adjacent to the canals and, idling on the bridges, beheld with affection the Venetians at leisure in that characteristically casual fashion of theirs so much admired by the English. Days and weeks passed pleasurably by in this strange, enchanting place. We were sad to leave this floating city, but alas depart we must.

CHAPTER THREE

Return Home

Our tour at an end, and with winter approaching, we made swiftly for Château de Saint-Cloud, for after making enquiries we had received notice from Saint-Germain-en-Laye that Minette was residing there. Fortunately for us, Monsieur was not at home and we were able to meet with Minette at our ease. And so I took charge of the miniature portrait, which I was to guard with my life until the time it was to leave my hand and be received into that of the King.

We made ready for our return to England, first and foremost arranging the shipping of more books and artefacts amassed on our further travels. I stowed in my personal baggage a small book of plays I had written, and a tiny bundle of private letters I had received during my absence, from family and friends enquiring of my well-being. The miniature, I hid ingeniously upon my person, only Balfour and I knowing of its whereabouts. Our journey to England was not without the usual inconveniences; conditions aboard the coaches were cramped and the wheels mercilessly sought every jolting rut and uneven boulder along the roads to the port of Dieppe. On arriving there, we boarded the *Sea Serpent* anchored at harbour, and the sea voyage was no more comfortable, for the swell of the waves, the listing of the ship and the company on board provided even less amusement. At last, the shores of England and the port of Rye came into view and, after some delay landing, we took coach to London where we endured a further rough ride.

After many hours upon the road, the coach at last halted outside a large inn of some thirty hearths. This welcome stop gave our shaken bodies time for a little respite from the gruelling torment of travel. The vittles were plain but wholesome. We had become accustomed to more exotic fare, such as abundant fresh fruits and mildly spiced meats, but instead we now ate heartily on mutton, beef and chicken. The landlord, apparently renowned for his good beer, did not however always take such care over his wine for we were presented with a bottle of his *best* claret having such an ugly, bitter taste that I promptly spat it onto the floor. At this, he obligingly sought out a bottle of his finest claret from his own cellar and all was well with me.

We were joined at table by the four other travellers who had boarded our coach at Rye: a clergyman of somewhat dubious character, not to be trusted I feared at any price; a sad young saddler's apprentice who had visited his dying mother, with his father away at sea, and who was returning to Leather Lane; and a pretty young virgin, not above twelve years of age, chaperoned by her stern and uncompromising mother, both of whom had spoken very little in the close confines of the coach.

"We will take leave now," said the virgin's mother, "for we are both very weary and are apt to prefer the quietness of our room. Good evening, my Lord. And to you, Gentlemen."

As they parted our company, I smiled and winked at the girl, who giggled at my gesture and was severely scolded for her flippancy.

"I will also retire, my Lord. Sleep beckons my weary soul," said Balfour.

"Very well, Balfour. I will stay a little longer in this miserable company. Landlord! another bottle of your finest to share with these cheerless travellers."

Needless to say, the clergyman could drink his fill, and even I was hard pressed to maintain *his* level of consumption. The young apprentice was next to leave, clasping firm the table to steady his sway. He bade the two of us goodnight and shuffled upstairs in a melancholic stupor. In turn, I too welcomed restful sleep, and without a word left God's servant to sup alone. I staggered to my bed and, partly undressed, fell into a deep insentient slumber.

Morning drew up quickly. At seven of the clock, Balfour and I rose from our beds, drank small beer and ate a little stale bread. Our party once again boarded the coach and with fresh horses, we sped away.

৵৽

Nearing London Bridge, acrid smoke bellowed incessantly from the chimneys. We drove past the tanneries with their stench of dog shit and urine and bore the overpowering smell of glue and soap rendered from the decaying animal carcasses. The noxious fumes of these trades conspired to make the passer-by feel overwhelmingly nauseous. We now at the foot of the bridge, I peered out at the Bear Tavern, renowned for its good food, excellent ales, fine wines and unsavoury whores from the nearby stews. This was a welcome sight indeed, though as we now neared the archway of the bridge, our eyes were drawn skyward to the tips of the many poles above the gates. At their pinnacles were impaled victims' severed heads in various stages of decay, each of their expressions bearing witness to their intolerable sufferings. This was a grave reminder to all who entered London from Southwark Borough of the dreadful punishment meted out to past and would-be treasonable regicides and other villains. It was an intimidating sight to greet any traveller, but thoughts turned quickly to one's own survival in the negotiating of this precariously narrow and busy thoroughfare. The bridge, whereupon are built many large and many humble dwellings, houses hundreds of citizens, some of whom live and work their whole lives there. The structures are three and four storeys high. Most are the shops and living quarters of merchants of all descriptions. The crossing of the bridge is a hazardous journey for animals and humans alike, yet far less fraught than crossing the river by boat, where the currents can seize the unwary to be dragged to a watery grave.

To our great relief, we crossed the bridge in safety and arrived at Fish Street Hill in this densely populated part of the city, with its dreary, crowded streets and alleys and the stench of open sewers and all sorts of putrid matter and filth rotting under the very feet of the throng. Added to this, the shouts of people selling their wares, the clatter of iron-shod horses' hooves and the rumbling of coaches, wagons, hand barrows and all manner of conveyance shaped this city as a noisy, poisonous, polluted Bedlam.

The coach came to a respite halt outside The Sun Tavern, so allowing the rest of our party to alight at their destination. I was feeling not a little fatigued by now, so I stayed in the coach while Balfour entered the tavern for ale. I implored the landlord, who stood at his bar close by the door, to bring me claret wine and a small amount of beef. As I sat there delighting in my meat and drink, I spied a pretty young woman peering in at me. She smiled sweetly and I, beckoning her to join me, called the landlord again who summoned the potboy to the coach with another cup. I offered her a drink and, accepting, she asked my name and what business I had in London.

And I replied, "I madam, am John Wilmot, Earl of Rochester and have recently returned from the continent."

I enquired how this common wench earned her living.

"I am an orange seller, my Lord, at the Duke's Theatre, and one day I will be a fine actress upon that very stage," she haughtily replied.

Her aspirations were great and, like me, she had been seduced by the stage. She drank her fill and told me she must not be late for the selling of oranges. I bade her good day but requested a kiss before our parting. She eagerly obliged, neither trembling nor with shyness. I slipped my fingers down the front of her bodice and dropped a coin between her pretty breasts. She smiled, and left the coach as brazen as she had arrived.

Balfour paid our dues and returned to the coach and so we continued along our way, heading for the Palace of Whitehall where the coach finally halted. This labyrinthine maze, with the London to Westminster road running through its very heart, is a distinctly sombre place in comparison with the remote and beautiful Saint-Cloud we had left just days before.

We alighted, announced ourselves, and were shown to our lodgings. Our room was small but there was a welcome blazing fire in the hearth and candles lit the room as dusk descended. It was the evening of the Twenty-third of December. Christmas preparations were nearly complete, ready for the seasonal revelry, which would culminate in Twelfth Night, the ever-popular climax to the festivities.

On Christmas Eve, The King summoned Balfour and me to meet with him. We entered the crowded hall and I walked across in the direction of the Monarch, bowing graciously to this lofty, imposing figure. His majestic gaze and calm manner drew me to him in warm submission. As I neared, he looked decidedly older than my recollections, though he was even now a handsome man and cut a fine figure in the finest fabrics wrought in the French fashion, complemented by a stunning black periwig that cascaded over his broad shoulders. I noticed a leanness in his face, his cheeks hollow and set with deep lines, the hardships of his exile now only too evident. His once generous lips had narrowed, but his warm and radiant smile had not deserted them. His alluring dark eyes commanded attention, but with an absence of sincerity. He was the tallest man there, and an imposing regal figure.

The King welcomed me courteously and was eager to receive the cherished miniature I carried. I silently offered it to him and smiling he took it.

"Thank you, John. This is most welcome and I am forever in your debt," said the King.

Bowing, I stepped back from His Majesty and, with tears in his eyes, he retired alone to a small closet to gaze reflectively upon Minette.

There was a small crowd of people gathering at a large window and much jostling for a sight of the clear night sky. I walked across towards the window and heard distinctly the word *'comet!'* Even this heavenly body had welcomed my return, I pondered.

The King's close confidante and boyhood friend, George Villiers, Duke of Buckingham acknowledged me and invited me to join him and other rakish courtiers of his set. Commonly known as *The Merry Gang*, these courtly rogues would sooner piss on your shoes in an act of shameful defiance than doff their hats and they were avoided with caution by many a man, unless he thought himself invincible. Some of their number: Charles Sackville, Lord Buckhurst; Sir Charles Sedley; Sir George Etherege; and Sir Henry Savile, the younger brother of the Marquis of Halifax, were all loitering in the hall. None but dearest Henry became an intimate friend to me.

Balfour had left the hall and was busying himself in and around Whitehall meeting his own circle of associates. His aversion to sharing with me in the company of these *gentlemen* was made obvious and he tried civilly to dissuade me from joining their ranks.

I resided at Whitehall for a further week and had the frequent company of *The Gang*, visiting playhouses on two occasions. At the end of each play, we had made our way backstage to the tiring-rooms and there we congratulated the actors and actresses on their talented performances. The rooms were small and cramped, with costumes and props scattered all around. We took presents of wine for the performers, who readily opened the bottles, and heavy drinking bouts ensued. Our fervent interest in the actresses was very clear. They in their turn were good-humoured and at ease in our raffish company. A couple of them were already mistresses to two of our party and proudly wore bejewelled tokens of their lover's appreciation.

On the second of the two occasions, an exquisite young woman brushed past me. As I turned, gazing upon this delightful creature, a gentleman rushed by in chase and as he passed, he eyed me with such contempt.

"Henry, who was she?" I enquired.

"Elizabeth Pepys." Henry replied, "That lady who you have a mind to, is the beautiful half-French wife of Samuel Pepys Esquire, Clerk of the Acts to the Navy Board, whose patron is none other than Edward Mountagu, Earl of Sandwich, a trusted and esteemed commander in His Majesty's Fleet."

I was now aware as to who had imparted such a stern glower. Mr. Pepys was a most fortunate man to have rodded such a beauty and so secure her in his net.

Balfour and I together left London and returned to my home at Ditchley. My mother and servants were very happy to see me safely home and marvelled at how I had left but a mere youth and, to their astonishment, returned a Gentleman. With Balfour's guidance, I had evolved from a young impressionable boy into an educated, self-assured man of eighteen. Ever aware of his status, this Earl meant to impress.

The Countess made Balfour most welcome and beseeched him to stay at Ditchley for as long as he would. He gladly accepted.

CHAPTER FOUR

Vowing to Marry

During my time in Europe, my mother's ambitions to betroth me to a rich heiress had been to the forefront of her mind. The Countess's determination was unceasing, and not a moment was lost in her writing to the well-informed, questioning the likelihood of available heiresses.

After four weeks' stay, Balfour left Ditchley on the long journey to Edinburgh to continue his studies of medicine. I too was eager to leave for London and my friends at Court. Since my return to England, the tedium of country living in Oxfordshire had been decidedly dull and so I soon left the quiet of Ditchley for the splendours of the City.

In London, I rented lodgings in Portugal Street, conveniently adjacent to Lincoln's Inn Theatre, which I frequented on many occasions. I also took lodgings in Whitehall, which served me whenever I was called to Court for business with the King or when I would wish to languish with the rakes and ladies there. One such lady was Barbara Palmer, Lady Castlemaine, His Majesty's Maîtresse-en-titre. She was the most renowned beauty of the Court, indeed in all probability in the whole of London. She had great influence over the King, who lavished upon her houses, money, jewels and anything else her greed desired. She had amassed a vast fortune and was greatly admired by some, yet scorned by others. One who showed a particular disdain was my mother's close friend Edward Hyde, whose appointment as Lord Chancellor gave rise to a constant battle with Barbara. He deplored her ambitions and resented His Majesty's excessive generosity to his lady of the night.

Barbara's sexual dominance with the King's affections often overrode Edward's authority over the Monarch's coffers. This remarkably forceful woman is fortuitously a cousin of mine, so I myself was well favoured by the King through her influence.

The subject of my marriage prospects had reached the Sovereign's ear and his personal recommendation was a young thirteen year old heiress, Elizabeth Malet. Her ancestral home, Enmore Castle in the county of Somerset, has been the seat of the Malets for centuries. Elizabeth is well loved by her mother Unton, as she had been by her father John Malet III who, dying young, had left a large portion of his estate to his daughter. Her widowed mother in time married Sir John Warre who lavished much love and protection on his prized and only stepdaughter.

Elizabeth's revenue from her Enmore estate amounted to two thousand pounds a year, a tidy sum by any standards, and naturally there were others eagerly pursuing this eligible young lady in the hope of securing a profitable marriage. Most were young, titled and rich, but none possessed my charismatic charm and irresistible wit.

Having been given the Royal approval, I commenced my amours towards this beauty, but alas my pursuits did not go favourably. Whenever the lady made an appearance at Court, she would be engaged in conversation with other suitors and, despite my best endeavours to converse, she blatantly ignored my advances.

With the King and Castlemaine urging on the betrothal, I resorted to writing poems of love, which I believed she would not oppose. How could she? I was the handsome Rochester, a courtier to Charles II, friend of many prominent persons and above all the author of such liberated, passionate verses of ardour she would ever have chance to read.

A quandary of the most delicate nature marred my way to success. I was involved in a liaison with a young woman who had now become my mistress. She was no more than a common street whore, but a beauty nevertheless. Her wit and lewdness appealed to me and we spent many a night's intercursus in my room at Whitehall. But the affair had to cease if I were to stand any chance of gaining Elizabeth's affections, for I knew that the appearance of a good reputation would incline her towards me.

Over the weeks and months, though not for the want of trying, my frustration became unbearable. I made no headway with the *Heiress of the West* and, with the King urging the match, I felt the need for drastic measures. I hatched a plan so ludicrous that failure would for certain put me in the gravest position.

Elizabeth was spending the evening at Whitehall with her close companion Frances Stuart, another of the Court's dazzling beauties. La Belle Stuart later eloped and married the Duke of Richmond, after a clandestine rendezvous at the Bear Tavern. This was to infuriate His Majesty greatly, for he had relentlessly pursued La Belle for his own but, to her credit, naught had come of it.

At the end of the evening, Elizabeth, accompanied by her grandfather Sir Francis Hawley, a man of extreme wealth and close friend of the King, was being driven by coach to his London abode. As the coach approached Charing Cross, the planned abduction took place. My men on horseback halted her coach, whilst another was stationary nearby. Elizabeth was snatched and swiftly conveyed to the waiting coach, whilst Hawley protested helplessly. Two ladies received her within, and it sped off at great speed. I had given orders that the coach be driven to North Oxfordshire and to Adderbury House, a property of my late father's, now in the keeping of my mother, though not often occupied by her. I had done this in the hope of impressing Elizabeth with such a daring and romantic intrigue. Regretfully, the outcome of the escapade was quite to the contrary, for the King's anger on receiving the news from the irate Hawley was unsurpassed and Elizabeth was soon tracked down and reunited with her grandfather, she apparently none the worse for her adventure. A Royal warrant for my arrest was issued directly, and I was conveyed to the Tower to wait on the King's pleasure.

Cousin Castlemaine pleaded for my release and begged the King to be lenient, for these were the actions of a young man profoundly in love's wake and who, after months of patient wooing, had alas resorted to such a reckless act. Unusually, the King had stood resolute and ignored Barbara's pleadings.

In the course of my imprisonment, there was rumour of plague deaths in St. Giles in the Fields, a poor, squalid outlying parish. Thankfully for me, the threat of the plague arriving in the city persuaded the King to show mercy and he released me from my confines. The pestilence soon took its hold across the city with such dreadful voracity that the entire Court moved to Oxford to escape its terrifying consequences. I too fled quickly and made for Adderbury, leaving London and its remaining citizens to their abysmal fate.

CHAPTER FIVE

All at Sea

Whilst incarcerated in the Tower, the long hours had given rise to my reflecting on the madness of my actions. I knew I must somehow make redress to the King and, after long and hard consideration, I resolved to join His Majesty's Fleet as a Gentleman volunteer.

The English and Dutch were once again at loggerheads, and I perceived the time was right to prove my worth. I begged the King to allow me to join his fleet and he agreed. He instructed the Earl of Sandwich, whose flotilla was moored off Flamborough Head, to accommodate me in going to sea. Accepting, he wrote back to the King and I was aboard the Admiral's vessel by July. My accommodation was cramped but adequate, unlike that of the poor pressed beggars who served on the ship. Their quarters below deck were appalling, yet they had no choice but to be on board, risking sacrifice of life and limb for their Sovereign. In their dark, airless quarters, the sailors' hammocks were so close confined that arms and legs jostled with those of neighbours. The heat below deck that humid summer was appalling, and often men took ill with sickness and disease. Their life on board, if life you could call it, was dire.

The chance to prove my loyalty to the King came quicker than I anticipated. The Admiral gained knowledge that the Dutch fleet had anchored at Bergen. Orders were given and we sailed there to engage them. As we neared the impending skirmish, morbid fears of death occupied my mind during occasional solitary periods when the hustle and bustle aboard this fighting machine abated. I had not been alone in volunteering, for other young men had too. Having in common our tender ages, and with no experience of naval life, we were soon companions in arms braving our dreadful fears together.

Sooner than was envisaged, the battle was upon us. Up on deck, we held steadfast valiantly as our ship opened fire along with others of the English fleet. The Dutch returned fire and a living hell ensued. Acrid smoke filled the ship's confines and splinters of timber and metal flew about in all directions. The screams of the injured and dying filled our ears until we became deaf with the horror of it. With the decks swimming in blood, and with flesh and bone lying about, I watched as the badly wounded among us were carried below deck to the horrors of the ship's surgeon. Many a poor soul travelled that route, and following the surgeon's often futile butchery, met their end in the deep.

My two companions and I held fast at our duties, but then, as I stood just yards from them, a cannon ball struck and in an instant my friends were fatally cut down. For a moment, I stood motionless. Then trembling overtook me, but somehow I found courage to stay at my station. My friends' mutilated bodies soon joined the dead of the abyss, poor souls, never to return to England's shores. Before long, the battle ceased, with heavy casualties on both sides and our fleet headed back to Flamborough to await further orders.

Sandwich gave a good account of my conduct to the King, who welcomed me back at Court where many now regarded me as a young hero. But the horrors had left my mind in turmoil, tormented with nightmares of my friends' gruesome deaths.

In the month of June 1666, the English fleet had further encounters with the Dutch and I for my part felt compelled to volunteer once again. The bloody and fearsome battles that ensued took many lives of every rank. During one mêlée, it became necessary for a volunteer to convey crucial orders to the captain of a nearby ship. I, for reasons beyond even my comprehension, offered my services for this perilous task. Finding myself in crossfire,

I delivered the orders and miraculously returned unscathed with the vital reply. This action of bravery, or stupidity, for I have never been able to decide which, was viewed by witnesses as a very valiant feat indeed.

As a favoured courtier once more, I was bestowed the honour of Gentleman of the Bedchamber by order of His Majesty. This privileged and sought after position assured a yearly pension of one thousand pounds, together with tied lodgings in Whitehall during my continuance of the duty. The obligatory attendance was just twice a month, which allowed me freedom of the Court and opportunities aplenty to rally with the rakes. Their stakes were high and many a fortune had been won and lost in their ephemeral company, but the hand I'd been dealt was destined to win the hearts and minds of many.

CHAPTER SIX

Hearts Resigned

Over a year had passed since my ill-fated abduction of the lovely Malet, she now a marriageable sixteen and still keenly sought after. But none could match my forthright determination. This much prized lady was often seen at Whitehall and the theatres, accompanied by her grandfather, who was known to have a keen eye for the actresses. I seized all likely opportunities to be in the presence of this fine lady, but was never able to surmount the wall of protection that accompanied her whether at Court, at the plays or taking the air in the parks.

On an evening in late July was to be held, at the Banqueting House, a masked ball to celebrate His Majesty's safe deliverance from the recent plague; a privilege denied many poor souls who had not the chance to flee to Oxford and who had suffered the gravest hardships, abandoned and often alone.

Grand preparations were underway for this noble occasion, and decorative invitations on fine parchment with illuminated script were sent out to the illustrious people of the city. I received mine early, being lodged at Whitehall. The City's Guilds: of industrious drapers; Spittlefields silk weavers; the tailors, dressmakers, and periwigers of the Exchange; leatherworkers crafting boots, shoes and finely stitched gloves; and the hordes of embroiders throughout the city were all in great demand from those who could pay for their services.

I myself made a special effort and visited my tailor Will Norton, where I bespoke a coat and matching vest in the new fashion. I chose dark blue silk embroidered with fine gold thread and I also chose gold buttons, each subtly engraved with two entwined hearts. With my low hung, pale blue, ruffled breeches, just visible below the coat, I made a very handsome show. To complement this costly outfit, I took the momentous decision as to the wearing of a peruke and had one commissioned from a renowned periwiger in the Exchange on the advice of George Villiers, whose long curled, golden wig no man living could wear with such elegance as he. On the eve of the masquerade, I walked to the Exchange and there, having collected my wig, summoned courage to go and confront the barber. He began by shaving my face and then proceeded to cut my long natural locks. I watched sadly, as the tresses fell silently upon the cold stone floor. Finally, he shaved my exposed head. These horrors were not unlike my time at sea, and though far less fraught with danger were endured with the utmost nerve. At last, the peruke was carefully crowned upon my head, and in an instant was born a handsome hot-headed courtier.

The evening warm and humid, impatient masqueraders queuing around Whitehall sat frantically wafting fans in their airless carriages, akin to butterflies entrapped in cages. Hot and tired liveried servants and their sweating horses plagued by flies, slowly yet patiently edged ever nearer to the entrance. Footmen were kept busy opening and shutting doors as the throng of masked passengers, with thus impaired vision, jostled and fought their way to the hall.

The interior was brightly lit with a thousand shimmering candles illuminating the splendour of the Rubens ceiling. This was a rare vision indeed, which few privileged eyes could feast upon, for only daylight ceremonies were normally permitted so as to avoid damage to the precious canvases from smoke. I made for a good vantage point from where I observed the coming of the King, Queen Catherine, the Duke and Duchess of York and certain fortunate courtiers. Cousin Barbara being one such, and charismatic amongst their party, was masked in green silk encrusted with rubies and wore a crimson velvet dress embellished with emeralds and diamonds, shamelessly displaying her dominance in securing the King's generosity. How dissimilar Her Majesty looked, by contrast dejectedly barefaced in pale blue satin and only moderately jewelled. His Majesty, on the other hand, was predictably clad opulently, sporting a smooth satin vest of emerald green, richly embellished with the finest diamonds and rubies and, with matching coat, the very embodiment of kingliness. He held to his face a mask covered in fine gold leaf, with black pearls encircling the eyeholes thus enhancing those dark, captivating eyes. With the King enthroned, the stage was set for the most lavish display London had witnessed for many a year. The expense of the clothes alone would have fed the London poor for a month.

As music sounded, the Royal couple promenaded to the centre and began the Bransle, the assembly watching and applauding their every step. The King then beckoned onlookers to join them and presently a sea of dancing couples waved past.

My interest then turned to the heiress Malet. I spied her talking with Frances and others, with two gentlemen vying for her attention. As I was making my move towards Elizabeth, I was halted, as trumpets hailed servants entering the hall, each holding in front enormous pewter platters, which were heavy laden with the banquet's feast. The platters were piled high with all manner of exotic tropical fruits especially imported for the occasion, together with the more familiar from the rich soils of Kent, Surrey, Berkshire and Essex. There were eight courses in all; fruits, dishes of sweet sugared flowers, almond paste fancies glazed with sugared rosewater and many more delights that whetted the appetite. Anon, cellar servants brought into the hall decanters of Venetian glass filled with sweet Florence wine, dry Muscadine from Spain and the Canaries, and the most delectable of all, French claret. Sipping a glass of wine whilst tasting the exotica, some recognizable from my time abroad, a chance occasion arose to approach Elizabeth, who now stood alone, her companions and would-be suitors absent for a moment. The way ahead seemed clear.

"Good Evening, madam," I said.

"Good evening, my Lord Rochester."

I continued boldly, "You are by far the most captivating and indeed the finest looking woman in the hall."

She *was* a beauty, unlike the false painted, be-patched women gathered there. Her features held the charm of innocence. Her rosy moist mouth turned teasingly upwards, her bashful smile revealing small but good even teeth. Her light brown hair, entwined with pearls, hung gently in soft curls around her face with a glint of auburn encouraged by the candlelight. Fine pearl earrings hung from delicate lobes. Her face exhibited a pale, smooth and flawless complexion; no May dew or puppy dog water required for this fair skin. But, with the rising heat of the crowded hall and my ardent attention, her cheeks submitted to a pink hue. Her nose, with its slight upward turn, gave her an air of haughtiness, yet her bewitching hazel-green eyes, so clear and bright, surveyed my face with a soft sincerity. These delightful features perched upon a slender neck, her soft white shoulders and her delicate expressive hands aroused me with such vehemence.

"Your persistence does you credit, my Lord. I have heard tell of your gallant bravery at sea and I am resolved to a favourable opinion of you. Why, I am led to believe you now have no further attachment to a recent female acquaintance, hence I am willing to consider your friendship."

The ploy of concluding my affections towards a certain lady of the street had certainly paid dividends so far, I mused.

"Madam, my friendship proffered is truly sincere."

"Very well, my Lord, I am disposed then to accept your sincerity."

Elizabeth was wearing a dress of fine yellow silk trimmed with gold lace. Upon her bodice were embroidered flowers of blue velvet, and at the centre of each was placed a radiant sapphire. Smooth white pearls hung around her neck, but the gems of delight were her firm young breasts, barely concealed by the securely laced bodice.

"May I be so bold as to address you as Elizabeth?"

Smiling she replied, "Yes, my Lord, you may."

I held out my hand and begged she accompany me to the vittles. She agreed, and placed her warm delicate hand upon mine. Walking together, I was in no doubt that her hand would tremble and that her step would be hesitant, but I was taken aback by her self-assured manner.

Choosing fruits from the refectory table, many of which Elizabeth had never tasted before, we delighted in their succulent sweetness. Her appetite for them equalled my own for the wine. As she bit into a large and very ripe peach, its juice squirted onto my coat and dribbled slowly down to the buttons.

"Oh! My Lord! I do apologize."

Napkin in hand, she hastily wiped the front of my coat and at the same time I placed my hand upon hers and gently, but firmly, guided hers slowly over this most fortunate of stains. At that point, I brought her hand to my mouth and gently kissed it. Smiling, she lowered her eyes and blushed a little.

Composing herself, she remarked, "What striking buttons, my Lord."

"Elizabeth, I believe that the two hearts entwined thereon may soon reflect our own."

"Perhaps before long, my Lord," she replied, smiling sweetly.

Grasping the lowest button firmly in my hand, I ripped it from the coat and handed it to her. She took it readily, hiding it discreetly from view in a concealed pocket in her dress.

The King, who had been mingling with guests, spied us together and advanced. We thanked him for his generous hospitality on this so auspicious an occasion. He replied, saying how delighted he was to see us so enraptured, at the same time gently kissing Elizabeth's cheek. *I must possess this girl before the old rogue's pintle takes a fancy to her*', I thought. I bowing graciously and she curtsying, we moved swiftly in the direction of cousin Castlemaine who was holding court encircled by admiring gallants.

Barbara greeted us enthusiastically and complimented us on our attire but eagle eyed, she remarked upon the missing button. Mindfully, I explained that on my entering the hall amongst the bustling crowds, it was torn accidently from my coat, trampled underfoot and lost. At this, Elizabeth turned to me with a knowing smile. Barbara, whispering, then took her to one side, I perceiving by Elizabeth's giggles and girlish blushes that my cousin was, in her familiar crude manner, enlightening this innocent girl as to the subtleties of pleasuring a man.

It was late in the evening and, with the Royals retired to their private apartments, the weary but happy guests took to their carriages and headed home by way of the poorly lit and inhospitable streets of London. I escorted Elizabeth and her friend Frances safely to their coach and attendant liveried servants. Before taking my leave, I gently kissed Elizabeth's hand entreating that we should meet again. I stood as if in a dream as the coach vanished into the gloom. Triumphant, I marched towards Whitehall and my barren bed.

Early in the morning, the noise of palace servants attending to their duties awoke me abruptly. Whilst the Royal party slept on, His Majesty rose early and took his usual morning's brisk walk with his dogs and four servants trailing far behind. This took him through his gardens and down to the Thames' edge. I fell to sleeping again, and drifted into dreaming of Elizabeth lying naked and warm beside me.

Elizabeth was residing at her grandfather's house here in the city and, eager to make contact, I wrote her a short letter expressing my desire to meet at the Mall and to take a carriage ride through St. James's Park. Attached to the letter was a poem I had penned specially for her…

❧

Song

❧

Give me leave to rail at you,
I ask nothing but my due,
To call you false and then to say
You shall not keep my heart a day.
But alas, against my will
I must be your captive still.
Ah! Be kinder then, for I
Cannot change and would not die.
Kindness has resistless charms,
All things else but weakly move,
Fiercest anger it disarms
And clips the wings of flying Love.
Beauty does the heart invade,
Kindness only can persuade!
It gilds the lover's servile chain
And makes the slave grow pleased again.

❧

The letter was delivered forthwith and, to my astonishment, Elizabeth replied swiftly, agreeing to a clandestine meeting the next day at eleven of the clock in the morning.

In the close confines of the carriage, a loving intimacy blossomed, I capturing Elizabeth's heart and she in turn stealing mine. We were alone for one short hour before her return home. At our parting, we embraced, kissing each other with gentle but passionate lips, earnestly agreeing to meet again soon.

We artfully sustained our secret liaisons until the end of January the following year. Even the riotous devastation of London's ferocious fire could not surpass the burning love in our hearts. Our attraction for each other was now so powerful, we could not wait a moment longer to pledge our love, determined to become man and wife. We furtively planned, foolishly perhaps, to elope and marry in secret, contrary to the wishes of our families.

೭~೪

Early on the morning of the Twenty-ninth of January 1667, and with the utmost secrecy, my darling Elizabeth and I eloped. In a hurried ceremony at Knightsbridge Chapel, some two miles from Whitehall, in what was to be our *first* clandestine marriage we took our vows and were married lawfully in the eyes of God. Then, in a fantastical flight, we boarded a coach bound for the south west, leaving behind the inevitable wagging of tongues at our devilish elopement.

Our journey proved unromantic and inhospitable and was folly in the extreme. The makeshift accommodation, which we reluctantly shared with others, was cramped and repugnant and offered the meanest of vittles.

Cold, tired and hungry we arrived at the small town of Milton, which lies deep in a Dorsetshire valley. With our light baggage, we sought accommodation for the night. Here, luck was on our side, we having made the acquaintance of Emmanuel and Jemima Clenston, an elderly and needy couple. We introduced ourselves as brother and sister, John and Elizabeth. Manny and Jem, for that is what they affectionately called each other, had worked their whole lives toiling on the land. They had not been blessed with children, and lived on their own to the east of the town. They graciously offered two cramped rooms in their starkly furnished tied cottage, welcoming equally our companionship and our money for lodging.

Naturally, we were eager to consummate our marriage but the

temptation alas was sublimated, as our tired and wearisome bodies welcomed only sleep.

Morning broke with a white mist shrouding the quiet town. Nearby stood the splendid Abbey of Milton, and to its east a wooded hillside where, upon its ridge, stands the secluded ancient Chapel of St. Catherine. I had learned of this sacred spot when a scholar at Burford. An elderly tutor, who had been baptized at the chapel, believed his passion for study and his remarkable longevity were St. Catherine's doing. As an impressionable boy, and inclined to an adventurous spirit, I had vowed to one day seek it for myself.

As the Abbey bell pealed eleven of the clock, we began our climb of the steep grassy steps leading heavenward to the chapel and stole unnoticed through its hallowed portal. We, all alone and hidden from prying eyes, pledged our love in our covert *second* nuptials in this the most romantic of settings and at last placed rings upon our fingers.

Returning to our lodging, we told Manny and Jem of our secret and, although still ignorant of our true identity, they vowed never to tell a soul of our veiled marriage. They were overjoyed at our news and insisted we celebrate our union in the sharing of their meagre supper before we should retire to our marriage bed; the very bed Manny and Jem had shared throughout their wedded life, and which they had offered most generously. We awoke late in the morning, our spent, naked bodies entwined in blissful contentment, wishing never to depart this peaceful tranquillity, but alas, we were obliged to leave this Dorsetshire haven. Anon, we took leave of dear Manny and Jem and set out on our journey to London. Arriving late in the darkness of night, we hurried unseen to my lodgings at Whitehall.

చ౼ఠ

At the earliest opportunity, we made our way to the Duke's Theatre and, to the utmost astonishment of all there, barefacedly announced our titles… *'Lord and Lady Rochester'*.

CHAPTER SEVEN

Holy Matrimony

After our revelation as husband and wife, we later left London and were initially compelled to reside with my mother at Ditchley. Her disdain for Elizabeth was well known, and she was not overjoyed with our impulsive marriage. Bitter wrangles ensued over marriage settlements, conducted by the Countess and my wife's family. Naturally, I had hoped that my mother would consent to Elizabeth and me residing at the Adderbury estate, but my mother intended soon to move there herself.

For the time being, our living at Ditchley was most unsatisfactory for all concerned, so Elizabeth and I left Oxfordshire and made for her estate at Enmore in Somerset in the hope of a more convivial atmosphere.

Our time at Enmore was idyllic in comparison to that at Ditchley, but I longed to return to Oxfordshire, and this was to be sooner than I had envisaged. It came to pass that her necessary involvement in family affairs thwarted my mother's proposed move to Adderbury, and so she would be staying at Ditchley. As a consequence of this unexpected good news, Elizabeth and I would be moving direct to Adderbury, and so we might hope to avoid maternal meddling.

❧❦

Adderbury House is large and imposing, built of the rich local ironstone that gives forth a warm golden glow in the evening sunlight. It is located at the eastern boundary of the village, a short distance from the Oxford Road. The estate is farmed by local tenants, and so secures a modest income towards the upkeep of the house, but I envisaged the income from Elizabeth's large Somerset estates to be most opportune in supporting the heavy outlay demanded by this large residence. Once there, Elizabeth at last seemed contented with her new rôle as Lady Rochester and thought the house a splendid building very much to her taste.

My mother, however, soon arranged a short stay at Adderbury, barely two weeks after our arrival there. Her intention for this sudden visit was never clear but her meddling, as usual, was all too evident. To my bewilderment, Elizabeth, for all her young years, showed an amicable restraint on mother's arrival and welcomed her to Adderbury with much friendship and kindness. Nonetheless, Elizabeth's upbringing and education on a well-run family estate had prepared her, it seemed, for the overseeing of such a large household and so she would tolerate no meddling from the Countess.

The Countess, a shrewd lady at all times, was civil and attentive to Elizabeth and mercifully, after a brief period of just one week, returned to Ditchley resuming the supervising of her two young orphaned grandchildren; their father, Henry (Harry) Lee my half-brother, had died of the smallpox, like their grandfather Harry, and left his wife Anne a widow with one infant and the imminent arrival of another. A cruel twist of fate then overshadowed the birth of this second child, for only a short time after giving birth, the mother too had died, leaving my own mother the Countess as guardian.

Our life together at Adderbury was initially idyllic. We spent hours idling in the gardens, discussing the intended planting of many different species of trees, shrubs and herbs. Elizabeth had a great interest in nature and, for one so young, she was very knowledgeable as to the many species of trees and flowering plants that grew in abundance at Enmore. She held a passion for the growing of herbs, and the hitherto neglected kitchen garden at

Adderbury would in time become her haven. We often times walked to the lake at the far end of the gardens, this despite a bitter cold winter with the lake a mirror of ice, and we longed for the warmth of spring for to catch fish and cook them fresh to eat at our table.

❧✦

"Must you go?" Elizabeth shouted with resentment.

"You know I must. The King commands it!" I replied angrily.

Here in the middle of March, the King had ordered me to my bedchamber duties, and the news of the need for me to depart had greatly distressed Elizabeth. I dismissed her annoyance and prepared for my return to London. The coach was made ready for my journey and we parted on less than favourable terms. As we kissed goodbye, I felt a pang of guilt at leaving her forlorn at Adderbury, and with sorrowful tears, she implored my swift return.

"My return madam, will be at the King's pleasure, not yours," I replied sharply, as I stepped aboard the coach.

On my arrival at Whitehall, my guilt at leaving Elizabeth weighed heavily on my mind. I wrote a letter to my mother asking her to visit Elizabeth to account for the magnitude of my duties at Court and to reassure her of my undying devotion. My mother replied, but made it perfectly clear as to the inconvenience of my request. However, she assured me that she would honour it and travel to Adderbury, if only to please me.

Six weeks had now passed since my abrupt departure and during that time, I wrote letters to Elizabeth, receiving her several replies. She enthused that the kitchen garden was starting to flourish in the warm spring sunshine, and that she was eager for me to glimpse the young shoots of her labour. She acknowledged my mother's short visit and, although now a little more understanding of my duties to the King, she imparted that she still felt aggrieved by my absence. In her loneliness, she prayed for my return so as to lay with the warmth and comfort of my body and declared that she could endure no longer the cold sheets of her empty bed. At last, my duties at Court came to an end and I returned home to a joyous welcome.

రావ

The warmth of spring gave way to the heat of summer. It was now July 1667, our first summer as man and wife, and we were blissful in our domestic rôle, turning Adderbury into our home. As well as the further planning of the kitchen garden and the stocking of the lake, we employed local craftsmen to re-plaster and decorate various rooms in the house that, over the years, had fallen into disrepair. For our hall, we commissioned a fine oak dining table and ten chairs from a renowned cabinetmaker at nearby Banbury.

రావ

In early December, intruding upon this tranquil life, came the sad news of the death from smallpox of my half-brother Frank Lee, this the same fate that had befallen his brother Harry eight years earlier. My mother was devastated by this latest loss, and went into deep mourning for her beloved son. She found herself once more as the head of the Lee family, caring for Frank's widow Eleanor and her two infant sons Francis and Edward Henry. As a consequence of Frank's death though, I was to succeed as Ranger of Woodstock, a position held by the Lees for generations. With this rangership came the right to reside whenever I pleased at High Lodge within the park. This turn of events, sad though it was, permitted me unbridled liberty from tedious domestic rankles of both wife and mother.

As Christmas approached, and our house looking very fine indeed, arrangements were underway and invitations delivered for our Twelfth Night celebration at Adderbury. On that cold frosty morning, our servants were busy making all ready for the arrival of the guests. Fires were lit in the hearths of all the rooms, with plentiful coal and logs piled high at each fireside. Wine was brought up from the cellar and, most significant of all, the Twelfth Night cake was revealed. In the making of this cake, the vital bean and pea had each been placed meticulously, before the baking in our oven, warranting a chosen King and Queen for the evening. Two crowns of parchment had been made and painted colourfully in readiness for this custom.

It was six of the clock in the evening and Elizabeth and I were now ready to receive our guests. Lit candles, cheering our house in their warm glow, illuminated the welcoming rooms. As the first of the guests arrived, the servants greeted them and led them in to our festive room. By seven of the clock, all the guests had arrived and stood with well-charged glasses of our best claret or sweet Florence wine, or mulled spiced wine, which was more to the liking of some. On a table in one corner of the room were laid two large venison pasties together with cold beef, mutton, three capons, a plentiful dish of oysters, a dish of cream and a large dish of sack posset. Guests helped themselves to food, and copious amounts of wine were served to each guest by two of our servants whose main task it was for the evening to ensure that no guest's glass was ever found wanting.

As the hour of nine of the clock drew nearer, I invited the company to take to their seats for the welcoming of the cake. In great anticipation, all heads were turned towards the opened doors as it was carried in to the applause of everyone. The cake was carefully placed at the centre of the table and fine pewter plates were then handed to all. With great excitement, I took a sharp knife and divided the cake equally to ensure a generous piece for everyone, I being party to the whereabouts of the bean and pea from our cook.

"It's me!" exclaimed Lord Folgate, "I have the bean and so shall be crowned King for the evening!"

At that, everyone applauded his lucky find. A short time passed before the pea was found, and this by Lady Hepsibah Wroxton. Great excitement now filled the room as the newly proclaimed King and Queen of Twelfth Night took their seats at the head of the table. After the crowning ceremony, the strong men of the party raised the King and Queen aloft and chaired them serenely around the room. As they passed, everyone drank their good health. Then all around danced, cheered and some to song, as their Majesties were carried back on their thrones to the head of the table, where the King and Queen together drank the health of everyone.

It was near to midnight and our guests prepared to leave, calling for their servants to make ready with the carriages for their journeys home in the cold, frosty night air. We wished them all a safe voyage and thanked them for attending. They in turn thanked us for our generous cordiality. As the last of them left, Elizabeth and I, now very tired but ecstatically happy, made ready for bed, whilst our exhausted servants tidied the rooms and snuffed out the candles.

At last in our bed, we talked and laughed over the antics of some of our drunken guests. We had witnessed them staggering to their waiting coaches, unable to clamber aboard without the aid of their attendants. Anon, in a warm embrace, we drifted into slumber.

࿏

"Are you awake, John?"

"I believe so," I replied.

We had both lain long and could hear the servants busy at their work. We washed our hands and faces, dressed ourselves and then down to the little parlour on the first floor, whose windows overlooked our garden. It was mid-morning, so we drank a draught of small beer and ate the remainder of a venison pasty left over from the feast.

࿏

As winter grudgingly relinquished its icy grip, we walked hand in hand through our garden in the welcome spring sunshine. We inspected the preceding year's plantings to assess their condition after a particularly fierce frosty spell. To our great delight and relief, all was well, they proudly displaying vigorous buds and shoots. We again conversed over the planting of the kitchen garden. I for my part, although interested in such matters, had no knowledge of what to plant where or when. Elizabeth was well informed in these things, so she alone would oversee our gardeners in the husbandry of vegetables, fruit bushes, trees and all else.

≥∘≤

After a further absence of a few weeks at Whitehall, I returned home again to Elizabeth at the beginning of July. She greeted me with that degree of coldness I had lately come to expect. I thought that, in the fullness of time, she would come to understand that my duties at Court were imperative and could only benefit our status and wealth. But, on each time of my return after such an excursion, she grew more and more displeased and for days on end would sulk, not speaking a word to me. She often retired to her bedchamber for two or three hours at a time, and there would sit weeping and bemoaning the injustice in my leaving her alone and isolated at Adderbury. She insisted she had not a friend in the world when I was absent, and relied solely on our household servants for any small measure of conversation, which with their lack of education and lowbred simplicity was limited in the extreme. My patience was now wearing thin and I demanded that she join me in the parlour. This she was reluctant to do, but in anger I shouted that if she did not come of her own free will, I would be obliged to drag her there and she would be the butt of all the jokes of her simple servants. I waited patiently for her to arrive, and after a few minutes she came into the room. I asked her to sit down and proceeded to chide her over her ridiculous demeanour. I told her forcefully that I would not in any circumstances allow this disrespectful behaviour to continue and that she must present herself with the conduct expected of someone of her class.

With tear-stained cheeks, she shouted angrily, "You never take me to London. Are you ashamed of me?"

"Ashamed of you? Why should I be ashamed of you?"

"Because you are often amongst the beauties of the Court who wear the latest fashions, so I must look very drab in your eyes, rarely having occasion to wear fashionable clothes, living constantly in the country."

I was most annoyed at this sudden outburst, but my heart softened as I looked into this sweet girl's face and so held my repose. I walked over to her and held her in my arms suggesting that we both visit London early the following week.

"John, my sweet love, I would enjoy that very much."

"Then make preparations and we will travel to London on Tuesday next."

On the Tuesday morning, we took coach. His Majesty would be delighted that Elizabeth was returning to the City after her long absence from Court.

On the journey, I told Elizabeth that I had arranged for the making of a new garment for her from the dressmaker Madam la Roche.

"Madam la Roche! John, is this true? I am to have a dress by Madam la Roche?" she questioned, for she was overwhelmed by this and wept with joy.

"Yes, Elizabeth. *The* Madam la Roche."

"But John, she is the most sought-after dressmaker in the whole of London. Oh, John! You are the most thoughtful, kind and loving husband any wife could wish for."

"There is no need to wish, Elizabeth, I am yours and will be always."

Presently, we were summoned to His Majesty, who welcomed our arrival. His attention swiftly turned to Elizabeth, for I was merely an inconvenience in this charade.

"Lady Rochester! As entrancing as ever I see. It has been far too long since I set my eyes on this feast, John. Your Lord should not keep you hidden away in Oxfordshire, my dear. It is not good for one so beautiful to be left alone and deprived of admiring company," said the King, then kissing Elizabeth softly on the cheek.

"I am honoured, Your Majesty," Elizabeth said, blushing from his attentions.

"I will make every effort in future to bring Lady Rochester to London, Your Majesty." I said, "And rest assured I will be mindful to stay close by her side at all times, to ensure her virtue from the ever present licentious distemper that breeds so prolific in this city."

"I am content you will, John, for you are only too aware of the temptations that befall so many in this ungodly Garden of Eden," said His Majesty as he turned and walked away.

The following morning, Elizabeth and I took coach to Madam la Roche, and we were very pleased indeed with the cream coloured silk taffeta dress, which already fitted Elizabeth extremely well. She was by far the most beautiful and innocent darling I had ever seen. After the fitting, Madam la Roche promised that the dress would be finished for collection the following morning.

❦❧

With Elizabeth attired in her new taffeta we, by personal invitation, ventured to a play at Whitehall. At the close of the play, we were invited to dine with friends in the evening, where we ate a very good dinner, drank excellent wine and played at the cards until late. We were offered a room for the night by our hosts, which was most welcome, we having neither the wit nor direction of our lodgings after much imbibing of strong liquor. Our hosts' servants had prepared the bed with crisp, clean sheets and soft pillows. The windows were open, letting in a fresh breeze, and arranged in the room were dishes of rose petals and dried peel of oranges and lemons whose sweet smelling fragrance perfumed the air. Elizabeth and I retired to bed, and as she unclothed I sat gazing at her.

"Why are you looking at me in that curious manner?" Elizabeth asked.

"Just admiring the most beautiful woman in London. I have not seen you look so happy and bright as you have this evening since our secret liaisons and carriage rides in the park, before we were wed."

"Please forgive me, John, for my despicable behaviour at times, but I am so lonely when you are away, and not a little jealous."

"Come here and sit on the bed," I beseeched her.

She came to me half-undressed. I gently removed the rest of her clothes to reveal her beautiful naked body and invited her to lay beside me. This she did and, with a girlish giggle, covered herself with a sheet. I too unclothed and slipped under the sheet and we kissed and embraced passionately. I kissed her beautiful white breasts and gently licked her rose pink nipples, and as my hands caressed her soft, supple body she sighed, urging me enter her aroused cunny.

As we lay spent and in silence, I looked at my darling Elizabeth, now sleeping contentedly, and I a happy man.

❧❧

With the weather set fair, we made our way by river with friends for a turn in the new Spring Gardens close by Fox-hall. This riverside garden of several acres, with its shrubs, flowers, tree lined avenues and discreet arbours, is a much-favoured place of many Londoners. The hot July day had lured crowds of people there. Many fine ladies were to be seen but I was not fooled, for most were but common whores and doxys who frequented the gardens plying their licentious trade among the many gentlemen who gathered there willing to pay handsomely for the quenching of their carnal thirst.

We strolled the avenues and there met acquaintances who joined our company. Feeling a little fatigued in the heat of the day, we took refuge in the shade of a covered arbour, close to where wine and vittles were for sale. There with our friends we drank cups of costly cheap wine and partook of oysters, hoping not to be poisoned into the bargain.

As the night drew in, revellers in liquored high spirits grew more boisterous and obnoxious. Fights broke out between the gallants and rakes vying for the attentions of those ladies of dubious quality, whose sole purpose there was to relieve a gentleman of his purse.

A particularly vicious brawl between two men erupted and, with swords drawn, they fought each other until one of them struck the other in the groin. Screaming, he lay in agony with copious blood pouring from a severed artery. No one dared go to his aid for fear of reprisal. The rake whose sword did the terrible damage walked away with his prize; a dark-haired, painted and, for sure, pox-ridden lady. The despicable rogue seemingly had no feelings for the poor fellow writhing on the ground a dying. My terrified wife, who witnessed the whole affair, begged that we should return to our lodgings. To this I agreed, and we parted from our friends, who intended to stay longer in the hope of more, dubious excitement. We called for a boat and travelled along the river returning to Whitehall. Back at our lodgings, my poor wife was still shocked and shaking from the incident.

"John, please stay close by my side, as you promised the King you would. That licentious distemper you have talked about, I have now witnessed with my own eyes, and it is indeed rife in this city. Could His Majesty not bring order and punish those responsible?" Elizabeth asked.

"He could, but would first have to clap *himself* in irons." I said, with some irony, "You see, Elizabeth, this city of our great and gracious realm feeds on greed, and the more one devours, so increasingly sick one becomes, and there is no known cure to be had," I added, with great sadness.

Elizabeth looked perplexed and a little startled at my answer, but I told her not to concern herself over such things.

The next morning we made ready for our return to tranquil Adderbury.

જ્જ

Soon, a month had elapsed since our journey to London and our days at Adderbury were passing peacefully by. Elizabeth and I were the best of friends in most things and our lives together concurred most agreeably.

"Elizabeth, are you ill?" I enquired, for my poor wife looked most pale.

"I feel wretched, John," she said, as she rose from the bed and rushed towards the washbowl on the table.

Clutching at her stomach, she was violently sick. As she retched uncontrollably over the bowl, I rushed out of bed, went to her side and held and comforted her until the sickness had passed. I implored her to lay on the bed and called our servant Martha Bodicote to come to our aid.

"What's all this fuss about, my Lord?" asked Martha.

"I do not know. Elizabeth felt very ill of a sudden and has been violently sick."

"Leave it to me, my Lord. I will attend to it," she assured me.

I took my leave of the two women and went into the garden for fresh air.

Half an hour had passed and Martha called to me asking that I go to Elizabeth. I walked into the room and saw her sitting upon the bed. The colour had now returned to her cheeks.

"John, I am so sorry for what happened this morning," she said.

"Do not worry my love. I am so pleased that you now look so much better than when I left you."

"Martha was so wonderful, John. She is so wise and understanding."

As tears streamed down her face, Elizabeth declared to me that she was with child.

"Elizabeth, this is wonderful news!" I smiled and, embracing her, cried with joy, "No more trips to London for you. You need complete rest and I order this of you."

"Yes, John. I understand, and I will try to be most patient in the condition I find myself."

With this, we sat and talked most agreeably about our new child to be born the following April.

I travelled to Ditchley next morning to inform my mother of our most happy circumstance. She welcomed the good news somewhat coldly and yet she wished Elizabeth well for the safe arrival of our child, saying that she hoped the outcome would be an heir to the Rochester title.

Elizabeth was now very ill with sickness for the next few months of her pregnancy, but as time passed, she grew stronger and flourished. She was then able to resume her duties organizing the household, and also took to embroidering beautiful crafted covers for our baby's cot.

"John? If it is not a boy will you be disheartened?" Elizabeth asked one evening, as we sat alone in our parlour.

"Of course not, Elizabeth. All I wish is that you and the baby are delivered safely to me."

What could I say? I hoped the child would be male, but the safe survival of both mother and infant were uppermost in my thoughts.

❧

"You cannot go, John. You cannot." cried Elizabeth, "I need you here with me at such a time."

Elizabeth sat crying bitterly at the news that the King had asked me to travel to France on crucial business and to deliver in person vital documents to his sister Minette.

"I too am upset, Elizabeth, and I will try my utmost to persuade the King to relinquish his demand. But it will not be easy."

"Why now, John? Why now? You know the birth of your first child is very near."

"Elizabeth, I will see what I can arrange."

I sent word to the King and explained my plight at such a critical time. His answer was cold and without feeling; I was to travel again immediately to France as his envoy, with a Gentleman usher of the Court. I left Adderbury and Elizabeth the following morning. It was now March. Elizabeth was distraught at my leaving, but I implored her to be strong. I held her tightly in my arms, kissing her tear-stained cheeks and promising to return as quickly as duties allowed. I boarded the waiting coach and did not look back, for my heart was heavy laden at our parting.

రావ్

The intended short period abroad in France, as events would have it, kept me away for more than four long months. Elizabeth had been safely delivered of a beautiful girl who was named Anne after my mother, for we had agreed this should the child be of the soft sex. My cruelly enforced duties in France had wrenched me from my wife at this most vulnerable and dangerous time. My daughter's baptism had gone ahead at Adderbury Church in the absence of her father. I had written many letters during my time away and Elizabeth had replied most bravely, yet urging my return home for us to be together with our most precious daughter.

At the Court of France, I and my companion had delivered the documents to the King's sister as ordered. As usual, Minette was charmingly witty. She was most appreciative that I had taken the time and trouble to bring the documents to her, and was genuinely happy to hear of the birth of our first child. Minette, heavily pregnant, prayed she too would be safely delivered of a healthy child.

The French Court had given many opportunities for me to become acquainted with several fine-looking women. Many an evening was spent in private apartments in their company, gambling at the cards or feasting and drinking to excess, and so giving rise to amorous adventure.

Unfortunately, during my stay, Louis had received knowledge of a disagreement I'd had with Tom Killigrew, manager at the King's Theatre, in sight of our Monarch, when I had set-to and hit Tom. This disrespectful act of lese majesty was more than Louis could stomach, and he remarked that Charles's leniency towards me served to confirm the rumours he had heard; that he was a weak and easily led king surrounded by rakish upstarts such as I. As a consequence of this news, my companion and I were asked in no uncertain terms to leave Louis' Court, and so we made our way to Paris. We stayed there for several weeks, at which time I was re-introduced to the city's theatres and in times of weakness, fuelled by too much drink, I had visited those brothels renowned for their sexual extravagances. Throughout these periods of excess and illicit carnal adventure, it was as though Elizabeth was no part of my life, I succumbing to over-indulgence and pleasure. This evil in me was out of control, and nothing could impede its diabolical path.

CHAPTER EIGHT

Fatherhood and First Signs

A Dirty, filthy rat had entered my soul in Paris and its sharp teeth gnawed deep into my heart on my way home to Elizabeth and my newborn daughter. It was a long and painful journey, more agonizing than I could ever have imagined. I was soon to arrive back at Adderbury and in moments of panic, I fought for composure.

An overjoyed and excitable Elizabeth walked briskly towards me with Anne in her arms, welcoming my return. I looked down at this little bundle and spied there the sweetest little face I have ever seen. Tears filled my eyes.

"She is every bit as beautiful as I imagined, Elizabeth."

"Thank you, my Lord. Could she be anything else, being the daughter of my beloved John?"

I put my arms around my dear wife, first kissing her and then the child and we made our way into the house. Elizabeth then handed our little Anne to Beatrice Leafield; a trusted and dependable wet-nurse who had attended the child since the birth and who now took Anne into a private room to suckle her.

We entered the dining room just off the hall, where Elizabeth had ordered that dinner be served. I was ravenous from my long journey and tucked in to wild duck, and roast leg of lamb from stock reared by one of our tenant farmers. As we sat eating, Elizabeth asked me about my time in France. I raised my glass and toasted Louis XIV as the most pompous and foppish King I, or anyone, could ever have the misfortune to meet.

"But you liked Louis the first time you met, John."

"Yes I know, but I was much younger then and most overawed by the splendour of the occasion."

"Why then, John, did you not approve of the Sun King this time?"

"Sun King? His piercing rays blind most in his presence, but not me," I declared.

And so, I was obliged to tell Elizabeth of the foolhardy incident with young Tom Killigrew when I had been in the presence of King Charles. This she frowned at, and showed great annoyance at such unruly behaviour. Her ensuing silence at this news put me ill at ease again for a while, but after a time we set to talking again, putting the whole nasty incident behind us. We sat conversing at great length about our dear child. I could see in Elizabeth's face that she was a most proud mother and loved Anne very much, as too did I.

Beatrice came into the room and told us that Anne was now in her cot, so I went with Elizabeth to the nursery where our daughter lay. We knelt beside the cot and gazed at our dear child with such contentment.

"I hope you are not ill-pleased, John, at her being a girl."

"No, Elizabeth. She is so precious to me."

We left the nursery, and Anne to her slumbers, and I feeling particularly tired prepared for bed. Elizabeth said she would join me before long but had one or two duties to attend before she retired.

As I made my way to our bedchamber, I felt a sudden, sharp stab of pain and became aware of a soreness in my cods and an uneasiness of my prick. I quickly undressed and inspected the offending member and found an inflamed ulcer, which surprisingly was not sore to the touch. I knew immediately the route by which my thing had become infected. The Paris brothels had offered pleasure, but at a price. I climbed into bed and wondered how I would tell Elizabeth so soon after my return that I must travel to London. I knew that I must secure early treatment and until cured, my love for my dear wife would prevent me bedding her for fear of passing on this evil and disgusting pox.

Two days later, I made arrangements to travel to the City, and to my great surprise, Elizabeth was quite calm and happy about my going. I believe the arrival of our daughter now gave Elizabeth a more contented mind. She kissed me goodbye and expressed her wish for my speedy return.

తొ౸

I arrived in London making straightway for Whitehall and my lodgings there. I met with my friends Henry Savile and George Etherege, and we made our way to the Dog Tavern in New Palace Yard to drink and talk after my absence abroad. We discussed the comings and goings of the King's courtesans. George said that Barbara still ranked high in His Majesty's favour, but others now had become part of his intrigue, in particular his lovely Nelly. Mistress Gwyn had left the gilded stage and become another of the King's mistresses. This transition from her performing on stage to performing in the King's bed had taken place during my absence abroad. Barbara had been unperturbed at this new rival, but we all knew that, sooner or later, young, pretty chestnut haired Nelly, whose comic wit and dainty breasts no man on earth could resist, would charm the King to her favour. She had captivated her audience as comedienne with her witty prologues or the dancing of jigs, which could not be bettered by any actress. We all raised our cups and drank a health to our dear sweet Nelly; our tragic loss but the King's most pleasurable gain.

"I must take leave of you now, gentlemen." said George," I have an urgent matter to attend."

"Would this pressing matter concern a woman, George," I said.

"What other matters are there in this world that can impede a meeting with a wench?" smiled George, on leaving the Dog.

I winced at a sudden stinging in my prick.

"John, are you in pain?" enquired Henry.

"Yes. I have come to London sooner than anticipated. I am needy of treatment for my ulcerated cock."

"Is your dear wife aware of your predicament, John?"

"No, Henry, she is not, and I'll make damned sure she neither knows of it, nor in fact is diseased by it. I am in dire need of a cure, and quick, so I can bed my wife without fear. She must never know of this, Henry," I implored.

"I understand, John. Your secret will be safe with me, for I will breathe not one word on the matter. But heed this, my friend; the pox can be very volatile, and you may never be entirely free of it."

"That's as may be, Henry, but my pressing inconvenience is uppermost in my mind."

"Well, John, I know just the man to help you."

And so, Henry told me of a house in St. Martin's Lane which was well known to a select few, and discretion at all times was the mark of the establishment. I arranged an appointment and took coach there two days later, arriving at eleven of the clock in the morning. I rang the bell at the door and was welcomed by a gentleman dressed in fine clothes who escorted me to a room on the ground floor. As I entered, I was asked to sit and await the arrival of the physician. The room was large and well carpeted and plush hangings covered the windows. The seats were comfortable and candles lit the room. There was a desk of the finest oak, and around the walls hung paintings depicting miraculous cures being performed on individuals whose dress illustrated their quality. It was not long before the physician entered and introduced himself as Dr. Valentine Loveall.

"I believe, my Lord, that you are here for the cure."

"I hope for as much."

"Accompany me then, my Lord, and I will begin."

I was taken to an upstairs room where I was undressed by his servants and clothed in a robe of fine crimson silk. I was then escorted downstairs to a small room and invited to sit on a low stool.

A wooden bucket was placed at my feet and I was then asked to drink a cup of liquid, blue in colour but tasteless. After imbibing this seemingly harmless fluid, I was taken rapidly with a profuse sweating accompanied by unbearable cramps in the stomach and within a short time was violently sick, vomiting stinking blue matter into the waiting bucket. After a short respite from this nauseous attack, I was escorted to a very hot, steamy room at the back of the house. In its centre was set a large, round bath, sunken into the floor and filled almost to the brim. I was asked to disrobe and walk down three small steps into the hot bath. As the water found my feet and legs, the sensation was most pleasant, but as it reached my privies, an excruciating pain seared through my whole body. I shouted out in agony. The doctor's assistants held me down.

"Let me out! For pity's sake let me out!" I screamed.

But to no avail. I was held firmly by their cruel, strong arms.

"The pain will soon subside." said Loveall, "Please be patient, my Lord. All will be well before long."

As I lay there in my agony, I tried to close my mind to it and to think of Elizabeth and our child, but the pain overwhelmed even those thoughts. As I found myself drifting into unconsciousness, I was pulled clear of this hot steamy hell, laid upon a couch and wrapped in warm soft sheets. I was then left to gather my senses. After a short time, I was given another draught of liquid and was taken to a further room where my clothes were laid out. The physician's two servants dressed me. Loveall entered the room and asked how I was feeling.

"Better than in that damned bath!"

"Well, my Lord. That damned bath, as you call it, will hopefully be your eventual cure of this pox. After two more sessions, over the next two weeks, we shall see a miraculous return to health for your Lordship," he concluded sternly.

"Two more sessions of hell?" I protested.

"Yes, my Lord. Two more sessions should suffice."

He then handed me an account for his fee for this my first visit. It amounted to one pound and one shilling, including the use of after bathing sheets and medicinal drinks of what poisonous concoction I was never told.

I handed Loveall my guinea piece with a rather shaky hand, for I had still not fully recovered from that vile but necessary treatment.

I left his establishment and "chairio" I called for a sedan to take me to Whitehall and to my lodgings where I lay my weary body on the bed and fell into a deep but troubled sleep.

❧❦

"John! It's me, Henry."

I awoke to a loud knocking and a familiar voice. I rose from my bed and opened the door. There stood my very good friend.

"How was it, John? You look tired and pale."

"A steaming hell! I am to have two more sessions, Henry."

"You poor fellow," Henry said sympathetically.

"Why should such a gratifying pleasure, and one I find so irresistible, lead to such a fearful and disgusting condition?" I asked.

"Well, John, the more you allow such pleasures to ravage your body, the more the threat will hang over you. The disease and its repugnant legacies may sooner or later drown even *your* buoyant spirit." Henry replied most gloomily, "John, let's walk." He added more cheerily, "The air will lift your spirits, and no doubt a glass of wine will lift them even higher."

We left my lodgings and walked through the garden at Whitehall, then on down to the river. We took boat and alighted at nearby York House, then making our way by the New Exchange. We arrived at Covent Garden and entered Chatelin's French eating-house. By this time, I was particularly hungry, so we ordered a fine French dish and a bottle of their best claret.

It was now late in the evening and, after two further bottles, we made ready to leave and return to Whitehall. We beckoned a linkboy and walked back in a steady but drunken manner. On arriving, we paid the linkboy his meagre fee. He thanked us for our payment and as he turned to walk away into the darkness, I asked him if he would like to earn a further threepence.

"Threepence? I thought you had no further to go, my Lord."

"John, it's late. Leave the boy alone and let us get to our beds," said Henry.

"What do you require, my Lord, for this further threepence?" said the boy.

"Just a kiss of those young lips of yours."

"A kiss, my Lord!" he cried.

"Yes, just a kiss, and the coin's yours."

"Very well, my Lord," the boy answered shyly.

With the boy standing there, holding his lanthorn aloft, I placed my hands around his trembling body and kissed him softly on his lips. The poor lad stood there in shocked amazement, yet not unhappy with the experience. I placed threepence in his hand and said, "Be off with you."

"The bath of hell is far removed from your thoughts then, John."

"I give not a fig, either for the bath or the boy," I replied drunkenly.

Henry saw me to the door of my lodgings and said, "Goodnight, John. Try and reflect, if you are willing, on your chosen life and all it brings, for your natural brilliance is being extinguished by the lure of a dark, seductive pit where there is but little light and no sanity."

I closed the door and lit candles in my room. I sat and watched the flames flicker and my eyes were drawn to dark shadows on the walls swaying hideously and dancing menacingly about me. They seemed to be laughing and sneering, in anticipation of my inevitable fall.

The whole episode put me in such melancholy, I began to write down the thoughts in my head. I scribbled furiously the following lines…

꙳꙳

A Song

꙳꙳

Absent from thee I languish still;
Then ask me not when I return.
The straying fool 'twill plainly kill
To wish all day, all night to mourn.

Dear, from thine arms then let me fly,
That my fantastic mind may prove
The torments it deserves to try
That tears my fixed heart from my love.

When wearied with a world of woe
To thy safe bosom I retire
Where love and peace and truth does flow,
May I contented there expire,

Lest, once more wandering from that heaven,
I fall on some base heart unblest,
Faithless to thee, false, unforgiven,
And lose my everlasting rest.

꙳꙳

I sat and stared, reflecting on the verse before me and saw the image of a gaunt, weary face with sadness in its eyes. This pale reflection eyed me from a looking glass on the table. It was a man of but two and twenty years.

CHAPTER NINE

The Heir Apparent

Late in the year 1670, Elizabeth's screams resounded around the house and chilled the already cold winter rooms at Adderbury. I sat close to the large open fire in our parlour, longing for the screams to cease and for all to be well. Finally, after many hours of torment, and the constant toing and froing of the servants and midwife, silence filled the house. Silence that is but for the cry of a newborn baby.

Martha came running down the stairs, her white smock covered in blood, but with such a happy smiling face, that I knew all was well.

"Mother and baby are fine, my Lord," Martha assured me.

I ran up the stairs to the room where Elizabeth lay exhausted but with tears of happiness in her eyes.

"John! Oh John, it's a boy!" she cried.

I ran over, held her in my arms and kissed her flushed cheeks.

"Let me see my son," I said to the midwife.

She gently picked up a small bundle wrapped neatly in a soft white sheet and walking over to us placed the child in my arms. I was overcome with joy at the birth of this, my first son.

"All is truly well with him?" I asked of the midwife.

"Yes, my Lord. All is well. He is a very healthy little boy."

I decided on the name Charles for my heir and arranged his baptism at Adderbury Church for the Second of January. I had informed the King of my son's birth and had invited my closest friends to the christening. I had asked Henry Savile and Charles Sedley to be godfathers, and they had gladly accepted. Charles

Sackville was to attend as the King's representative. To my great disappointment though, Henry had later given a disappointing excuse for his not being able to attend, which saddened me greatly. My wife too was absent, for she now embraced the Catholic faith for reasons of her own choosing. Following the birth of Charles, Elizabeth's moods were most unpredictable and she was either inclined to melancholy, or to irritated quarrelling. To rid me of this tedious difficulty, I proposed that my wife visit friends in London and there to enjoy a play or two, or whatever inclined to her fancy. Anon, Elizabeth left Adderbury, and I was at peace for a time.

Before her return, I had already departed for London myself, travelling with Sedley and Buckhurst after their sojourn at Adderbury. My own stay in the city proved, as often, to be an extended one.

๛

Soon after my arrival, I visited the Pall Mall studio of Mary Beale, as I had a whim to a portrait of myself. This I would send to Elizabeth, instructing for it to be hung in our bedchamber, in the hope that my presence in our house, if only on canvas, would be of comfort to her in my absence.

I found the artist at work in an upstairs room of her charming house, where its large windows let in a clear, north light. The overwhelming stink of oil paint and all manner of concoctions fumed into my nose and throat but, in the course of time, I became oblivious to this inconvenience. There were many paintings placed along a wall, all in differing stages of completion. Mary introduced me to her husband Charles, himself an accomplished artist who, after abrupt dismissal from his post at the Patents Office, now worked tirelessly for his wife. He would purchase the materials of her trade and spend many hours crushing and mixing with precision the costly pigments. Charles also kept a keen eye on the family's finances and maintained his daybook and ledger meticulously.

Their two young sons, Bartholomew and Charles, were also employed in their parents' trade. At an early age both of them had shown a natural aptitude for art. Charles showed the greater interest as an artist, but Bartholomew's foremost passion came to be medicine and, in time, he was apprenticed to an eminent physician.

On viewing Mary's work, I had been greatly impressed and could see she was a fine portraitist. Compared to the work of her very good friend Sir Peter Lely, Court Painter to His Majesty, her paintings demonstrated a subtle softness and realism that appealed to me. An appointment was made for early the next morning.

પ્ર

"Please, Lord Rochester. Do try to sit still for a further few moments and I will have the preliminary sketch finished," insisted Mrs. Beale.

"I am not the most patient of men madam, and find it most difficult to sit motionless for more than a short time," I retorted.

At that, she, with her grubby, blackened hands, placed the piece of charcoal on the ledge of her easel.

"Well, my Lord, I think that will be enough for today. I believe a further sitting tomorrow will be sufficient for me to complete the portrait without further inconvenience to you. I will send word when it is finished, so that you may arrange payment and collection, provided you are fully satisfied with it."

"Madam, I have no doubt in my mind that the portrait will prove worthy of display."

On the painting's arrival later at Adderbury, with my strict instructions as to the hanging of it, Elizabeth was not pleased. She wrote an angry letter to me and in it protested that my portrait was no comfort to her in her barren bed, and so was no substitute for my absence.

ھے

In early summer of the following year, Elizabeth received pressing news regarding her estate at Enmore. We were compelled to travel with our two young children on the long journey to Somerset. The children found the travelling most arduous and were constantly irritable. The interior of the coach was stifling, and the incessant jolting and bumping over dry rutted roads had done nothing for their comfort, the poor accommodation each night at the inns only adding to their distress.

At last we weary travellers arrived at Enmore. Elizabeth's trusty family retainer, Old Shepherd, and the servants welcomed us and attended to our needs with plentiful food, drink and all comforts. Our children's bedchamber was very pretty, with bright tapestry hangings on two of the walls. There was a carpet covering the dark-stained floorboards, woven in fine wool and dyed in rich colours of blue and red. The window hangings were of crimson red silk. In the corner of the room was a half-sized, oak four-poster bed. It was furnished with pale green silk hangings and embroidered thereon were red and pink roses. This exquisite bed had been commissioned specially for Anne's earlier first visit to Enmore. At the opposite end of the room was, for our son, a beautifully carved large oak cot that, like Anne's bed, had been specially crafted. The carving upon the cot was of the highest quality: intertwined oak leaves and acorns adorned its sides; the canopy had been set meticulously with galloping horses and hunting dogs giving chase to stags; and at its foot were two small pinnacles each topped with a beautifully worked miniature pineapple. The pillows and sheets were of the finest white linen and there were quilted silk top covers, red and pink for Anne and blue for Charles.

The children were soon fast asleep, and looked most contented in their new surroundings.

Elizabeth and I made our way downstairs to the large hall and sat awhile talking with dear Old Shepherd. The children were the main subject of our conversation and he remarked particularly on Anne's exceptionally kind nature and intelligence, rare in one so young. Our daughter was a beauty, with fair hair falling in tiny curls around her face, and her large blue-green eyes were ever bright and full of life.

Charles was only eighteen months old, but was already showing signs of becoming a bright and studious boy. When awake he was never still, always alert and walking and talking, or playing with his tiny wooden dolls and small wooden bricks. Some of the bricks were carved with castellations and with these he would create a child's Enmore. During his miserable time of teething, Elizabeth would sit him on her knee and hold a small piece of pink coral for him to bite upon, so as to encourage the tooth to pierce the gum. This was the only time Charles sat quietly and although in pain, often shedding a few tears, he bravely accepted his ordeal.

The months ahead were hectic at Enmore. Elizabeth's estate duties kept her very busy. She also had need to travel and visit the various tenanted farms, for the rent had not been increased for the last five years and a review was long overdue. The tenants and their families showed no welcome for what was but a small increase, but Elizabeth in her formidable, persuasive manner had them agreeing to her demands. The rent that each family paid was governed by the years each had resided and worked on the estate. Service ranged from twenty down to three years, and the longer the time served the less the rent, and so too the increase. However, this unexpected expense had not arrived at the best of times for any of them. The previous year's very hot, dry summer had unfortunately made for slow growth of the crops, particularly the hay forage for the farm animals. As a result had come a harsh winter shortage of animal feed and of food for the tenants' tables. Much of their livestock was of necessity undersold at the nearby Bridgwater market to enable their families to survive the long winter months. The spring of 1672 had proven more favourable and the summer was set fair, so the harvest was likely to be plentiful. Nonetheless, the tenants were working very hard to ensure recovery from the last year's heavy losses.

As a result of my marriage to Elizabeth, and with the Malets' eminence in Somerset, I was to be appointed Deputy Lord Lieutenant of the county. I would thus be expected to travel around Somerset meeting various dignitaries and wealthy landowners. The appointment was most felicitous, for I was becoming ever more fractious by the confines of Enmore and family life, and so I decided to introduce myself before my official appointment.

I was away for two weeks of unshackled freedom, travelling with two companions throughout the county, passing the villages of Curry Mallet, Sutton Mallet and Shepton Mallet, these all bearing testimony to Elizabeth's ancestral roots and wealth. In time, we made for Glastonbury, our destination being the slopes of the Tor. The coach halted as near to the foot of the hill as was possible, where we alighted and walked to the very top of the Tor itself. We were all very breathless by the time we reached the summit, and not a little dizzy, but the view was well worth the effort. We stood looking out as far as the eye could see, with the Polden Hills in the distance to the southwest and the imposing Mendip Hills to the north. At length, we made our way down the hill, climbed into the coach and travelled on towards Bridgwater. Dusk was soon descending upon us and so we stopped at a village on the Bridgwater Road. Here we would stay for the night and travel on the following morning.

We were made welcome at the village inn, where I for one wished to keep my identity unknown, and so gave a fictitious name. There were only two rooms available, so my two friends shared one and I took the other. We ate heartily, and fortunately the innkeeper kept a good cellar, and so we fell to drinking each other's health.

The innkeeper's two daughters served at table. Both were young, very pretty and very naïve. I set a wager with one of my friends as to who would be the first to bed one of these pretty creatures. The third of our company showed no interest at all, for he preferred the company of men, and was already busy making the acquaintance of a young fellow who had been sitting alone at table. I for my part knew I had already won the gamble, for my other friend, although a man of older years with an eye for a pretty lady, had not the skill that my younger years had gleaned me in the art of wooing women.

Of the two, I had my eye set on the dark-haired sister called Constance. Before long, she was happily sitting on my knee and telling me about her hopes and dreams of marrying a rich Gentleman, so ending her days of drudgery as an innkeeper's daughter.

Her father, smiling, looked on at her innocence and remarked, "Constance daydreams all day long, Sir, of some handsome Lord abducting her and stowing her away in his castle. Her imagination often interferes with her work. Leave the gentleman be Constance and get on with your duties."

I gazed across to the innkeeper and said, "An innocent daydream for Constance, but a most hazardous undertaking for any Lord, I fear."

My competitor, sitting at the opposite end of the table looking somewhat dejected, had barely caught the attention of the other sister, who also seemed content to be in my fun-loving company.

Smiling, I looked at him and said discretely, "You might as well pay me now."

Laughing, he said, "Not until morning, Sir."

Later in the evening, I feigned tiredness, so I wished goodnight to my friends and made way to my room. I undressed, climbed into bed, snuffed out the candle and waited for the expected knock at the door.

The knock came and I called, "Enter."

To my great surprise, both girls, with flushed cheeks and giggling uncontrollably, stood in the doorway.

"Come in and shut the door," I said.

What then followed were hours of such sexual pleasure that even I could not have imagined. During the act of intimacy with one girl I wondered how I would find the strength to continue with the next, but strength I found and enjoyed each girl in turn and turn again. At last, we grew tired and exhausted and we fell to sleeping, with legs and arms entwined like a pit of resting snakes.

Early morning came, and the creaking of my bedchamber door awakened me. There stood my two male companions peering around the doorframe at the heap of debauched forms on the bed, and I will never forget the look of sheer astonishment on their faces. "Good morning, gentlemen," I said in a quiet voice.

"Good morning, my Lord," echoed one of them.

Fortunately, the girls were still fast a sleeping, so they did not hear the term 'my Lord'.

"I shall be down shortly, gentlemen." I said quietly, and whispered to the one, "So have ready the fruits of our wager that you owe, only doubled if you please, sir."

I arose, washed my face and quickly dressed. I quit the room and left the two pretty maids sleeping very contentedly. Hurriedly, we paid the landlord, thanked him for his generous hospitality and boarded coach.

As the coach pulled away, we heard the innkeeper shouting for the whereabouts of his daughters who, after sleeping late, were not at their usual duties and were in grave trouble indeed. My friend, although poorer in his purse, remarked on how privileged he was to be travelling in the company of such a magnificent debaucher.

My business in Bridgwater concluded, and our travels together being at an end, I bade farewell to my friends and boarded a coach back to Enmore, Elizabeth and my beloved children. On my arrival, Elizabeth rushed out and greeted me with the grave news that Charles had not been well these past two days. The child had become feverish and at first they had thought it to be another tooth breaking through but when one had not appeared, they had realized his fever was more serious. A physician had been brought in to attend upon the boy and Elizabeth had been advised to bathe the child at regular intervals to cool his burning little body. We held vigil all that night in great anguish for Charles, for the fever would not abate. Elizabeth prayed in earnest throughout, while I sat solemn next to the boy. Thankfully however, by morning he seemed a little eased and was able to sip a drop or two of warmed milk infused with honey and sage. By mid-day, the poor boy's fevered sweating had subsided, and to our great relief he started to make a steady recovery.

Guilt weighed heavily on my mind over Charles's illness. As the child had lain in the arms of his loving mother fighting for life, I had lain in the arms of two filthy whores not knowing the plight of my son, who I love dearly above all things. The cause of his malady was not known but alas, it was to become all too apparent on his progression into boyhood.

With our visit to Enmore at an end, we prepared to travel back; Elizabeth and the children to Adderbury and I to London to resume bedchamber duties and to meet with friends so sorely missed these past months.

CHAPTER TEN

Fooling and Duelling

On arriving in London, I first made for my secondary lodgings in Portugal Row, which I seldom used, and only then for illicit purposes.

Unfortunately, saddled with an increase in rent, I would soon relinquish these rooms, with some reluctance. The lodgings were dreary and damp, so I ordered my servant, who lived there during my visits, to light fires and candles to make all warm and wholesome again.

"With what coal?" the servant asked impertinently.

"The coal in the cellar, you fool."

"But that was used up long since, my Lord."

"Then replace it immediately, before I replace you."

The servant left the room to comply, and jibing replied, "Credit as usual, my Lord?"

"Of course credit, you damned fool. Do you think I would trust the likes of you with coinage?" I scowled as I left, telling him I would be back in a couple of days.

I travelled on to Whitehall to find Henry and George, and I came across the two scoundrels walking the matted gallery, conversing on the latest plays at the King's Theatre, and on how puffed up Killigrew was with his latest play's success.

"I hope your talk is not of me, you dogs," I said, tongue in cheek.

Startled, they turned and, laughing, Henry replied, "There are no words foul enough for you, Rochester."

"How was your new appointment in Somerset?" George asked.

"Almost incessantly dull. Though it did have certain attractions," I answered, with a wry smile.

"To the Harp and Bull then!" declared Henry.

"And you can tell all!" said George.

"Very well then, gentlemen. Indeed I have a tale to make even you gasp."

In the tavern, we drank each other's health and discussed the latest news: my revelatory tales; the goings on at Whitehall; and how well, or otherwise, the public were receiving the plays at the King's and Duke's. Henry and George lamented how dull the theatre had become these past two years, since Nell's retirement from the stage and her subsequent service in the King's bed. They told me of a party they had attended only a week before at Nell's sumptuously decorated house in Pall Mall, her permanent residence since becoming the King's highly prized mistress.

"'Tis a pity you were not back a week ago, John. You would have enjoyed the evening immensely. Nell's beauty and wit abounded, and the guests included handsome Monmouth and the flamboyant Buckingham," Henry imparted with great relish.

George added, "Buckingham arrived half-drunk with the smelliest, ugliest whore in London on his arm; the evening's entertainment was secured. We left in the early hours, but heard that the guests had continued their revels until six of the clock in the morning, when all left for their beds to sleep for many hours that following day."

❧

With my current bedchamber duties at and end, it was now October and time for me to leave the warmth of London society for the cold isolation of Adderbury. I arrived home on the fifth day of the month and was greeted with the usual enthusiasm of my beloved family.

Elizabeth's journey home from Enmore had been without incident, and my son Charles now seemed fully recovered from his fevered ordeal. Anne was so pleased to see me that tears streamed from her eyes as her tiny arms hugged me so tightly around my neck.

She whispered in my ear, "Father, I have missed you so very much."

Martha having put Anne and Charles to bed, Elizabeth and I retired to our parlour. She had missed my company over the last four weeks and we talked at length. She was, as usual, curious of the latest Court gossip, which she loved to hear on my returns: who now held the King's favour? who was his latest mistress? was the Queen still as solemn as ever? and whose play was the best in town?

My ever-resourceful wife had wasted no time on her return and ensured that food and other provisions; wine, coal, candles and bed linen, were all in order for my arrival. She eagerly showed me an invitation we had received from Lady Wroxton to her Twelfth Night celebration at Wroxton Hall. Elizabeth had responded that the Rochesters would attend, for she knew that I would endorse her decision, I rarely turning down an invitation to a gratis drink.

The following week we travelled to Chipping Norton and after a night's rest at the Norton's Falcon, a coaching inn renowned for its very good fare, we made our way to Stow. There, the shopkeepers were making busy for the Christmas festivities with their shops well stocked in seasonal fare.

In the square at Stow, there was a toyshop. Although small and unassuming, this shop and its owners were famous throughout England. There was no other toy maker in the country with talent enough to produce such exquisite work and they received commissions from notable families from far and wide.

These famed proprietors were Samuel and Dinah Notgrove together with their two sons, Willersey and Draycott. This illustrious family crafted magnificent hand worked toy horses, carriages, dolls' houses and dolls. Although costly, their wooden toys were the most beautiful I had ever seen. The Notgroves were an interesting and eccentric family. Their likely wealth was never evident, for they lived simply, being completely absorbed in their craft and seeming to have no interest in material gain. A large part of their earnings must have gone by way of purchasing the very best seasoned woods money could buy.

They made us most welcome as we entered the tiny shop and proudly escorted us to their workshop at the rear, where the two sons were sat at a long wooden bench surrounded by their razor sharp carvers' tools. These implements were used so skilfully to create, from solid blocks and planks of wood, amazing works of art. This was all the more remarkable for the fact that the elder of the sons, Willersey, had years before, when a young boy of only nine, been tragically trampled in the square by a runaway horse and cart. His left arm had been badly crushed in the accident. Fortunately, he had survived the ordeal but it had left him with little use in his arm and hand. He made best use though of the damaged arm, by it aiding to guide his right hand through the more intricate movements of the chisel, with the piece he was working on held firmly in a vice. The finished articles belied this young man's physical disadvantage.

Draycott, on the other hand, was a very strongly built young man, the tallest of all the Notgroves. It was his job not only to carve occasionally, but also first to saw and then to prepare the chosen pieces to their preliminary shape, with mallet and chisels, in readiness for the more intricate work.

Samuel had taught his sons their craft from an early age, just as his own father had taught him. Sadly though, his sight was now impaired through age and the constant strain of many years' close work, often in candlelight and late into the evening, although he still managed with the aid of a water-glass magnifier to produce fine work.

Presently, we were shown into the finishing room, a small chamber off the workshop, where Dinah worked. She meticulously smoothed the wooden objects, and then polished them to a high lustre with beeswax infused with a secret ingredient known only to the Notgroves.

We commissioned a small toy coach and four for Charles, and a doll for Anne. Dinah then showed Elizabeth a pattern book with hand painted designs of clothes, to be fashioned especially for their dolls in a fabric shop further around the square. The proprietor there was a French seamstress who employed three young women working in a backroom of her shop for many long hours each day. They would cut out, using intricate patterns, the parts for small dresses from an array of hand printed silk, satin and cotton fabrics. The dresses were carefully hand-stitched and were as perfect in every detail as any full sized garment.

"Pink or yellow, John?" asked Elizabeth, looking through the book.

"You choose, Elizabeth. You have far more idea than I do when it comes to women's attire."

"Pink it is then." And she ordered a pink satin dress, together with matching hat and with calf leather gloves and tiny boots, for Anne's doll.

Before leaving the shop, we secured our commissions by a deposit of fifteen shillings, the balance of two pounds nineteen shillings to be paid on delivery. These toys were expensive, with the coach and four at two pounds eight shillings and the doll at one pound six shillings, but these superior, unique toys justified their expense. The toys were to be delivered to Adderbury during the first week of December, and we expressed our wish for the parcels to be well disguised, in case the prying eyes of our children might spy their arrival. The parcels would be safely and secretly stored in a lofty cupboard until Christmas, when Anne and Charles would receive their exceptional gifts.

On leaving the Notgroves', we continued along the square and Elizabeth purchased a pie from the local cook shop for our supper. I, in the meantime, crossed the square to Porter's the stationers to purchase paper, ink and quills, for London stationers are outrageously expensive.

Our business concluded, we boarded coach back to Chipping. With the weather now turning cold and wet, we looked forward to reaching there, to a warm and welcoming fire in our room and to a supper of venison pie.

❧

Christmas at Adderbury and Twelfth Night at Wroxton Hall proved to be most enjoyable. The sight of Charles's and Anne's excited faces, when we presented them with their very special presents, was the true highlight of our festivities. The children were so delighted with their toys that, when it was time for their beds, they begged not to be parted from them. We reluctantly agreed that they would be allowed to sleep with their presents for just two nights. After that time, the toys were to be placed carefully in the oak chest in their room when bedtime came.

Since my return at the beginning of October, Elizabeth and I had been most agreeable to each other, and a special closeness and intimacy had returned over this time. As my cure was long since secured, I now felt content to lay with her.

❧

By March 1674, my wife was five months into her pregnancy with our third child. She bloomed with health, and was so looking forward to the birth in July. Preparations were being made for an upstairs room to be decorated and furnished for the arrival. The nursery bedroom, in which Charles and Anne slept and played, would prove far too crowded with a third child. In time, on Charles's fourth birthday, this newly decorated and furnished room would become his, and our third child would be moved to the nursery room to share with Anne, who would then be nearly six years old and have begun her education at home at Adderbury. As a girl, in preparation of a future good marriage, she would begin with light domestic duties under Elizabeth's watchful eye, including helping to care for her young sibling.

One Monday morning, Elizabeth lay long in bed after a restless and uncomfortable night, she now feeling tired with her swollen belly and with her back continually aching from the strain of it all.

A letter arrived for me from the Marshall at the House of Lords, summoning me to a meeting with him on the following Friday. This summons was not one I could think to ignore, for I knew full well the reason for it. I made some furtive excuse that I was required there to vote on some urgent matter and the following day I left for London.

The reason for this secrecy was that my summons pertained to my impending duel with Robert Constable, Viscount Dunbar. Our paths had seldom crossed until one evening, during my last London visit, an argument and scuffle had taken place between George and the Viscount outside the King's Theatre. George being of a gentle, passive nature had tried his utmost to calm down the situation but Dunbar was having none of it. In a rage, he had run his sword clean through George's left arm. George, collapsing in agony, was bleeding profusely and I had rushed immediately to my friend's aid. Then, as passers-by were helping George, I confronted the bastard Dunbar on this rash and injurious action. Dunbar had taken offence at this, and announced that the prig deserved it.

"So you are judging George by your own standards," I had said.

"You impudent rake!" Dunbar had retorted.

Hence, the duel had been set, with time and venue to be arranged. Then, with George staggering back onto his feet, clutching his wounded arm and looking pale and shocked, he and I had taken coach to Whitehall and to his lodgings there. I had summoned one of the Court physicians, Dr. Bartholomew Morall, to attend him and to stitch the gaping wound in his arm.

"You are a lucky man." the physician had sneered, "Fortunately for you, the bone was not shattered. The healing will take time, but you will eventually mend well enough."

Dr. Morall is well known for his abhorrence of injuries caused unnecessarily by men's vanity and anger. It has been known for him to attend the victim of a duel then, when becoming aware of the circumstances of the injury, he would bluntly refuse to help. The wounded party would be told to summon some other physician whose ethics were perhaps agreeable and who would be prepared to make good the consequences of man's egotistical folly. Meanwhile, the casualty often as not bled to death whilst awaiting the assistance of another.

Once in London, on the appointed day, I attended the Marshall and was ordered to abandon the duel with Dunbar. He informed me that if I did not adhere to this demand, I would be duly arrested and imprisoned in the Tower. The choice was simple, as I had spent more time than I cared for in that damnable place before, and the duel was abandoned.

CHAPTER ELEVEN

Elizabeths All

On the Thirteenth of July 1674, as the bells of St. Mary's pealed out across Adderbury, I entered the church with family and friends, where we sat in our pew to await the arrival of the vicar. We were there for the baptism of our third child who was to be christened Elizabeth after her mother, but we would lovingly call her Lizbet, so as to avoid the confusion of having two of the same name in our family.

During the long drawn out service, I found some difficulty in focusing my eyes to the reading of the prayers. I grew more anxious as the service progressed, but trusted that it was due to a trick of the candlelight.

At length, the baptism at an end, we all walked to my home on the far side of the village, where all attended the baptismal dinner. On this occasion, although not attending the baptism itself, Elizabeth was at the house to welcome guests each in turn as they arrived.

At six of the clock, when all the guests had left, Elizabeth and I spent time with Charles and Anne. We watched them playing happily with their toys, whilst Beatrice our wet-nurse attended to baby Lizbet's needs. The children soon grew very tired after their long day, and so were put to bed after we had kissed each of them in turn, wishing them a peaceful night. We then crossed the landing and entered baby Lizbet's nursery.

"She's a hungry child." said Beatrice, "She's sucked so hard on my milk breasts that my nipples are red raw."

"That's what you are paid for Beatrice. And I wager many a man has nibbled on those ripe cherries and made them red with pleasure."

Beatrice blushed and left the room giggling, with a sideways glance at me.

"John! Enough of that improper talk." chided Elizabeth, "For God's sake, remember you are at home with your family and not in some bawdy tavern with your debauched friends and common serving wenches."

An air of dreariness now filled the nursery. As I stood, Elizabeth knelt quietly by the cradle and offered a short prayer of thanks for Lizbet's safe arrival and for her continuing good health.

※

In the following January, freezing conditions gripped the country. Many of the roads were treacherous for weeks, either due to drifting snow or to such frozen rutting that neither horse nor carriage could negotiate them.

Our house at Adderbury was extremely cold, and coal fires burned continually in the fireplaces of every room in the endeavour to keep all warm. Even so, our hands and feet were forever ice cold, despite the wearing indoors of gloves and extra thick stockings.

The lake to the rear of our house was so thickly frozen that it became impossible to break the ice for the winter stocking of the icehouse, until perhaps at length we might be blessed with a thaw. My health was in decline during these bitter cold weeks and I came at first to believe that the bleak conditions must be the cause of my malady. After a time, I was plagued with a tormenting ache in my cods accompanied by pain whilst pissing, and this alarmed me much. It became all too apparent after all these years that I was once again in urgent need of Loveall's baths, but alas it was not possible to travel during these unrelenting freezing conditions. Elizabeth grew deeply concerned at my illness and begged for me to allow a visit from our local physician. This I adamantly would not agree to and made some feeble excuse that I possessed a morbid fear of country quacks. I told her that as a small boy I had often experienced the terrors of my mother's physician who, rather than alleviating my sickness, had made me altogether worse. I insisted that I would not be troubled with them. Mercifully, during the next week, my condition improved. This was entirely due to Elizabeth's care and herbal medicines she had given me in my infirmity. Along with my recovering state of health came the long awaited thaw, allowing the roads to be used once more. Travel nonetheless was still very precarious, for the frozen ruts now turned to runnels of deep, sticking mud.

With the freezing conditions now behind us, the household at Adderbury began to function quite normally again. The lake had now thawed sufficiently for ice to be gathered and placed in the icehouse, in readiness for the hot and humid summer months.

I was now feeling well enough to travel, with the ache in my cods thankfully eased. Nonetheless, I still felt pain when pissing, and to my alarm discovered a small red patch on my prick, which was very sore to the touch.

Over supper that evening, I told Elizabeth that I would be travelling to London the following morning. She looked perplexed and not a little angry at my unexpected announcement. I explained that, after being stranded at Adderbury by the weather for these several weeks, I was in urgent need of attending to business there.

"Then make sure you say goodbye to the children, John, before you leave, since we are never quite sure how protracted your stay will be," Elizabeth said with suspicion.

"Of course I will. You know how dear our children are to me."

"And your wife, John? Is she also dear to you?"

"More than you can ever imagine, my darling."

"It's my imaginings that worry me, John," Elizabeth replied, with sadness in her voice.

As I crossed the threshold of Loveall's doorway, my face and hands were clammy and I shivered with trepidation.

"Lord Rochester! It is many a year since I have had the pleasure of your company, but not so for others I fear, for that is the reason behind your return, is it not?" said the pompous Loveall, seated at his desk.

"Yes, Loveall, I am here for the cure. The root of my ill ease is no business of yours. I pay you handsomely to cure me, so I will have no more of your damned impertinent remarks."

"Well, my Lord, you know the procedure. Please undress, put on the robe and I will closely examine the offending part."

I lay on the bed at the back of the room, close by the window. From there I could view the garden, in which grew many species of plants and herbs, but here in the depths of winter, the garden looked without a doubt very dreary. He scrutinized all the parts of my body and seemed most concerned when I shouted out in pain as he pressed upon my lower bowel.

"And how long have you had these cankers on your member, my Lord?"

"Cankers? But I thought there was just the one!"

"No, my Lord. There appear to be three. To the bath then."

Loveall summoned his bully-boy attendants who escorted me to the bath and held me firm in the hot and steamy, mercurial hell.

As before, there was the need for two further sessions. Each time I entered the bath I pondered on the ensuing pain, and each time there vowed never again to lay with any pox-ridden whore whose enticing but fouled cunny ensured pleasure and disorder in equal measure.

I was forced to rest at my lodgings for three days until the nauseating effects of the potent mercury had subsided.

Feeling rallied in body, but ill at ease in mind, I was in dire need of distraction, so I dressed in my finest clothes and made way to the Duke's, to a play. As I entered the theatre and walked along its dimly lit corridors a voice rang out. I stopped and, turning, smiled at the woman standing there.

"So you do remember me, my Lord, though I am surprised that you do. After all, eight months is a bloody long time. I am older now and am no longer a silly girl of tender years, but a woman who knows her own mind, and what she wants from a lover," she chided.

"Mrs. Barry, my dearest. How could I ever forget such beauty and grace?"

"Pox on you, my Lord. I venture that you have not thought of me once during all this time," she replied with venom.

'What a fitting comment', I thought, and stepping closer to Beth, I embraced her and kissed her gently on the lips.

She smiled and said, "Well you are here now, and against my better judgement I will forgive you, though my head warns me not to."

After the play, Beth and I went by river making for the New Exchange. From there we walked to Covent Garden, taking a turn in the Rose Tavern. The Rose, situated conveniently adjacent to the Theatre Royal in Drury Lane, is a favourite of playwrights, actors, actresses and the like and is one of the most enjoyable taverns I know.

As we sat drinking and talking, Beth asked, "Will you be in the audience tomorrow, John?"

"Why?"

"Because I am in a play. It is only a small part, but I would be interested of your comments afterwards."

"Very well, Beth. I shall be at the theatre, and afterwards I will walk you to your lodgings and give you my considered opinion on your performance."

She left the tavern and made her way to the Duke's Theatre to continue rehearsals. I rose from my chair, but had the need to sit down again as a dizziness and sickness overcame me. The room seemed to darken and my eyes would not focus, no matter how hard I tried. At that moment in walked Thomas Betterton, co-manager with Henry Harris at the Duke's. Before long, Thomas spied me sitting in my dark corner in the most melancholic state.

"Rochester, my Lord. How do you fair?" asked Thomas, as he sat down next to me at the table. I raised my head, and he glancing at me with such sadness added, "Are you ill, my Lord?" he knowing full well the condition I endured, since my symptoms were becoming more than obvious to anyone but a blind man or a fool here in London, for the place was rife with the distemper.

"No, Thomas. I am quite well. Cured you see, quite cured."

"I have just spoken with Mrs. Barry in the street, Rochester, and she says you are attending the play tomorrow."

"Has her acting much improved, Thomas?"

"Well, a little. But I must be honest, not nearly enough. Her progress is very slow. She is no natural, and if she does not improve greatly in the next few weeks I am afraid it's the pit for her, and a basket of oranges."

"I am sorry to hear that. I truly believe she has something special, and with patient coaching could become the best," I replied.

"Her tuition as your mistress has not helped thus far." Thomas conjectured, with a hint of sarcasm in his voice, "It will hinder her performance greatly if she becomes ill as a consequence."

I was not only sick in body but also of this tedious conversation. As I stood and turned to leave, my dizziness had subsided, and turning to Thomas, I said, "She will do it. She will be great."

I left the Rose and took coach to my lodgings at Whitehall. Feeling drained and fatigued, I lay on my bed and fell into welcome sleep.

Morning came, and feeling somewhat refreshed and in far better spirits than I thought possible, I made my way to the Exchange, for I was in great need of a new pair of boots. The soles on my present pair had worn so thin that walking over the cobbled and loose-pebbled streets had become most hazardous and equally painful. I was on my uppers, and they were little better. I entered the shop of Nathaniel Stepping, the finest boot maker in London, and took to trying on various pairs for their fit. At that very hour, George walked by and chanced to look at the boots displayed in the window. Spying me, ill-balanced and struggling to put on one of my chosen new boots, he entered.

"Let me give you a hand, John. You seem to be having some difficulty."

"It's my balance, George. It just doesn't seem right this morning."

With George's help, the new boots were firmly in place and reluctantly poor Stepping agreed credit for the goods. George and I left, and by coach made our way to Dorset Gardens and to the Duke's. On entering, we paid the doorman and took our usual box. With time on our hands, we sat eating oranges, discoursing upon the present state of the King and his Court and how, at the old age of forty-four, he still had prick enough to satisfy his mistresses. Notwithstanding the abrupt absence of the troublesome Castlemaine, now honoured as the Duchess of Cleveland, there were still Nell and French Louise. With the Royal pimp Chaffinch busy as ever providing a never-ending supply of young gullible women by the back stairs, and with the hordes of bastards brought forth into the world by the King's own whores, there must surely be a fearful drain upon the Royal purse. And yet we agreed that his open display of dutiful love and affection for all his offspring must surely be commended.

"I think you will be disappointed, John," said George.

"Disappointed at what?"

"Mrs. Barry. There is a modest improvement in her acting, but in all honesty the audiences are never pleased with her, and if the house is half full this afternoon we shall be lucky."

"I shall see for myself, George. I have plans; plans to make her a great actress."

"It's not plans you need, John. It's a bloody miracle!"

"Then a miracle I shall perform."

George was not wrong. The small part that Beth played was quite frankly appalling. Fortunately, she had finished her piece as cruel heckling erupted. He turned and looked at me with knowing eyes and said, "You are not God, John."

"No. Not God, George, but bloody determined. Am I the only one who can spot the potential in Mrs. Barry? Believe me, George, I know she will soon be celebrated."

"John, your efforts will be wasted on such as her. Just keep the poor wretch as your mistress, and be satisfied at that."

I left, and met Beth backstage in the dimly lit, cramped and airless tiring-room.

"John, what do you think? Have I improved since the last time you saw me?"

"Yes, a little, Beth. Come, I will walk you to your lodgings and we will sup there on a pie and a bottle or two."

We ate the pie and drank the wine and discoursed over her shabby performance.

"But surely, I am more than a little better?" she asked.

"A little," I repeated, "but a very little."

The disappointment on Beth's beautiful face was as disheartening to me as my comments had been to her.

"You believe I love you dearly?" I said.

"Yes, my Lord, of course I do."

"I would like you for my mistress."

"I thought I already was."

"No! What happened months ago was mere lust on my part."

"But you said you loved me."

"Yes I do. I do truly love you above all things, Beth."

"I will willingly become your mistress, John, but I will not, at any price, abandon the stage and become mistress alone."

"I do not wish you to leave the stage, Beth. You can be both mistress and actress. The first requires no accomplishment, for you are a natural lover. But to become a talented actress? Now that is more of a challenge."

"But I know I can become great, John."

"Yes, I know it too, Beth. I always have. That is why I am willing, and not a little able, to help you achieve greatness with my instruction. But it will take time and patience."

With tears in her eyes, Beth flung her arms around me and kissed me with such sensuous emotion that I alone could know.

"But first, Beth, I must find new lodgings for you. I will attend to it tomorrow, so be ready to move your possessions, what few you have, by the day following. I will, when circumstances permit, reside there both as your doting lover and as your unfailing mentor."

∾∾

I turned the key to the door of Mrs. Barry's new lodgings in Wych Street. Although not lavish, the rooms were marginally more spacious than her previous quarters.

"Well here we are, Beth. Here is your small palace, madam. What think you?"

"Well, it's an improvement, but it is far from a palace," she replied.

The rooms, though small and cramped, were four in number and in need of decoration. There was a front sitting room and a back parlour and narrow stairs led to the first floor where two bedchambers were to be found, one of these overlooking the street, and the room at the rear looking out over the narrow alley beyond. The furniture was sparse, but I promised that in due course new furniture including a bed would arrive. However, for the time being she would needs be content with the interior and furnishings as they stood. Beth seemed pleased enough with the lodgings, particularly as they were so close to Dorset Gardens and but a short distance from the Duke's. Presently she busied herself unpacking and arranging her possessions, which though meagre soon gave the rooms a homely feel.

"Is there a cellar, John?"

"Yes I believe so, but only a small one."

"In keeping with the rest of the rooms then, John." she sneered, "Well, small or not, I hope it's full of coal."

"I will arrange for a delivery." I assured her, "I do not want my darling freezing to death in the winter now, do I?"

I persuaded Betterton, against his better judgement, for use of his stage for two hours a day, in pursuance of Mrs. Barry's tutelage. He still insisted that I was wasting my time on a so-called actress who was devoid of talent.

Nevertheless, I was a ruthless, unyielding taskmaster and very soon had driven Beth beyond the limits of even her endurance. Because of this, she fell ill with exhaustion and needed rest for two days. My training methods were bitterly opposed by both Betterton and gentle George. They were present at several of these gruelling sessions and mockingly remarked that I would surely snuff out any spark in Beth's performance, if indeed a glimmer could be found. I realized I had pushed her to the brink, so I tried a more subtle approach. I became ever more patient and not too overbearing. This new method worked surprisingly well, with Beth mistakenly assuming I had lost interest. She became aggressively self-confident and flew into rages, changing her conduct on stage capriciously, displaying such emotion at last and exposing her natural brilliance.

Betterton and George were decidedly shocked at this unexpected revelation. George in particular was spellbound.

"If I had not witnessed it with my own eyes, I would never have believed it, John. She is truly exceptional, remarkable in fact, and you alone could see it," he admitted.

"I see many things George, and my eyes are never deceived."

The elation I felt with her transformation was soon dampened by a jolting return to reality. I had received a letter from my wife, she expressing her sadness by my absence, and informing me that she had taken leave of Adderbury to travel with our children to her estate at Enmore. This sudden departure, she went on to explain, was in large part due to her annoyance and great anger at my mother's persistent meddling, which she could tolerate not a moment longer. My mother, who is well connected, with friends in London, had received word of my apparent liaison with an actress. She had, by means foul or fair, managed to obtain the name Mrs. Barry and, vindictively, had intimated this grave situation to Elizabeth. She not only blamed me for my infernal weakness for the female sex, but also chided Elizabeth for not being a good wife to her son and thus entirely incapable of preventing her husband from straying to the arms of an actress who was no more than a common whore.

I wrote immediately to Elizabeth at Enmore, expressing sympathies for her plight at my mother's outrageous behaviour. I assured her of my love and devotion and that the actress in question was simply being trained in the art of the stage, and no more. I wrote with such passion and tender love, begging her to travel back to Adderbury, where I would be returning shortly. I enclosed with the letter a short poem…

I am by fate slave to your will
And shall be most obedient still;
To show my love I will compose ye
For your fair finger's ring a posy,
In which shall be expressed my duty,
And how I'll be forever true t'ye;
With low-made legs and sugared speeches,
Yielding to your fair bum the breeches,

I'll show myself, in all I can,
Your faithful, humble servant,

Jan.

⌘

I also wrote to my mother at Ditchley and admitted to being in contact with a certain actress. However, I suggested that I was only directing the girl on her acting, and that such malicious rumours of infidelity on my part were not true. It was four weeks before she was inclined to write back, informing me of Elizabeth's return to Adderbury and from the tone of her letter, whether true or false, all seemed well there again.

My mind was now in a state of unrest. I had spent many weeks with Beth, and my great passion for her was becoming so overwhelming that her training for the stage was suffering. I was spending more time in her company in bed than out of it and her tiredness on stage during performances was all too evident. The guilt I was now feeling for the neglecting of my wife and children gnawed deep in my conscience when I was not in Beth's company.

It was now due time for my return to Adderbury, and so to face with courage what might still prove to be the wrath of a disbelieving mother and a wife tormented and saddened at the suggestion of my infidelities. I wrote to each of them to inform them of my intended return, but intimated that I would first be travelling to my residence at High Lodge for a few days, for I had business to attend to there.

I informed Beth of my imminent departure to Oxfordshire. She was saddened at the news of it, but agreed that it was inevitable, my having been parted from wife and children for such a long time. On the day of my going, in her little parlour in Wych Street, we held each other in a long and desperate embrace. Beth, by far the stronger, held back her tears but my own flowed uncontrollably.

"I will return very soon my sweetest love. I will be true to my word, if you be true to your heart," I said with deep sadness in my voice.

"I will be as true to your love as your heart desires, my Lord."

At that, I handed her a note and turning swiftly I left the room. On the note was written a poem…

❧

Why dost thou shade thy lovely face? Oh, why
Does that eclipsing hand of thine deny
The sunshine of the sun's enlivening eye?

Without thy light, what light remains in me?
Thou art my life, my way; my light's in thee;
I live, I move, and by thy beams I see.

Thou art my life; if thou but turn away,
My life's a thousand deaths; thou are my way;
Without thee, love, I travel not but stray.

My light thou art; without thy glorious sight
My eyes are darkened with eternal night.
My love, thou art my way, my life, my sight.

Thou are my way; I wander if thou fly;
Thou art my light; if hid, how blind am I.
Thou are my Life; if thou withdraw'st, I die.

My eyes are dark and blind, I cannot see;
To whom or whither should my darkness flee
But to that light? And who's that light but thee?

If that be all, shine forth and draw thee nigher;
Let me be bold and die for my desire:
A phoenix likes to perish in the fire.

If my puffed light be out, give leave to tine
My flameless snuff at the bright lamp of thine;
Ah! What's thy light the less for lighting mine?

If I have lost my path, dear lover, say,
Shall I still wander in a doubtful way?
Love, shall a lamb of Israel's sheepfold stray?

My path is lost; my wandering step does stray;
I cannot go nor safely stay;
Whom should I seek but thee, my path, my way?

And yet thou turn'st thy face away and fliest me,
And yet I sue for grace, and thou deniest me;
Speak, art thou angry, love or triest me?

Display those heavenly lamps or tell me why
Thou shad'st thy face, perhaps no eye
Can view their flames and not drop down and die.

Thou art the pilgrim's path and blind man's eye,
The dead man's life; on thee my hopes rely;
If I but them remove, I err, I die.

Dissolve thy sunbeams; close thy wings and stay;
See, see how I am blind and dead and stray;
Oh, thou that art my life, my light, my way.

Then work thy will; if passion bid me flee,

My reason shall obey; my wings shall be
Stretched out no further than from me to thee.

ॐ∙৯

Journeying home, I thought of my dearest Beth reading the poem and hoped it would bring some contentment to her sad and breaking heart in my damned enforced absence.

ॐ∙৯

Arriving at High Lodge, I felt alone and wretched, but my melancholy soon lifted, spending days out hunting with friends, and in the evenings drinking and gambling with them at Woodstock. They never missed the opportunity of a soirée with Rochester, for they were ever keen for his notorious wit, poems and satires; invariably of the King, his entourage of whores within and without Whitehall, the rakes, the pimps and the bawdy licentiousness of the Court.

Ensconced in the lodge, I soon received a letter from Elizabeth begging me either to return to Adderbury very soon or to oblige her by inviting her there. The latter would have been most disagreeable, and so I replied in a most husbandly affectionate manner. I told her of my regret for my time spent at the lodge, of my determination to return to Adderbury as soon as possible and how much I looked forward to seeing my beautiful wife and children, from whom I had been estranged for far too long. Two days later, I travelled there by coach and, as it drew up to the house, I peered out of the window and took a deep breath, ready for the onslaught in prospect.

CHAPTER TWELVE

Plays the Fool

"So you have arrived at last, John, and left your whore of an actress," said Elizabeth, as I entered my hall at Adderbury.

My return was on the First of April 1675, the day of my twenty-eighth birthday. Although not planned, it seemed as good a day as any to come back. I had hoped that Elizabeth would be pleased at my homecoming but alas, this was not the case. Her anger and scorn at recent events made for the most unwelcome of welcomes.

"Madam, I have returned to you and the children. Surely that merits some enthusiasm on your part."

"Enthusiasm for what, John, when you are rarely at home, and spend more time in London and at High Lodge than in the bosom of your family?"

"You know I have pressing matters in London and at Court and, together with my duties as Ranger at Woodstock, they leave me precious little time to spend with my family. And when I do so, as now, I expect to be welcomed back to my home, and not to be chided by a wife who should know better the minute I enter the house," I said, more calmly.

At that, I kissed Elizabeth and shouted for the servants to bring my children to me. I threw my hat and topcoat to the floor and made my way across the hall into the opposite room where were lit a welcoming fire and candles. Food and wine were already set on the table. I heard Elizabeth crying mournfully in the hall. She ran swiftly up the stairs to our bedchamber and slammed the door.

I sat alone at the table partaking of food and drink, when in walked Martha and another servant with the children. Little Anne ran across the floor, smiling with excitement. She jumped onto my lap and, as she always would, flung her arms around my shoulders.

Kissing my cheek, she said, "Oh, father, it is you! It is you! I have missed you so very much."

The two servants then walked over with Charles and Elizabeth, our two youngest.

"Let me see my son. Is he well? He looks well enough."

"Oh yes, my Lord." Martha replied, "Charles is very well."

I set Anne down and Martha placed Charles in my arms. I sat gazing at my beautiful son, for beautiful he certainly was. Charles was growing into a stunning boy, with clear, bright eyes and a perfect skin. He was by far the prettiest boy I had ever set my eyes upon.

"Hello, Charles, how are you my son?" I spoke softly.

His little arms reached out and touched my face and he smiled so sweetly, and replying said "I am very well father. And you, sir? Are you well too?"

"Yes, Charles, I am well."

'When I again forsake Adderbury, for leave I must and tear myself away from my darling boy, it will without doubt cause me much torment', I thought.

"And how is young Lizbet, Martha?"

"She is fine, my Lord. A very robust baby. See for yourself."

Martha then took Charles from my lap and placed Lizbet there. I had seen but little of Lizbet since she had been born, but I could see now that she was growing into a very pretty child and seemed far sturdier than either Anne or Charles had been when they were her age.

Presently, it was time for the children to be taken to their beds, so I kissed each in turn and said my goodnights.

I, glass in hand, sat by the fireside supping wine and stared into the fire's flames. Were they the flames of hell or the flames of passion? As wine flowed through my veins, desire ignited and, unable to resist its potency, my thoughts turned to Beth: 'was she on *her own? was she with company? was she in despair at my absence? or was she quietly laughing with friends at my expense and confiding in them every detail of our intimacy?'*

The hour was now getting late, and the flames had drawn back to shimmering embers. Feeling weary with remorse I retired to bed, not as I had hoped to the warmth of our bedchamber with my wife, but to the loneliness and singular coldness of the adjoining room.

Next morning, I lay long in bed sleeping off the effects of excessive liquor. With bright morning light piercing the window, I awoke and could hear the muffled sound of voices. It was Elizabeth at her morning's toilette, talking with her maid.

A knock came upon the door and I bade whoever it was to enter. The door opened slowly, and in walked Elizabeth.

"Good morning, John, I hope you slept well?"

"Yes, surprisingly I did, Elizabeth. And how did *you* sleep, my dear?"

"A troubled sleep, John, with my mind in turmoil."

She closed the door behind her. She was wearing a fine embroidered silk cream dress. Her hair fell in attractive delicate curls upon her pretty face. Smiling, she walked over to me and kissed me softly on the lips.

She whispered, "Let us pretend that last night never was. I have prayed for the return of my dear husband for so very long. Trusting that you would be willing, I have arranged for us to take coach tomorrow to Burford. We will be away for some three days, so as to spend a little time together. I thought you would like to visit the Grammar School, and I hear tell that the church there now has a wonderful new stained-glass window. John, please say you are willing."

Smiling, I kissed her and said, "Of course I am willing. I too have longed for us to be together."

I then asked her to summon the servants to prepare the coach for our journey ahead, and called others to make ready my clothes and to dress me.

ও৲ও

It was a beautiful spring morning. There was welcome warmth in the sun, and in our garden spring foliage was bursting forth.

Our coach pulled out from Adderbury at nine of the clock in the morning. The day was set fair for a most pleasant journey to Chipping Norton where we were to stay for the first evening. We travelled through the tiny hamlet of Bloxham, then on to Milcombe, then on further to Hook Norton passing though Great Roll Rich and on again towards Little Roll Rich. The journey was most pleasing, reminding us of our covert coach rides many years before through London's parks.

We ordered a halt to the coach some half a mile distant from the village of Little Roll Rich, giving our coachman, servant and horses a welcome rest. There, Elizabeth and I alighted and walked a short distance to view the famous circle of the Roll Rich Stones. These ancient standing stones, some of them taller than a man, were an enchanting sight to see. Their history is nowhere clearly defined, but it is believed they have stood there in all their majesty for many centuries. It is said locally that their number can never be counted, as they are thought bewitched, but Elizabeth and I were determined to prove the contrary.

"Shall we walk around the stones and count them together, John?"

"No. We shall count them separately. I shall stand in the middle of the ring and you start to count from a stone of your choosing. When you return to that point, tell me how many you have counted."

"Very well, John."

Elizabeth walked slowly, carefully counting each stone in turn and on completing the circle she announced, "Sixty-three, John! There are sixty-three stones. It's your turn now."

So then Elizabeth took my place and I started to count them, commencing at the tallest. I walked on purposefully, making sure I would not miscount any stone. As I arrived back at the tallest stone I shouted, "Sixty-four, Elizabeth. I have counted sixty-four."

"But I counted sixty-three, John."

"Well count them again. You must have missed one."

So again I stood in the centre while she counted with deliberation each stone in turn. This time she came to the conclusion that there were sixty-five. This was a mystery to us both, and so I now repeated my journey around the circle, and finished on sixty-two.

Eventually, tired-out with walking and counting and with no harmonious conclusion, we settled that the legend concerning the tallying of the stones must be true.

Walking back to the coach, we laughed upon the event, I believing that neither of us had ever felt so happy and contented as we did then.

"You look so well today, John. I declare that I have not seen the warm hue in your cheeks and the brilliance in your eyes for such a long time."

"Madam, I feel as well as I have for many a day. The clean country air has no doubt played its part, but your company is the best of tonics for me. Not until my wife imparts a kiss with those sensuous lips of hers will I walk a step further."

Elizabeth and I kissed, and afterwards stood motionless holding each other close and I could feel Elizabeth's heart pounding in that intimate moment. We walked slowly back to the coach, uttering not a single word. We were happy and content in the hush.

We climbed into the waiting coach and continued our journey, through Little Roll Rich and on to Chipping Norton. The horses, well rested, made good pace for many a mile, until brought to a gentle walk to ease their tired limbs. As the coach now trundled slowly along the narrow Oxfordshire lanes, I spied a young boy with his ox and plough in a field, turning a strip of land, and I ordered our coach to a halt.

I alighted and walked over to this most handsome of boys, who must have been no more than twelve. I thought how hard the boy must toil for his meagre living, for I at that age was entering Wadham. Yet his physique was so extraordinary for one so young, reflecting that of an older man.

He ordered the ox to stop and bade me, "Good day, Sir."

"And a good day to you, young man. A fine hornéd beast you have there. When did you begin your labours today?"

"By six of the clock, Sir, I was in the field ploughing my furrows."

"And very straight and neat they are too." I replied, "At what age did you first labour on the land?"

"When I was eight years old, Sir, but now that I am eleven, I am a grown man and well used to my toils," he replied boldly.

I liked the look of this youth, with his large trusting eyes and innocent smile, but alas, I had not time to prolong the acquaintance. The boy asked where I was travelling, he apparently never having stepped more than a mile or two down the lane beyond his village. I told him I was journeying to Chipping Norton and at this, I opened my purse and gave the boy six pennies for which, with sheer delight and not a little shyness, he gratefully thanked me. We both knew he would needs work many a long hour at the plough to have another six pennies safely in his pocket.

Before parting company, I looked into the boy's large, clear eyes and softly spoke, "If only there were time enough."

Smiling, I turned and walked back to the waiting coach and boarded it, commanding our coachman to continue.

Elizabeth, inquisitive as ever, questioned why I had troubled to go over to the ploughboy. I replied that I had a mind to speak with the youth, being simply curious as to where he lived and to how long he had worked upon the land.

"He was very handsome, was he not, John?" Elizabeth suggested.

"As handsome as ever I have seen for one so young," I said distantly.

I looked wistfully out of the coach window, gazing back at the boy striding behind his beast's hazy vapour, until their mist grew faint and disappeared forever.

In course of time, we pulled up alongside the Norton's Falcon, and we made our way inside. We requested of the landlord that he show us the best vacant room, where we would take bed for the night.

The first floor room was well enough, clean and in good order. The landlord handed me the key to the room and our servant placed our belongings therein. I then asked him to have our supper prepared and brought to our room, I willing to pay a small additional charge for this service. Before long our supper arrived, and it did not disappoint. The meat was fresh cooked and the syllabub that followed was the best we had ever tasted. The wine too was of excellent quality and I called for a second bottle. The first, we had emptied swiftly, for we had not drunk awhile, and after our Roll Rich adventure we had an extreme thirst for the quenching. With our bellies full, and we not a little intoxicated, we were soon overcome by drowsiness and so retired to our bed, falling at once to a deep contented sleep.

ॐॐ

"John? John, are you awake?" Elizabeth quietly called, whilst at the same time shaking my shoulder, "John? John, are you awake?" she repeated, whispering.

"Yes, Elizabeth. Just. What is the matter?"

"I can hear a rat in the corner of the room. It's gnawing away at a floorboard. Please, John, find it and kill it. I cannot possibly rest with that damned thing in the room."

"You have encountered rats before, Elizabeth. Go back to sleep. It will soon slink off to its filthy nest."

"Yes, John, I have come across many rats but rarely in our bedchamber. Please, John, I beg of you. Kill it."

"Very well, Elizabeth."

I dragged myself out of bed, lit a candle and staggered as quietly as I could across the room, with the wine still running in my veins, all the time knowing that my reactions would be far slower than the rat's. I unsheathed my short sword and crept slowly to the corner where Elizabeth had heard it. Presently, I spied the filthy creature with my half-closed, bleary eyes. It was facing the corner and so was unaware of my approach as I crept stealthily towards my prey. At one point I saw two rats, this deception due to my drunken state, and in the blink of an eye, the pair became one again. I crept now as close as I dare and, taking a deep breath, I brought the sword down swiftly upon the rat, which gave forth a chilling squeal. I had sliced its body clean through, and as it lay there in two separate halves the damned rat was no more.

I wiped the blood from my sword with the lining of the window hangings and replaced it in its sheath. Staggering across the room, I fell into bed, where Elizabeth had buried herself under the covers.

"Is it dead, John?" she enquired timidly.

"Yes my dearest, it's dead. It has a large gap between its arse and its head. Sleep well, Elizabeth. And in the meantime if you hear any more rats, I suggest you grab the sword and deal with them yourself."

At this, I shut my eyes and fell back to sleeping.

Morning came all too soon. Elizabeth woke and crept out of bed trying not to disturb me, wishing to let me sleep on. The rat incident had been far from her thoughts until she now stumbled across its remains in the corner of the room. Shocked at the sight of this rather large, divided rat with its stinking entrails oozed out, she shrieked in horror and disgust. I woke abruptly to her screams and asked what ailed her.

"Sorry, John. I had forgotten the rat."

"Get back into bed, Elizabeth, and I will deal with it."

I dragged myself up and walked over to the window, picking up its two halves on my way. I opened the casement and threw out the rat's remains.

"Thank you, John. You know how I detest those dreadful creatures. I am afeared that they will bring some vile disease."

"I know, my love. They are evil, disgusting creatures. Let us not dwell on it, but rather make ready for our journey to Burford."

Presently, a maid brought us water to wash and also small beer, bread and ham, which were most welcome after such an eventful night. We ate well, prepared to depart and settled our account.

෴

Leaving the inn, we boarded our coach and made our way to Burford. The coach made good time, as we had taken on fresh horses at Chipping, where we were to collect our rested horses on the return journey.

About a mile from Shipton-under-Wychwood, we came upon a milkmaid milking her cow at the side of the road. We stopped and bought two cups of the cream that she was selling to passers-by. It was warm, and sweet to the taste and most agreeable.

Continuing our journey, we passed through Shipton. Three miles further on, the coach slowed down as the horses tackled the long inclines of Fullbrook hill. A mile or so later, we passed through the tiny hamlet of Fullbrook itself. Presently, turning left and crossing the ancient stone bridge spanning the Windrush, we entered Burford.

The town had changed little since my days at the Grammar School. It was still a small but prosperous market town, where the wool merchants' wealth was evidenced by their fine houses. We passed through the town, the horses climbing steadily up its steep hill and we then turned right towards Little Barrington where the coach came to rest at an inn a few miles distant from Burford. The Spotted Boar was large and most welcoming. It possessed fifteen hearths and the room we acquired was spacious and well furnished. Our servant brought up our belongings, and a maid was summoned to unpack our small trunk and to lay out a fresh change of clothes.

We were tired and uncomfortably hot after our journey. Although it was only early April, the weather had been exceptionally dry and warm of late, making the road unusually dusty for the time of year. Jugs of hot water were brought to our room and we revived ourselves with the washing of our hands and faces casting off our dusty, grimy clothes for fresh apparel. We then descended the stairs into the smoke filled inn, where a handsome fire was burning in the hearth. We took a table, ordered our supper and wine and, after partaking of the vittles, were contented and refreshed.

"Elizabeth, my darling?"

"Yes, John?"

"Do you not find the inn a little crowded and noisy? Shall we not depart this rabble and away to our room?"

Elizabeth, smiling agreed.

The comfortable oak bed, bathed in warm candlelight, beckoned. Elizabeth undressed to her under garments, but I wanted her naked.

"My Lord! Will I not catch a chill?"

"With the warmth of my body lying next to yours, no chill would dare to enter this bed."

Elizabeth, unclothed, slipped swiftly between warm sheets and I, as naked as the day I was born, joined her. We lay in the sensuous freedom of nudity, a far cry from our usual bed attire. Kissing Elizabeth, I felt the strong beating of her heart. I held her trembling body close to mine and drew my lips over her slender neck and down over her shoulders, anon, kissing her soft white breasts and aroused nipples. I arched my body over hers and she, groaning with pleasure, gently placed her trembling hand upon my already erect piece. Sighing, she begged for me to enter her restless cunny, and I with great satisfaction obliged.

ঠ৵৹৶ঠ

A cock crowing loudly in the yard awakened us.

"Good morning, Elizabeth. Did you sleep tight?"

"I did, my Lord, but now awake, I have the most unbearable toothache."

As my poor Elizabeth turned to look at me, I could see that the right side of her face was most swollen, and the pain she was suffering was great. Her tears fell freely as she cupped her aching cheek.

"I am so sorry, John. I have felt a little pain for some five days, but I believed it would come to naught."

"Well, Elizabeth, this is most inconvenient. We shall need to seek the services of a tooth drawer at Burford."

Elizabeth kept to her room, for she had not the stomach for vittles, whilst I went downstairs for an early morning draught and some cold beef.

After paying the landlord, I ordered that the coach and our belongings be made ready for our departure. Poor Elizabeth was by now feeling quite faint with her tormenting agony. As we journeyed to Burford she was greatly distressed, the jolting of the coach adding to her misery.

We arrived at ten of the clock in the morning and I left Elizabeth in the coach while I went to seek a tooth drawer. I was directed half way down the main street and was told of a man by the name of William Pullworthy, situate next to the Apothecary's shop at the sign of the Pincers and Hammer. I located him presently, and he was readily available to draw my wife's tooth on the payment of a shilling.

I returned to our coach and we made our way to Pullworthy's

residence. He met us at the door and escorted us to a room at the back of the building. His appearance gave neither of us confidence in his ability. He was a slovenly specimen, dour and thin featured and a half-closed watery eye left a clean streak on his begrimed face. His trembling hands fared no better, for they patently had not been washed for many a day and were soiled with the filth of his trade. The shabby room was poorly lit, and in the middle there stood a large, stout chair with a sloping back and with strong leather straps to render the poor patient motionless. To one side of the chair was a table, laid upon which were various torturous implements. Also on the table was an earthenware bowl in which lay an alarming assortment of bloody, black and stinking, rotten teeth drawn from many a poor soul in toothache torment. The atmosphere of that dark and dismal room, together with those frightful instruments, would cause the stoutest of hearts to falter.

The tooth puller instructed Elizabeth to sit in the dreadful chair. Shaking uncontrollably, she sat courageously and slowly reclined, as he tightly buckled the straps around her arms and torso. She closed her eyes, opened her trembling mouth and placed her faith in Pullworthy. Faith indeed must be a comfort when faced with the pain to be inflicted for sure by those evil devices. Elizabeth's cries chilled me to the bone as he located and, with great strength, pulled out the infected tooth. Although she was in agony during the operation, the drawing of the tooth brought instant relief.

"When the tooth worm invades, there is nothing to be done but for the tooth to be drawn," said Pullworthy.

Elizabeth's mouth was bleeding profusely and she was given a small pad of white linen to bite upon until the bleeding should subside. Our visit concluded, we thanked the tooth puller and made to proceed hence, but before we left, he offered us two small pots of tooth balm. We accepted his dubious assurances that this miraculous balm would guard against future infections and so would avert the need to have teeth drawn ever again. Despite being sceptical of the paste's warranty against rotting teeth, we purchased it, and most expensive it was too at sixpence a pot. Elizabeth was now feeling rather weak and tired after her ordeal, so we re-joined our coach, and there she rested to regain her strength before we embarked for the Grammar School.

The two of us arrived at the main entrance of the school. I knocked loudly on its old, solid oak door and a servant opened it enquiring of my name and the purpose of my visit. On my answering "Lord Rochester," John Martin, my old headmaster, rushed out of his study, surprised and delighted to see me.

"Welcome back to Burford School." he said enthusiastically, "We are most honoured by this unexpected visit, my Lord."

"Thank you, Martin. May I introduce you to my wife, Lady Elizabeth Rochester. The poor soul has just had a tooth drawn, so please do forgive her if she appears a little pale and withdrawn."

"Your Ladyship, welcome to our school," said Martin, "I am so sorry that you required the services of the butcher Pullworthy. He is an uncouth and altogether unpleasant man who, unfortunately, I myself had need to visit only two weeks ago. I still cannot pass his house without a shudder. You see, he is the new practitioner in Burford, and since the death of kindly old Jewbone, we have no choice but he. Some of the older boys of the school, whose teeth are already being attacked by the tooth worm, endure their agony for days rather than resolve to visit that house of horrors. But alas, the pain overtakes their fears and to Pullworthy they submit. Now, please follow me to my study where tea will be served forthwith."

"Tea, Martin? This headmaster has grown rich on spoils from the school's benefactors," I remarked.

"My Lord, you know me to be a sober man who has ever resisted the evils of strong liquors, so surely I deserve this small luxury. I find it a most refreshing and wondrous drink which calms the soul and enlightens the mind."

At this, Elizabeth turned and looked at me and, although still in some pain, her expression suggested… *'Now there sits a man of virtue.'*

After our taking of tea and reminiscing on my time at the school, Martin escorted us around the building. On entering the main hall, he announced our arrival and the pupils stood to attention. Martin instructed them to sit, and they obeyed as swiftly as they had risen. Observing the hall, its dimension was strange to me, for I had remembered it to be much larger. I gazed at the fresh, young boys at study and wondered how long it would be before immorality would seduce their innocence.

Our visit concluded, we made to take our leave of Martin, and I pledged him the generous sum of five pounds towards the school's continuing good work.

"Thank you, my Lord. This is a most unexpected and welcome gesture. The bursars of the school will be honoured to accept your most generous gift," Martin enthused.

We walked to the nearby Church of St. John the Baptist, where I had sat through many an agonizing sermon as a Burford boy.

Elizabeth asked wryly, "John, how is it possible that you have become so persuaded by drink, despite your sober tutor?"

Ignoring her trite remark, I continued to the church in silence.

We entering the church, I questioned Elizabeth, "Whilst we are on the subject of propriety, why are you allowing yourself to enter a Protestant place of worship, with your all too Catholic leanings?"

"Well, John. For a time now I have agonized over my beliefs and will be returning to the Protestant faith." Elizabeth said surprisingly, "I had the need to enter Adderbury Church whist you were away and there, in the true house of God, I felt such calmness and serenity. I shall declare my wishes to the vicar of Adderbury on my return. Perhaps you will wish to accompany me when I visit him, John?" she added, "Your family's pew stands empty unless for weddings and christenings. Surely, its occasional use of a Sunday would be welcomed?"

"You know that will not be so, madam, and I will hear nothing further on the subject."

As we walked towards the ancient font, Elizabeth pointed to the new stained-glass window directly behind. The old window had been damaged viciously during Old Ironside's occupation of the building. The colours of this new window were beautifully illuminated, and it brought vivid memories of my time spent in Venice. But the world outside this vision of beauty was so very different, dull and lifeless by comparison. I showed Elizabeth a sad inscription on the font, which read *Anthony Sedley 1649 Prisner'*. He was one of the incarcerated Levellers.

"I had been told, Elizabeth, that there are to be found, somewhere on the walls outside, marks from bullets which had pierced the hearts of three prisoners executed there, but even as an inquisitive young boy, I could never find those marks."

"John, I would prefer not to see the evidence of such a terrible deed."

We made our way outside and walked around the perimeter of the church, I observing on the north wall several newer blocks of stone, which time had not yet weathered.

"Elizabeth, do you see those new stones in the wall?"

"I do, John. Why would they be of interest to me?"

"Well, Elizabeth, they must have been fashioned and set in place of the old damaged stones by Christopher Kempster. He was born in Burford and now has the important position of Master Mason to Wren on the construction of the magnificent new St. Paul's. I believe he has supplied vast quantities of stone from his quarry near to here for use in the rebuilding of fire torn London. The fires of hell certainly brought him good fortune in abundance. What the devil consumes, God rebuilds, all to the benefit of man."

We boarded our coach, and leaving Burford made our way back to the Falcon for the night, Elizabeth demanding that we should not stay in the room where we had encountered the rat. I agreed, but assured her that the possibility of another rat disturbing our sleep would be more than remote.

Our evening was most agreeable. A different room was secured and our night's sleep was most restful, proving to be without interference from any dreaded rodent.

ഷ്

Back at Adderbury, our children and servants were pleased to see us. The children had missed us greatly, for it was the first time they had been left for several days without their devoted mother, and Elizabeth's joy at seeing them again was all too evident.

Summer 1675 passed peacefully enough, though occasional excursions to Ditchley at my mother's behest were adhered to, I being forced to attend on interminable family matters. Duties at Woodstock were most delightful in comparison, allowing a welcome diversion from family turmoil and from the ever-increasing hostilities between the houses of Ditchley and Adderbury.

The passing of autumn, and winter's approach, gave rise to a change of mood in Elizabeth. She grew irritable and sullen, being great-bellied with our fourth child whose birth was approaching.

As winter enveloped Oxfordshire, my own health deteriorated again in the chill. At times, an overwhelming weakness entered my limbs that made walking any distance a trial. My sleep was disturbed nightly and I often awoke with a burning in my guts, accompanied by alternating bouts of clammy sweating and icy shivers. Elizabeth grew most concerned at my illnesses, which sometimes continued for three or four days at a time. She again begged me to see a local physician, but I adamantly would not. I tried very hard to hide the pain I was suffering, as I was all too aware that the anxiety I was causing Elizabeth could be harmful to her delicate condition.

During my enforced stay at Adderbury, I corresponded with Henry, only to learn that there was a vicious rumour at Court and at the theatres that I had succumbed to illness and was dead and buried a month ago. There were many who would have delighted in this news, and a few who would have been saddened by it. *'Not yet, you vengeful gossips.'* I thought, *'You have not seen the last of me quite yet.'*

With my dear wife's devoted care, and the administering of her medicinal remedies, I began steadily to overcome my latest malady. By the time the Christmas festivities were again enjoyed at Adderbury, my illness had subsided and I was thankfully well again. To my relief, Elizabeth seemed in better spirits too, though her swollen belly was causing her much aggravation. One morning, in the early hours, I woke Martha as Elizabeth's pains commenced. Her labour was mercifully short, and she soon gave birth to a beautiful baby girl. Elizabeth's lying in at an end, we arranged the baptism of Mallet for the Sixth of January.

❧

At the end of that month, I felt obliged to return to London to disprove those malicious rumours of my demise. On my arrival there, I was most disappointed to learn that Mrs. Barry had left to visit friends in Bath. This perplexed me much, for Beth had never intimated that she had friends there. It was not the season to take the waters, but ever the season to take a clandestine cure, so I enquired of my friends after her wellbeing. They all agreed that she had looked rather tired and pale of late, but they dismissed it flippantly as mere stage fatigue. However, their remarks alarmed me much. Was my darling Beth ill of the pox?

❧

I returned to Adderbury at the beginning of March, finding my wife and children in good health. Our first child Anne, now seven years old, had been thrilled at the arrival of baby Mallet and now helped Martha in attending to all her needs. Anne was allowed to sit in a chair and hold the tiny bundle in her arms. She loved her little sister with a passion.

Charles, now five, on the other hand had no interest whatsoever in this new arrival that demanded so much attention from her mother and servants. He and I were of like mind, for the overpowering domesticity in the weeks following the birth was neither to my son's taste nor to mine. As often as not, Charles and I left the house and went for walks around the garden and down to the lake. We spent precious time together playing *Hide and Seek* and *Soldiers on Parade*. Several times, we tried to catch fish with a crude stick and line, but without success. On one occasion we travelled to Banbury for the purpose of replenishing my quills, paper and ink, which I had used in abundance during my late sickness at Adderbury.

Sitting in my study one morning, I opened a letter from George wherein he wrote that he had been working for many months on a new play, *The Man of Mode, or Sir Fopling Flutter*, for which he had great hopes of success. The play had opened on the Eleventh of March, just after my return to Adderbury. Betterton was given the rôle of Dorimant, whose character George had apparently based upon me, with Mrs. Barry taking the part of Dorimant's mistress, Mrs. Loveit. George urged my return to London and Dorset Gardens to see his *masterpiece* enacted. His new-found admiration for Mrs. Barry as an actress was obvious, he telling me of her increasing success. She was gaining popularity with admiring rakes and men of quality who rushed to her tiring-room at the end of each performance, begging her audience and presenting her with money and jewels. Reading between the lines, it was apparent that George had become besotted with the woman, an emotion I could not deny him. The crowd's respect for her performances now reached such heights no actress before had experienced. As far as George was aware, she was still faithful to me but, with my absence, her temptation for illicit dalliances must have become ever stronger.

And so, my intention to travel to London sooner rather than later was easily resolved. I thought it better not to write to George, but rather to arrive in the city unannounced. The element of surprise in visiting Beth would settle my mind, for better or worse, regarding the remarks in his letter and my fear that she was ready to embark on securing new lovers. I left for London on the Friday, and although Elizabeth was, as usual, not happy at my departure, she accepted it gracefully and we parted cordially.

––

The weather turned cold in the grip of a bitter east wind and found me in a most miserable condition. In the coach, the wind blew icy cold through the gaps in the leather window blinds and chilled me to the bone, penetrating my winter clothes. It was as though my long heavy topcoat afforded no protection from these wintery blasts. As my fingers and toes became numb, my jaw, to the contrary, ached mercilessly. I thought at first that it was simply the cold air that was causing this continual pain, but soon I tasted blood. I prodded my mouth with the little feeling I had left in my fingers and found that one of my teeth had become loose. It fell with ease from my aching gum into my mouth. I spat out the tooth and blood into my hand and, as I stared at the black, rotten tooth, I knew that my disease, which I had hoped was abating, was not. I was now resigned in the knowledge that further visits to Loveall would surely be of no use to me. His treatment had stemmed the onset for a short while, but inevitably I was damned.

On arriving in London, I put morbid thoughts to the back of my mind and made for the nearest inn, after which I made my way to Wych Street. I knocked at Mrs. Barry's door and, to my great surprise, Nell opened it.

"Rochester, you old rogue. Decided to look in on Mrs. Barry have you?" Nell remarked scathingly, "Your love alone does not feed her. If it were not for her many admirers and their generous gifts of vittles and money, the poor wretch would have starved to death this winter passed."

At this, Beth appeared in the hallway.

"My Lord! I am most honoured at your coming. Loaded with gifts for your mistress, I see." said Beth sarcastically, "And where are the bloody coal and the new bed you promised me. Have you any idea how I manage on my meagre wage? I work day after day on the stage, and when I return to my lodgings, I have neither the warmth of a fire nor food to fill my empty belly. I see from your stance that you have already visited an inn; the best claret no doubt, for that is your usual drink. For the price of that bottle I could have eaten well tonight."

"I will be leaving now." said Nell, "There are many men of quality and wealth out there, Rochester, who would gladly take Mrs. Barry for their mistress and treat her handsomely with fine clothes, jewels and money." she snapped, "Beware, my Lord! Your meanness to my friend will drive her into the arms of another."

At this Nell left and, slamming the door behind her, climbed into her personal coach supplied by the Monarch himself for services rendered.

"Well there speaks a lady of breeding." I said to Beth, "If you wish for the finer things in life, then I suggest *you* whore yourself to His Majesty."

"I have never expected much from you, John, in the way of fine gifts and jewels, but a little money towards a comfortable existence would not be frowned upon."

"My darling! You know I rarely carry cash upon my person."

"That's true, John. It usually finds its way into the inns before ever it arrives at my door."

"Beth, my love. My sweet love. I have not come all this way to argue over trivialities. Please hold me tight and let me feel your warmth, which you have ever been eager to offer."

At this, Beth walked towards me and caressed my aching body. We sat down in her small parlour and were friends once more.

"I hear George's play is the talk of the town, with your exquisite performances enchanting the audiences." I said, "Surely your wage for the week has been most enhanced of late."

"When Etherege, Betterton and the other leeches have all taken their share, there is never enough left in the pot for this lowly actress," she replied with continued venom.

"This will change, Beth, I promise. When I have had words with those upstarts, your circumstances will be all for the better."

My arrival at the theatre the following morning was greeted with some trepidation. George and Thomas were most surprised at my appearance.

"John, you are back! You sent no word of your intention to return," said George.

"It was an impromptu decision on my part, George."

"Now, have you seen Mrs. Barry?" he asked.

"Yes George, when I arrived early yesterday evening."

"Is she well?" said Thomas.

"As well as can be expected, living an almost penniless existence."

"Penniless? But she earns a good wage now she has become the best actress in London," replied Thomas.

"Yet it is not enough." I said angrily, "You know she is worth more than you are paying her, and from what I hear of the packed houses, she deserves a damned sight more than the reward she is receiving."

At this, George and Thomas ushered me to an unoccupied tiring-room and opened a bottle of wine.

"Surely she cannot be as poor as you say, for, God's truth, she's your Lordship's mistress," said Thomas.

"My personal matters in regard to Mrs. Barry should be none of your damned business." I said abruptly, "Yet you are all making money from my sordid reputation. And George, if it were not for me, your successful play would never have been staged. So I believe my mistress, whose character is a large part of this production, deserves her fair dues."

George and Thomas frowned at each other and reluctantly agreed to pay her worth. And so I left the company of these *generous* individuals and said I would return later in the day to see the play for myself.

ℒℒ

I left my box, with the cheering and clapping of the audience ringing in my ears and made my way backstage to meet with George and Thomas.

"Well what do you think, John? It *is* good isn't it?" said George.

"It's remarkable, George. But Thomas… in playing me, do you think you could appear a little more worn and unwell? You see, observing my gradually degenerating true self, the audience will soon not recognize who you are supposed to be," I said, with a sadness in my voice.

"I did not think you were looking your best, John," said George.

"Best, George? I have long been the best, but now my feeble body is resorting to the worst. Let us not dwell on that damnation, but instead we must to an inn and celebrate your success."

With that, George, Thomas and I joined Mrs. Barry and we headed for the Devil in Fleet Street. The Devil seemed an appropriate place to drink I thought, as we made our way along the streets and alleys. The devil had used me pretty damned well and was even now contriving to spit me out into the filth and stench of the gutter outside his very house.

CHAPTER THIRTEEN

Disgraced, Despised and Disguised

We left the Devil's House late and made our ways home by separate conveyance, excepting that Mrs. Barry and I took coach together to Wych Street, on our way passing the late revellers of the city. There were whores in abundance loitering in dark alleyways, in doorways and on street corners, offering sexual favours and willingly obliging those gentlemen and rakes keen to pay for pleasure. There were also young men and boys all too eager to be part of this squalid trade since, for some, an adolescent boy gives more pleasure than an accomplished whore. For these poor wretches, born in the depths of poverty, uneducated and with no particular trade, this is the only way they know of earning a meagre living, the only alternative being death from starvation. These disease ridden filth-mongers, who themselves all too often are not far from death, give not a fig for the innocent man of pleasure who, as a consequence, receives far more than he bargains for.

We arrived at Wych Street and entered Beth's lodgings proceeding straight to bed and trying in earnest to make love, but our drunken minds and bodies would not allow this fulfilment, and sleep was the only conqueror of our desires.

In the morning, I awoke feeling most wretched. With eyes heavy-lidded and with blurred sight, I again tasted blood. The right side of my neck felt warm to the touch where was manifest an ugly and painful, weeping sore.

Beth woke some little time after, she feeling sickly and looking most pale. She stumbled out of bed and made her way across the room to a leather bucket that stood in the corner. She knelt down over the bucket and was violently sick.

"Must you make that stink in the room, Beth? What is wrong with opening the window and using the street below?"

"Open the window? I hardly had time to reach the bucket, my Lord. God, how ill I feel."

"Yes, you look dreadful, Beth. The vision of beauty I beheld on the stage yesterday has faded to present the poor wretch I now cast my eyes upon."

"Well, John, I suppose *you* believe you still resemble the handsome young Rochester. Have you reflected upon a looking glass lately? If you had, I do not think you would have been so uncomplimentary to me."

Beth left the room in anger to refresh herself at toilette, and after a short while shouted from the foot of the stairs that she was off to Dorset Gardens.

I got out of bed and found a small cracked looking glass lying on a table close by. With great reluctance, I held the glass before my face and stared into the eyes of a dead man. Again, I could taste blood in my mouth, and as I opened it, looking into the glass, I could see that my painful teeth were rotting in raw and corrupted gums. They were loosening in their anchorage and, with the merest push of my finger, yet another tooth dropped away into my mouth. The oozing sore on my neck concerned me much, but I was able to conceal this unsightly mark of the pox under my silk necktie. However, even the simple task of securing the tie became an ordeal, for my trembling fingers were numb to the touch.

I gathered my wits and, with what little strength I could summon, took coach most urgently to Loveall's.

"My Lord Rochester, you know I will do all I can to alleviate your misery." Loveall looked at me from the far side of his desk, with the knowing eyes of defeat, "The sore on your neck can be cured with the application of my cerecloth plasters and special paste. These must be renewed and applied fresh daily to the affected area for two weeks. This I can guarantee will heal. Your decaying teeth will also benefit from my tooth tincture, which you will find nowhere else in London. I am sure by now, my Lord, you have come to terms with the seriousness of your disease." Loveall remarked gravely, "With your illness so advanced, further submersion is out of the question, for it would no longer be of benefit to you, but only hinder your body's defensive humours."

With this devastating news, he handed me my cloth, paste and tincture and, after paying his fee, I left the room.

Before I had opened the door to leave, Loveall spoke in a most grave tone and announced, "My Lord Rochester. Refraining from over-indulgence in the drinking of wine could delay your decline a little longer."

At this, I opened the door and slammed it behind me. I took coach to Wych Street, and on my arrival applied the paste to my neck without delay. Afterwards, I swilled the tooth tincture around my mouth; the taste was disgusting. I promptly spat it out, and yet it numbed my mouth and tongue, leaving no feeling at all, this causing spittle to leak from the corners of my mouth uncontrollably. I went down stairs and sat in the small parlour, alone and desperate, with one lit candle and with the faintest shaft of light entering at the window.

After two weeks, as Loveall had assured, the unsightly sore on my neck had healed well. But alas, and not unexpected, the tooth tincture, with its professed curative properties, did not help this patient. To my delight though, my weakness of body had receded. I was feeling stronger and, my mind somewhat eased of the thoughts of death, I embarked upon my usual pleasures.

Guilt ridden, I felt bound to write to Elizabeth to enquire after my family. She replied swiftly, having grave concerns regarding my precious son's health. Charles had of late succumbed again to a fever, but Elizabeth assured me that he had been well attended by the local physician and was now much better, though still not eating well and having little interest in his toys. She had been advised to take Charles to her estate in Somerset where it was believed the air would be most beneficial for the boy's recovery. They were to travel two days hence. Concluding her letter, she intimated there would now be no immediate rush for me to return to Adderbury, declaring bitterly that the pleasures of London, of which I was so fond, would in any case no doubt thwart my return.

At first, I was viciously annoyed to learn that Elizabeth had not alerted me immediately to Charles's illness, though on reflection it would have been impossible for me to travel any distance in my deplorable state. This belated news now saddened me to the heart, knowing that my own self-inflicted, disgusting condition prevented me from my beloved son's bedside. What father could sink so low as I?

∂∞∫

Whilst Beth's fame was on the ascent, her amours towards me were on the decline. I was in need of diversion and earnestly craved excitement. During the warm month of June, I was enticed by my rakish friends to the spending of a few days at the races, in pursuit of gambling and wenching. We climbed aboard a coach bound for Epsom early one Saturday morning. I, along with most Englishmen, greatly admire the power and graceful beauty of the horse, but my purse has ever been the poorer for the wagers. The first day's meet on this occasion proved to be no exception.

In the evening, we entered Epsom village, intoxicated and unruly after many hours drinking and gambling. There was a young man in our party by the name of Downs, a likeable fellow whose beauty and youth I found most attractive. We had been formally introduced by Buckingham in Will's Coffee house, a week before Epsom. Downs was a close acquaintance of his, and our immediate attraction to one another was patently obvious, leaving Buckingham not a little resentful. I had a mind, if no whore was to hand, to invite Downs to my bed that very evening.

We enquired after the local whorehouse and were directed down a dark alley towards a small timber framed house at the sign of the Unicorn. The man who directed us hence clearly bore a grudge against the city rakes, for when we arrived and hammered at the door, it opened abruptly and to our surprise there stood the Constable of the Watch. Young Downs, who was very drunk and wished to impress me by showing his authority, demanded of the constable that the whores make an appearance and welcome us into their stew. The constable stood firm at the doorway and announced that the house was no stew but his home, and that he was appalled at the inebriated state of these *gentlemen* who had arrived at his door with such conspicuous skulduggery. Downs proceeded to antagonize him further and repeated that he wished to see the whores.

One of our party came forward and punched the constable on the nose and, as he fell to the floor, kicked him viciously. Again we called out for the whores to show themselves, and we all entered the house. The constable by this time had managed to stagger to his feet and shouted in desperation for the local watchmen, who promptly came to the house. On the belated realization that we had been duped, we returned to the street where we were in an instant surrounded by the watchmen. We now tactfully explained our plight; that we had been falsely informed of the stew. The watchmen, eager to settle the commotion, left well satisfied with our explanation. However, the constable, who reappeared out of the darkness, dazed and in pain, walked towards me with an air of disdain and, fearing for my life, I unsheathed my short sword to protect myself. At this he shouted, "Murder!" and the watchmen, hearing his outcry, hurried back to the house. Downs had foolhardily placed himself between me and the constable to protect me from harm. Then, during a confused skirmish, my guardian angel was struck viciously on the head. The young man's skull was split open and in desperation he took up a stick, but before any blow could be struck, one of the watch ran a spike clean through his body. Poor Downs keeled over screaming in pain and anguish as the rest of us watched in disbelief. The situation was grave and we ran frantically into the darkness. We knew Downs was done for.

Unfortunately, during this terrible mêlée, someone shouted, "Rochester! Run for your life!" and hence, my name was overtly connected with this hapless incident. As none other of our party was with certainty recognized, I was, as fate decreed, the only one there forced into hiding. I learned that Downs had died in agonising torment a few days later. What a tragedy I thought; the death of such a fine-looking young man endeavouring to protect from harm this worthless rake of an Earl. The anonymity of the other rogues gave them liberty to return to London without hindrance or suspicion. His Majesty ordered that I be found and brought to task for my part in the death of poor Downs, and so in desperation I contemplated the need for disguise. As will be seen, so effective was this deception that even I would not have known myself if we each had met in the street.

I took lodgings in Tower Street near London Bridge and seldom ventured out except for vittles and wine to sustain me in my isolation. Here I remained, a fugitive conniving an ingenious plan. The days were long and the nights an eternity. In vivid dreams, I recalled the bloody body of Downs and awoke in remorseful guilt. My mind in turmoil, I scribbled pages of meaningless prose, but then destroyed all but one...

❧❦

To the Postboy

❧❦

Rochester: Son of a whore, God damn you, can you tell
A peerless peer the readyest way to Hell?
I've outswilled Baccus, sworn of my own make
Oaths would fright furies and make Pluto quake.
I've swived more whores more ways than Sodom's walls
E'er knew' or the college of Rome's cardinals.
Witness heroic scars, look here, ne'er go,
Cerecloths and ulcers from top to toe.
Frighted at my own mischiefs I have fled
And bravely left my life's defender dead,
Broke houses to break chastity, and dyed
That floor with murder which my lust denied.
Pox on't, why do I speak of these poor things?
I have blasphemed my God and libelled Kings.
The readiest way to Hell? Come quick, ne'er stir.

Boy: The readiest way, my lord,'s by Rochester.

❧❦

Early one morning, I had woken from a disturbing dream. This
vision would become a reality, for it inspired a conspiracy of such
deception that no one would unearth my whereabouts. And so I
employed the help of two locally renowned villains who were all
too ready to earn an easy penny. Concealed in disguise themselves,
they assisted me in the grand illusion of Dr. Alexander Bendo. In a
subtle veil of cloak, buckram mask and beard, I, Dr. Bendo, would

offer all manner of medicines, potions, pills, pastes and liquids in a variety of colours to alleviate patients' troublesome symptoms; blues to cool the blood and reds to fire the coolness of heart. All would be cured who bravely entered my establishment.

I meticulously wrote out my introduction to lure unsuspecting patients. I carefully documented my qualifications from around the world. There was nothing I could not cure and make well again, even to the point of making fat people thin and consumptive persons to put on weight. Young women who craved to be with child would instantly bear fruit. Older women with sagging breasts and bodies, worn out from child bearing, would once again flaunt firm breasts and desirable bodies. All with rotting teeth would be free of the worm, and even white teeth the result. I would promise to cure everything from sweating sickness to agues and dropsy. Crooked bodies would be straightened and scabs, open sores, scars and blemishes would disappear, the skin thereafter becoming smooth as silk.

I had many news sheets printed expounding the virtues of the miraculous Dr. Bendo, and my villainous helpers distributed these among the populace. I set up a small stage outside my lodgings where crowds of people would daily attend to read my advertisement displayed on the door of the house. The news sheet was long and drawn out, but inquisitive passers-by took time in the reading and digesting of its contents. It began thus…

ॐ∙ঔ

To all gentlemen, ladies, and others, whether of City, Town, or Country, Alexander Bendo wisheth all health and prosperity…

And concluded…

They that will do me the favour to come to me shall be sure from three of the clock in the afternoon till eight at night at my lodgings in Tower

Street, next door to the sign of the Black Swan at a Goldsmith's house to find

Their humble servant,

Alexander Bendo.

୨୦⊷ଔ

For the first few days, business was slow, despite the hordes gathering outside. They were obviously inquisitive of this newly arrived establishment, yet most felt reluctant to step over the threshold and be confronted by such a mysterious and rather frightening spectacle dressed in cloak and mask.

But it took only one or two brave souls to confront their fear and enter Dr. Bendo's surgery, to start a tide of customers. The first patient I encountered was an aging man; a veteran of Naseby and a brave and courageous old soldier. His left foot had been badly crushed under a falling parliamentary horse. This injury had necessitated amputation to save his life, yet he recalled this frightful and agonising incident with pride. Being a cripple of sorts, he had found employment scarce over many years, but for the last ten had been happily employed as a pewterer crafting fine pewterware for the wealthy of the city. This labour was most agreeable to him as he was seated for many hours, thus setting aside his crutches. Observing my patient, I knew what illness afflicted him. By the shaking of his body and the pallid colour of his skin I guessed that this poor man was suffering from an accumulation of poisons from his craft, they having seeped into his body and humours after many years working the metal. I prescribed Dr. Bendo's red drops, which I declared would warm the humours of his stomach and bring colour back to his pale cheeks.

The red liquid would do him no harm, comprising as it did

merely water and red dye from crushed beetles, and yet it would not cure him either. I knew from his ill condition that this poor beggar had not long to live.

The old soldier thanked me and, balancing on his well-worn crutches, he fumbled in his pocket to pay for my services. I refused, saying that his dues had been paid most dearly in the service of the King. He hobbled out, clutching in his hand the small medicine bottle. A crowd quickly gathered about him asking who and what he had found indoors.

Word soon spread in the locality, and further afield too, that Dr. Bendo's cure-alls were proving miraculous to the many diseased wretches who walked through his door. To my astonishment, I was making a good living from the sale of my remedies and was able to pay my two helpers handsomely. Sworn to secrecy, they dared not tell of this deception, knowing full well that their bulging purses would soon empty if our secret was uncovered, and that they would find themselves back on the streets begging and thieving for a living. The patients I attended came from all parts of the city, both the impoverished of the east and the affluent of the west.

I recall vividly a day when a beautiful, well-dressed young woman attended my surgery with her companion. Both women wore masks so as not to be recognized. As she walked in, her attempted anonymity did not fool the all-seeing Bendo. I had seen her but twice before and, although fleetingly, thought what a lucky beggar he was. It was apparent from our conversation that her husband, who she did not name, would be vexed indeed should he discover she had visited this mountebank. I asked what help I could offer and she replied shyly that she had been suffering from a persistent toothache during the past two days. I sat this beautiful creature in a chair and looking into her mouth, I diagnosed the dreaded tooth worm therein. The lady seemed anxious, and asked if there was any help I could give her. I replied that Bendo's tincture would kill the pain and remove for good the burrowing grub.

I enquired if that was all I could help her with. To my utmost surprise, she asked with embarrassment if there was anything I could prescribe to help her bear a child.

The opportunity of examining her unclothed body was too great for me to resist. I asked them both to accompany me to a room at the back of the lodgings. In the room lay a small bed in a corner, enclosed by a leather-clad screen. With the companion present, I asked the lady to undress to her undergarments and, when ready, to lay on the bed and call for my assistance. This she did, and before long I was gazing at this fine creature whose voluptuous curves were as delightful as any I had encountered. My intimate examination caused her great anxiety, she averting her eyes at all times. On concluding, I asked the lady to dress and then join me in the surgery.

"Well, Dr. Bendo, what is wrong with me, for I long to conceive a child, but God has not blessed my husband and me with such a gift?"

"Madam, there is no possible reason that you should not be blessed with many children. To help your womb bear fruit, I prescribe this small pot of conceiving balm, to be applied to your privy parts for the next seven days, always after your first urination of the morning. Your husband will not detect it as it possesses no odour or colour."

The lady concurred with this and left the shop pleased with her purchases. As she and her companion entered the crowded street, I smirked, *'If Loveall could not oblige his wife, then I could all too readily offer my services.'*

CHAPTER FOURTEEN

Pretence and Reality

I continued my elusive masterpiece as the incredible and miraculous healer, Dr. Bendo, for far longer than I had thought possible. I sometimes cured, with sincerity attempted to cure, and occasionally made infinitely worse, all manner of conditions. Needless to say, the fees for my services to my more affluent clients were far in excess of those raised on many poor and beggarly souls hoping to be restored to health.

The days were long and arduous, and though the deception accommodated the immediate necessities of a man in hiding, it soon added further to the deterioration of my own fragile health. Often in the evenings, at eight of the clock, when the last patient of the day had vacated my surgery, I would sit alone and survey the many bottles of liquids, the powders, the pastes and all manner of concoctions that were Dr. Bendo's cure-alls. I knew all too well that not one of my miraculous elixirs could in any way begin to help ease the torments of my own diseased, ulcerated and wasting body.

I decided, reluctantly at first, that the time had come for Alexander Bendo to vanish as swiftly as he had appeared. I resolved to leave without trace the following evening, and in particular did not breathe a word of my planned escape to my trusty yet villainous accomplices.

The day after my unannounced departure, innumerable clients, after having paid handsomely for their remedies, would despatch their servants to the surgery to collect pills, potions and the like, only for them to return empty handed. Days after my disappearance, I learned of a hue and cry outside the goldsmith's house, where outraged clients had been told that Dr. Bendo no longer resided therein and had apparently vanished without trace.

Under cover, I had a message delivered to my most trusted and faithful friend Henry, begging him to meet me. He replied that we should meet in St. Bride's in Fleet Street at twelve noon the next day.

I entered St. Bride's in the guise of a street beggar and made my way to a dark corner of the church. There, I sat patiently awaiting Henry and it was not too long before he arrived. He walked by me with no more than a fleeting glance, whereupon I coughed. He turned to look back and I beckoned him to join me.

"John, your disguise is remarkable."

"It must be, if my closest friend would pass me by without a second look."

"It's good to see you, John. Well, to see the parts I can recognize." he offered with a wry smile, "How are you keeping? And where the devil have you been these past weeks?"

"I have been in limbo, Henry. I have bided my time as an elusive reclusive."

"Things have quietened down at Court now, John. The Downs incident seems to have passed without too much recrimination, and I believe the King is now eager to forgive and forget the whole sordid incident."

"Henry, I need to be away and back to Elizabeth and the children. The poor wretch has had no word from me for many weeks."

"Very well, John. If you do not yet intend to return to Court, you know you can trust me completely. I will not breathe a word of our meeting to any living soul."

At this, Henry looked upon me with great sadness and, putting his arms around me, bade me a safe journey to Adderbury. He begged me to take complete rest once back in the country, in the hope of me regaining my strength. My eyes filling with tears, I promised to heed his advice and we left St. Bride's, each going our separate ways.

In a deserted dark alley, close by the church, I discarded my beggarly outer clothes and hastily took a coach bound for Oxfordshire, arriving at my home fatigued after a long and arduous journey.

࿉

Although I arrived unannounced, my wife and children greeted me with smiles. I had not seen them for far too long and realized evermore how much I had missed their company.

My eldest children, Anne and Charles, ran to me with open arms shouting "Father! Father!" they both clinging to me like limpets upon a rock. I gazed across to my wife, who was smiling wistfully at this happy family scene.

"John, you look so pale and ill. What has become of you these past weeks? You have written only twice in all this time, and only then after my letter told of Charles's fever. Thank God he is now recovered. I was right to take the physician's advice and move our dear son to Somerset to convalesce in the sweet pure air there. The advice of his father would have been justly welcome, but you were too busy with your London life to put in an appearance at your home." Elizabeth said all this with a sad air of regret.

I did not respond to her resentful words, already remorseful and guilt-ridden over my infatuation with Mrs. Barry.

I entered the hall, observing the familiar chattels of home, and listened contentedly to the echoes of my happy and excited children at my side. I did not altogether relish the constraints of family life, but I was in desperate need of a complete rest in the warmth and tranquillity of the country, far away from the wearisome city. Adderbury in July offered this aplenty.

The first week after my return passed in amenable harmony. The children were still very excited at their father's return, but also with two very special presents which had been delivered for their amusement some time earlier, in my absence. My son had been sent one of the King's Water Spaniels, whose name was Omah. Anne's present was a beautiful French doll. Our other two children, Lizbet and Mallet, were a little too young for such presents, but the return of their father was my gift to them. My wife, I fear, had been suspicious, and not a little angry, that these gifts were sent by messenger and not conveyed by me. Unfortunately, her suspicions were well founded, for my involvement with Mrs. Barry had not allowed me occasion to travel home and deliver the presents in person.

My quietude at home was predictably unsustainable, particularly where my wife was concerned. Her distrust of me, though warranted, grew more and more irritating. I tried to calm the waters of our relationship by spending as much time as possible with her and the children. We would take coach rides to the town of Banbury, embark upon long walks through the Adderbury estate, picnic in our garden whenever possible and I would partake of fatherly duties with the eldest two children, playing such games as *Hide and Seek* and *Blind Man's Buff*. But the most memorable day for Charles and Anne was when I staged a marionette play.

I, unbeknownst, had commissioned a local joiner, one William Elm, to make a miniature theatre and some small wooden figures to play their parts. The prospect of this task he had relished, it being so very different from his usual work, and he set about it keenly, skilfully endowing the theatre with painted backdrops of various scenes that could readily be interchanged. The figures were to be clothed handsomely by his wife Suzanne, with scraps of material from her sewing box. As daylight faded into dusk, exquisite tiny candles would be lit at the front of the stage, and the whole scene would be magical.

Three weeks later, the theatre and its tiny actors were ready. I arranged with William that the play would be performed on the following Saturday evening at six of the clock. He assured me that everything would be ready, and I would arrange for him and his wife to enter the house covertly to set up the theatre in good time for the evening's entertainment.

On the morning of the performance, I whispered to Elizabeth to accompany me into our parlour. I closed the door behind us and we sat down at our small table.

"John, what is all this secrecy about?"

"A marionette show, Elizabeth, which will be performed on a miniature stage. When I was last in London, I visited the Duke's Theatre."

"Well, John, that is no surprise to me," she snapped.

"Please listen, Elizabeth. I am trying to tell you the purpose of that visit. During the morning, whilst the players were busy rehearsing, I made for the tiring-house. There I persuaded young Adam, assistant tire-man to the costume keeper, to loan me one of their costumes; a garment that would not be in use for many weeks and so would not be missed. He was reluctant at first, and said that if this came to the knowledge of the keeper, he would not only lose his living but also would be severely punished, for the keeper's reputation as a drunkard and bully was well known. But, as often in men, Adam's own weaknesses were drinking and the company of whores, so he gladly accepted a bribe that I offered. We then hid the costume in a sack, and I smuggled it safely out of the theatre."

"John, I do hope this will not be discovered, for the sake of Adam's living, even though he did do it for the most immoral purpose, the which I highly disapprove of." Elizabeth scolded, "But what does this costume look like?"

"It is a fantastical, long green silk cloak bedecked with red and gold satin ribbons, green matching hat and a deep red mask. Today, when all is ready for the performance, I intend to arrive in it."

"For what purpose? Surely, you are far too big to perform on such a stage," Elizabeth laughing replied.

"Madam. I am glad your sense of humour has not diminished as much as I feared." I said with a smile, "After my entrance, I will introduce myself as the Italian character *Scaramuchio* in order to announce the grand opening of the show. This will add to the mystical excitement of it all."

"*Scaramuchio?* Who is he?" Elizabeth asked.

"He is a colourful aristocratic braggart who some perceive, wrongly in my opinion, as being rather cowardly. He often gives such an impression, but under his disguise he is a man of immense complexity who sees the world in many colours, from the brightest yellow to the blackest black."

"Well, John, I believe his character will blend very well with your own, and you will appear most credible to your audience."

"Remember, not a word to anyone Elizabeth, and when all are gathered together in the hall, I will make my spectacular entrance."

The scene was set. The onlookers were spellbound at the small illuminated theatre with its magical flickering shadows, when suddenly I flung open the door and made my entrance. Everyone turned and gasped as I introduced myself as '*Scaramuchio the Puppet Master*' and swiftly but silently glided through the throng, making my way into the half shadows at the back of the diminutive stage and announcing the opening of the play. Everyone clapped and cheered. I looked down at Charles and Anne, whose sparkling eyes, full of delight and anticipation, were fixed upon my face, and I returned their gaze with a smile and a wink. Kneeling on a cushion whilst working the puppets, I caught a glimpse of the two of them, and I saw that their fascination at this spectacle was akin to mine when I had first encountered the marionettes in my youth. Our servants too were amused at the sight of these tiny wooden puppets so flamboyantly attired in their costumes. The four little characters danced and tumbled their way back and forth across the stage, whilst at the same time quarrelling with each other in a strange tongue, each vying for the attention of the gathering. Finally, after several set changes, the puppets bowed silently to their appreciative audience who erupted in laughter and clapped with joy.

I made to rise from the cushion, with difficulty due to numbness in my knees, and Charles and Anne ran towards me with glee in their eyes. They both hugged me tightly before I could stand, the three of us collapsing in a heap on the floor in pleasurable laughter. As we scrambled to our feet, I looked up and saw Elizabeth with tears of joy smiling at our frolics, and in her arms was dear Lizbet, her little face smiling at the wonder of it all.

అన్

That summer the weather was extraordinarily hot. One sweltering day would haunt me for the rest of my life in a vivid vision of death.

We had finished dinner at three of the clock in the afternoon, when my wife and I set to arguing regarding my prolonged absences in London and at High Lodge. Her renewed bickering rankled me, so much so that I stormed out of the room clutching a bottle of claret and a glass, informing her I was not to be disturbed. I walked outside and meandered across the gardens to the shade of our little arbour, where I have often found solace and peace in times of discord. A shimmering haze hung over the garden. I sat, shirt open to my waist, allowing what little air there was to cool my heated body, now fuelled not only with anger but also from liquor.

Although my state of pique had cooled, my temperature was rising by degrees, necessitating a calming walk under the welcome shade of trees, so I made my way towards the inviting water of the lake. Nearing the lake, I stumbled upon our part-hidden icehouse, in a thicket to the side of the path. It beckoned me to enter and, negotiating the slippery moss covered steps, I opened its door and scrambled inside.

With the unusually torrid summer, the store of winter ice had been in frequent demand. Bucketfuls had been brought up to the kitchen daily to preserve meat and fish, and the icehouse was now only a third full. The lure of this cooling bed seduced me, so I lay me down submitting to its crystal gaze. Heavy-lidded, I drifted into peaceful sleep.

Elizabeth's rancour had certainly not abated, as she chided our servants spitefully for taking far too long over their duties. In particular, those who toiled in the kitchen received her disapproval. Our young kitchen boy Tom's first chore of the day was to collect ice, but this had slipped his mind and he, poor soul, received a stern reprimand and an uncharacteristic lashing from Elizabeth. With both his pride and body bruised he, with head bowed, made his way with ice pick and bucket. Once inside this dark cavern he stumbled across me, finding his good master half frozen to death. Shaking in disbelief and horror, he dropped the pick and bucket and, in breathless panic, ran as fast as he could to the house, shouting for help as he went.

All at once, the burning heat of the sun was piercing the numbness of my face and body. Setting me upon a wooden board and covering me in a blanket, four of my male servants carried me back to the house. In my bedchamber, I was stripped of my icy wet clothes, rubbed down with warm oils, clad in fresh garments and laid upon the bed. My anxious wife sat by my side until my shivering had subsided. Elizabeth, in anger, questioned my sanity for such an irrational act. I explained that I had intended to be inside for but a few minutes but, to my horror, she informed me that I must have lain there for almost an hour. I held and kissed her hand and she then, kissing me tenderly, left the room. A shudder ran down my spine, I now fully aware of the gravity of my madness in entering that icy tomb.

☙❧

In the month of August, with my health vastly improved, I vacated Adderbury and moved to High Lodge, committed as I was to my duty as its Ranger.

I had asked of Henry, upon our closet meeting many weeks before in St. Bride's, that he address any letters for me to High Lodge. Now, on my arrival there, I was handed two letters from him. The first, which had been written three weeks before, was enquiring after the state of my health. He said that he hoped the clean Oxfordshire air and peaceful surroundings were proving beneficial. Nothing did he know of my domestic inflammations and my brush with death in the icy crypt. The second, written some two weeks after the first, informed me of his imminent departure to France on the King's business. This news saddened me for I would greatly miss my dear friend, though he assured me that he would soon be returning to his Rochester. However, there was *some* good news, for he confirmed in the letter that the Epsom incident was entirely forgotten and the King was indeed now happy for me to return to Whitehall. He said that he would write from France, to inform me of the happenings there at Louis' Court. He closed with a sorrowful goodbye, but trusted that before long he would be in my company again.

Word spread swiftly that Rochester was back at the lodge. Friends soon arrived, joining me for long hours of gambling, whoring and a good intake of wine.

I was annoyed to receive a letter from Elizabeth, asking for permission to visit me at the lodge. She had felt aggrieved that I had never requested her company there, and threatened to one day arrive unannounced. Her outrage angered me much and I replied in the strongest of terms that to arrive without my given consent would meet with my incensed displeasure, and would not be a wise move on her part.

There were no further letters from Elizabeth, but I did receive an angry and contemptible letter from my mother, who wrote of her disgust after hearing shocking rumours to do with High Lodge and its occupants who, by all accounts, cavorted naked in the grounds and worse. She had also become aware of my connection with the scurrilous incident at Epsom and the consequences thereof.

She informed me that Elizabeth, who was in a most sad and lonely condition, had left Adderbury and had taken the children to Somerset for the foreseeable future.

With the King's forgiveness and the assurance from Henry that the Downs incident was now a thing of the past, the stage was set for my long awaited return to London and to Beth.

❧

On arriving, I made straight for Wych Street and there found Mrs. Barry in the company of a seamstress who was adding the finishing touches to an expensive, fine satin dress that Beth was sporting.

"My Lord! You are back in London," Beth cried.

"Yes, I am back. You are looking very fine in your new dress. And who is the generous fop who has provided for such a rich garment?"

"Why do you presume it to be a gentleman, John? Just because you have been whoring in Oxfordshire, you deduce wrongly I fear, that I have whored myself across London to gain such finery." She replied angrily, "My good friend Nell has furnished me this dress out of the kindness of her heart. She has generously paid for the material and the seamstress's time. The shabbiness of my attire saddened Nell, she declaring that as a reigning actress I deserved more, much more. She also remarked that a fine string of pearls from Rochester would complement the dress most handsomely, but I suppose the token of a pearl, or any other necklace for that matter, would be out of the question from such an uncharitable lover."

The seamstress, flustered and embarrassed from our cross words, left promptly, so that the two of us were alone in the parlour. Beth, with an air of dramatics, and never faltering or seeming to take breath, demanded answers promptly. *What had I been doing? Who had I been seeing? Why, for weeks, had I neither written nor called upon her?'* God! I had taught her well.

"I heard the most dreadful rumours: some, that you are a heartless, cowardly rogue and that you had left a man to die at Epsom; others, that you had taken on many different guises so as not to be recognized and that you had fled abroad never to return; and worst of all, I heard you were *dead*! I was at my wit's end, though my mind was eased when I spoke with Henry at the theatre. He perceived my sadness at thinking never to see you again, and assured me that he had received a letter from Adderbury reporting that you were ill, but that you had returned there to convalesce."

"Beth, my antagonists at Court are many, and would banter the most evil untruths in the hope that I would lose favour with the King. Their hatred of me hath no bounds, and news of Rochester's death would give them more pleasure than any whore in London."

CHAPTER FIFTEEN

A Family in Crisis

I seldom lodged at Whitehall, habitually residing at Wych Street. I took to the theatre twice a week and watched Mrs. Barry weave her spell. At the end of the performances, her audiences erupted with rapturous applause and after bowing most gracefully, she would walk, smiling triumphantly, into the wings. Afterwards we, with our rakish friends, would cavort in the inns and taverns close by, where dwelt the illustrious company of wits, playwrights, artists and poets of renown. On occasion even *Drybob* Dryden ejaculated such wit as to raise laughter among our company. What gratifying diversions those evenings held, in contrast to the sober constraints of Adderbury.

ॐॐ

At the end of November, I received disturbing news from Elizabeth, she having returned to Adderbury. Charles was gravely ill again, so I travelled home immediately, and on my arrival was greeted by a most fractious and tormented wife. Charles had become ill only three days after their return from Somerset, despite having enjoyed the utmost good health in that fair county. A most eminent physician, who resided at Banbury, had been summoned to attend and he was gravely concerned at the boy's fevered deliriums. He had prescribed the usual bleedings and emetics, and my wife told tearfully of Charles's sufferings at the hand of those barbarities.

We entered the boy's dark and airless room, in which his mother had spent much of her time for three days and nights. His devoted dog lay at the foot of his master's bed, refusing to eat and whimpering mournfully. The few candles that were lit placed a pale glow upon the poor boy's ashen, angelic face. I sat motionless at the side of his bed, whilst Elizabeth knelt praying quietly for the life of our dear son.

In time, I left the room and went downstairs to our parlour. I poured a glass of wine, and sat sobbing uncontrollably.

Through the night, Elizabeth and I sat aside the boy's bed, mopping his steaming body with cool, damp cloths to alleviate his torment. At daybreak, to our great relief, Charles's fever was subsiding. Half waking, he opened his eyes calling "Father! Mother!" then closed them and slept contentedly for three more hours. Later, the physician attended him and was astounded at his recovery, declaring he had been convinced that the boy would not live. Charles was confined to his bed for a further two weeks, except for two short walks around his room each day with Omah.

The physician, making to leave the house had requested a private word with me. I had escorted him to a room on the ground floor, inviting him to sit close to the fire.

"My Lord Rochester. I am most anxious regarding your son's health," he had said gravely.

"But my son *is* recovering. You have witnessed it with your own eyes, have you not?"

"Yes, Rochester, he is recovering. But nevertheless, your son will suffer increasingly from recurrences of these fevers that will, I fear, be his demise before he reaches adulthood. It is a delicate matter, my Lord, which I find most uncomfortable to discuss. Recently, I have become aware from colleagues in London that you have had need to resort to the mercury cure. Although not common knowledge here, it appears so in London, and looking upon your own frail condition, I believe it to be true. Is this so, my Lord?"

"Yes. I cannot deny it. But my wife, as yet, has perhaps only a vague suspicion of it. I insist that no hint of this be given to her, for it is a grave matter indeed."

"Grave indeed, my Lord. I believe your son's infirmity is a consequence of your diseased humours at the time of his conception, which alas brought corrupted blood upon the boy."

After the physician left, I dwelt on how to broach this distressing revelation with Elizabeth. She soon appeared and sat down. She looked tired, and yet she was now becalmed for the first time in many a day. How could I begin to tell her of our beloved son's plight, with his young life held in the balance, and how he would suffer so miserably the inevitable consequences that would befall him?

"Is it not wonderful, John, that Charles will once again make a full recovery?"

"Elizabeth, I need to talk with you in earnest about Charles."

"About Charles?" Elizabeth said anxiously, "You look so serious, John. What have you to tell me?"

"As you are aware, my own health has fluctuated between good and bad this past year or so. Have you not pondered upon what might be the cause?"

"I believe it to be your drinking, John, for you do indulge to excess. But lately I have held other fears, too distressing to contemplate, that you are diseased with the syphilis. For pity sake, John, please tell me this is not true."

My heart heavy with the reality of my condition, I told her in great anguish that I had indeed been forced to take the cure of the mercury baths. She was so deeply shocked and sat trembling and crying bitterly.

"In all honesty, I thought I was cured. My condition abated and it appeared I was well again. But this damned elusive disease can assault the humours again years later. Dr. Loveall has concluded regrettably that, with its return, there is no more he can do for me."

"Years later?" cried Elizabeth.

"Its origin, Elizabeth, was, I fear, long before you and I were wed," I said with great remorse.

"What in God's name has any of this to do with Charles?" questioned Elizabeth.

"Charles's physician is under no illusion that the boy's illness stems from my own," I ventured.

"How can this be, John? Our three girls are in good health and have never succumbed to the maladies that poor Charles has suffered. And I myself am blessed with good health."

"I asked the same of the physician, Elizabeth, and all he could proffer was that at the time of Charles's conception, the sickness dwelt in my humours, but remained dormant during the conception of our daughters. He also conjectured that beyond his understanding, you too, by God's mercy, have avoided its curse."

"So our poor innocent child is as dammed as his father due to your weaknesses and debased morality. God only knows how many pox ridden whores you encountered before you lay with me," Elizabeth cried in great anguish.

"Believe me Elizabeth, I will do all in my power to help my son when he is inclined to fever, and will engage the very best of physicians to attend upon him."

There was a knock upon the door, and in came Martha, smiling. She asked us to accompany her to Charles's room.

As we entered he called, "Father, mother, look at me!"

He was kneeling on a rug with Omah, in front of the coal fire, which had burned continually throughout his confinement. He was amusing himself happily with his horse and coach. We were beset with joy and marvelled at his courage, and I wept.

As our Christmas festivities drew near our hearts were joyful, for our precious son had gradually gained his strength and now seemed well recovered.

Elizabeth and I made a visit to the Notgroves' and there purchased toys for the children. For our daughters, three exquisite dolls, dressed in the French fashion. These diminished in size, each to the other. The largest was for Anne being the eldest, the next was for Elizabeth, and the smallest for baby Mallet. The gift for Charles was a little more special, we buying for him a beautiful small wooden horse, which had been masterfully carved by old Notgrove. The steed sported a fine mane and tail of rich chestnut horsehair and was ridden by a male doll, dressed in the finest silks and satins, with leather top boots and fine tiny leather gloves that held the reins of the horse's bridle. This handsome fellow was adorned with silky black hair, which hung in tiny curls cascading to his shoulders and flowing over his fine velvet jacket, his head topped with a tall wide brimmed felt hat complemented by tiny feathers of many colours. When Charles received it, he cried out with wonder and he treasured it beyond anything he had ever owned, apart that is from his precious friend Omah, for he and his dog were inseparable.

Elizabeth and I declined invitations to Twelfth Night, for we felt compelled to be at Adderbury with our children throughout this our most joyous of Christmases. We asked our servants to join us for the evening's festivities and, although in complete contrast to our usual gatherings, the night proved most delightful. Upon the dividing of the ceremonial cake, Charles received in his portion the much-coveted bean and Anne in hers the pea. King Charles and Queen Anne relished their Royal rôles, laughing and giggling as they were held aloft and paraded to the applause of their parents and the servants.

Elizabeth attended the New Year service alone at Adderbury Church and in her prayers thanked God for his mercy given on the life of our son. On her return, she found me sitting in the parlour, most agitated and forlorn. "John, what is wrong? You look pale and restless. Are you not well?"

"If remorse is an illness, then I am suffering severely from its symptoms."

The guilt over my son's grave condition, for which I, and I alone, am responsible, weighed heavy. I was descending into a dark abyss of despair and was forced to London in an attempt to salvage my sanity, of which precious little I now possessed.

CHAPTER SIXTEEN

Deception and Hope

In March 1677, I returned to London and Wych Street in a most melancholic state of mind. I was in dire need of Mrs. Barry's intimate solace, for she would have the spell to raise me from my wretchedness. She greeted me with her usual complacent yet teasingly loving manner. Looking a little tired, she was now resting after her demanding rôles at the Duke's during the winter.

We talked at length of her stage success and now comfortable wealth, in her noticeably well-furnished parlour. She then asked of Adderbury during my recent stay there. I told her sadly of Charles's illness, and the physician's assumption for the poor boy's distress. She was surprisingly unperturbed at this, she having neither faith in quacks nor, as was quite apparent, any true interest in my family affairs, wishing to speak no more of them, for such talk only inflamed her hostility.

Beth had often intimated to me that she herself had the wish to bear me a child, and I had acquiesced in her pursuit of this desire, if only to keep her from straying out of my grasp into other amours. But *her* reason was so very different from mine, for she had a deluded ambition to be the equivalent of my wife, and no doubt to prosper by it. Yet all this had so far come to naught, for our union had proved fruitless.

"Well, John, what is the true purpose of your visit?" she enquired coldly.

"We two on a grand adventure, Beth. Two lovers to the realm of Venus and Cupid, in bewitching Dorsetshire."

"My Lord, tell of this intrigue."

And so I spoke of my elaborate plan, for us to pose as mystical soothsayers. Beth became excited at the prospect of our acting out these rôles and said she would secure, from the theatre's wardrobe, exotic silken garb for us both. Hooded cloaks would mantle our costumes whilst travelling.

Anon, with our deception, we carried two small bags of belongings and boarded a coach from the heart of London for the southwest. After several days' arduous journey, we skirted the downs and arrived at the ancient city of Winchester.

The journey had been tiring, my body altogether weakened by the experience. The sore on my neck was once more inflamed and my health was on the wane again. Resolute though, I steeled me to continue.

Making our way to a tavern in the heart of the town, we secured a room for two nights. Beth was under no illusion of my ill state, and knew that *The God of Love* would not rise to the occasion for many a day.

Morning arrived, and we ate a meagre morsel accompanied by small beer, then made our way into the streets of Winchester, a city of prosperous trade that supported many a rich merchant. Walking the streets and alleyways, we came to the splendid cathedral and entering, beheld the wondrous interior. On leaving this sacred place, we made our way back to the tavern.

Sitting in the corner of the largest room, we dined heartily on beef and bread, quenching our thirst with two bottles of modestly priced fine wine. Other patrons gazed upon us with intrigue and whispered, for we appeared quite against expectations here in this city.

Prior to our journey, we had discussed with great zeal in the parlour at Wych Street how we would tell of our spiritual gift, given to us by mystics in the east when we had roved the world. We would contrive to foretell a person's future by the stars, moon and planets and foresee their longevity, or otherwise, with the aid of our unique

Healthoscopic instrument bestowed upon us by a sage, many moons past. We were to be known as Hellawaits and Bethaven.

We had not sat long before two of the company introduced themselves, remarking on our unusual dress and asking what business we had in Winchester. I welcomed them to our table and informed them of our assumed names, saying our business was that of soothsayers. For a fee of sixpence, I would foretell the paths upon which their lives were to travel. For a further three pennies, if they were willing, they could each be tried with the aid of the Healthoscope to foretell the span of their earthly life.

The two men were most eager to know what the future offered, and were surprisingly keen to learn as to the length of time they would endure upon this earth. They each paid their ninepence and both sat transfixed but attentive.

I left Bethaven at the table and went to our room to collect a bag. Returning, I delved deep into it and extracted therefrom a rolled manuscript that had printed upon it colourful stars, planets and moons; supposed worlds beyond our own. With care, I unrolled it and secured it flat upon the table. I then took from the bag an unusual metal instrument, made of silver and hinged in the centre. When opened, it measured eight inches in length. Tubular in appearance, at one end was a metal ring and at the other a gilt pointer. It was patently a measuring device of sorts, but its true use was a mystery to me, it being a curio I had purchased as a young man on the Tour.

I asked who would be first and one of them nodded. I asked his name, his age and in which month he was born. He replied Edward, three and twenty years and that he had been born in May. With these scant facts, I proceeded to consult the chart and with the aid of the instrument, slowly and deliberately followed the pictorial stars and planets on the parchment until stopping of an instant covering a line of three stars and one solitary moon. Fixing my eyes upon his, I told him that I knew he worked hard for a living; I could see clearly from the calluses on his hands that this was true. I informed him that his labours would not be in vain and that he would prosper very well from them, foretelling that he was soon to be master of his trade and would take orders from no one. The young man smiled contentedly and seemed most pleased at the prospect. I continued that his sweetheart, whom he had yet to meet, lived but a short distance away and was a beauty, possessing the fairest skin and golden hair. He would one day marry this girl and make her a fine husband and they would be blessed with many children. I added though, that they would unfortunately not have a son, but only daughters. At this he looked saddened and perturbed, but when I assured him that his daughters would marry well, he was heartened afresh. There would be one daughter whose son would be apprenticed to him and, on his grandfather's demise at a very grand old age, he in turn would continue the business that his grandfather had striven so hard for. At this, the young man thanked me most gratefully, swiftly left the table, and was soon relaying his good news to others close by.

I then turned to his friend, who I believed to be at least ten years older. I could see from his hands and stature that he was not a manual worker and seemed to be a most educated man. I had the premonition that he was a scribe of sorts, and fortunately, I was not far off the mark. Having assessed his age, I asked his name and the month of his birth.

"Thomas, sir, and I was born in the January month," he replied.

I assumed he was already married and I proceeded. Again, I moved the instrument slowly across the parchment and stopped it, this time at an angle. Here were covered four stars and two moons. I begged the man to listen carefully, as I believed from a certain sadness in his eyes that a great heartache had recently befallen him. I had also come to this conclusion in the noting of a mourning ring that adorned one of his fingers, and so I assumed he had lost someone very close to him.

I then pronounced, "I believe that the great heartache you are now suffering will pass. I know there has been a sad loss in your life, but happiness will soon be upon you again. As a married man, your children will share a good, long life with you, void of tragic mishaps and of poverty. They, like you, will secure for themselves spouses of the most genteel nature and they will prosper. As to your work, which I perceive is not of a manual nature, you will obtain a position in the Patents Office working for the many merchants of this city. You are destined to have a long and fulfilling life, provided one peril is avoided at all costs; never buy, ride or hire any horse that possesses a blue eye."

Thomas seemed happy with the telling and thanked me heartily for it. He assured me that no such horse would ever come into his possession, and that hereafter he would look closely at the horses' eyes, before ever he boarded a coach.

I then closed my own eyes, bowed my head and sat perfectly still as though entranced. Bethaven informed Thomas that the reading had now come to an end. He thanked us both and left.

Raising my head, I turned to Beth with a wink and a smile, "Bethhaven, let's drink to our success and then retire to our room."

☙❧

In the morning, we left Winchester and boarded a coach heading for Dorchester. There were but few travellers aboard the coach, accompanied only by two coachmen. It was the first coach out of the city that morning and being early, not yet six of the clock, there was good reason for its dearth of passengers, the coachmen informing us that the good people of Winchester preferred to travel later, when daylight had pierced the sky. They knew all too well the dangers on the southern highways. To our relief the coach made good time, and we arrived at Dorchester, weary but unscathed.

Dorchester is a pleasant and agreeable town surrounded by rolling hills and luscious downs, where thousands of sheep, seen as white dots covering the land, graze the green slopes as far as the eye can see. This was a curious sight for Beth, she having spent her life confined to a crowded city, where sheep were noticed largely by their bloody carcasses hanging on hooks in slaughterhouses.

Making our way through the crowded streets in search of lodgings, we found a large, busy tavern along the main street where, fortuitously, we secured the last available room. Ravenously hungry, we ordered food to our room, not having eaten or drunk since our departure from Winchester. Then, taking a turn in the streets, we found the people of Dorchester not altogether unfriendly, and certainly not in any way alarmed at our bizarre attire. We enquired of an old man, who was leaning backwards against a wall in a cloud of smoke from his bacca pipe, as to where we might find the apothecary's shop.

"Down Sheep Street you go, to the Blue Bottle," he answered in his Dorset drawl.

We thanked him, trusting that he was not so drunk as to be oblivious to the shop's whereabouts. With a silly grin, a wobbly nod and the wall his only support, he bid us good day.

Locating the shop, I entered and there purchased cerecloths and paste, for the eruption on my neck was now uneasy; painful, burning hot and inflamed. Back in our room, Beth assisted me in applying the remedy. Wincing with pain, my face beaded in sweat, I removed my necktie. Then Beth gently peeled off the stinking, puss-covered dressing and shrieked in horror.

"Oh! John."

"Beth, it is an ugly sight I know, but the sooner you apply the fresh cloth the easier I will be," I assured her in a faint whisper.

"Should I seek a physician, John? Surely one could help?"

"No, Beth. None could help, believe me. My neck will soon ease. Do not concern yourself."

"You poor darling. No coward could suffer the torments you endure so bravely," she said gazing upon me, her eyes wet with tears.

We lay upon the bed, peacefully content in each other arms until evening came when, seated in the tavern, we once more caught the eye of the unwary who might be eager to know our business, as were those gullible souls in Winchester. Curiosity won the day for, by and by, ten individuals came forth and, with the aid of our parchment and the Healthoscope, each went away contented in mind but lighter in purse. Our little venture was proving most profitable.

⊱⊰

Anon, leaving Dorchester, we travelled north upon the road running parallel with the River Cerne, our destination Cerne Abbas which lies in a small valley in among the Dorset hills, the highest being Black Hill to the south. The road there was quite desolate, apart from three hamlets and the small village of Godmanstone.

The day fairing a little warmer enabled us to roll up the window leathers, thus giving view to the wide-open spaces beyond. There were two other travellers in our company; a man and his wife, both of great age. The wife studied us with a fixed stare, never uttering a word. In spite of this, her toothless husband was more amenable and entered into conversation, introducing himself as Woodcock Skeleton and his wife as Agnes. He apologized for her apparent impoliteness, saying she spoke very seldom, not through ignorance but due to her profound deafness, which silent world she has endured for many years. He enquired of our purpose upon the road, and was now keen to learn of our business in Cerne. With Beth asleep and his wife a near mute, Woodcock and I spent the journey in agreeable conversation. This old man held for me a deep fascination, his intellect quite rare for one so rustic.

They too were travelling to Cerne, from their home in Dorchester, to visit their son, his wife and their children. Woodcock said proudly that his son was well respected in his trade as a blacksmith and that he made a good living from his work, his wife and children never wanting for food in their bellies or clothes upon their backs.

On arriving, we bade farewell to Woodcock and Agnes, and headed to the Giant Inn, highly recommended by him. Although its name belied the smallness of the building, the cost of accommodation was large enough for any man's purse.

We were shown to a small, cramped room at the back of the building, which housed a large bed and one stool, there being just room enough for our baggage. We were brought clean, cool water in an earthen bowl and we refreshed our hands and faces. Famished, we slaked our stomachs with bread, cheese and copious beer, and then took a turn in the village.

"John?" began Beth.

I interrupted, whispering, "I am not John, am I, Bethaven?"

"So sorry, my Lord Hellawaits."

'My Lord Hellawaits! The devil himself would be proud of that title', I thought.

Beth went on, "I feel uneasy. These folk do not appear welcoming. Do you sense it too?"

"Yes, I do. I certainly do."

We continued walking the narrow cobbled streets, ignoring the evident hostility shown by passers-by.

Returning to the Giant, we found the inn teeming with inhabitants whose favoured drink is apparently locally brewed cider, the potent ferocity of this piss coloured drink soon leaving the customers in a drunken frenzy. As we entered, they were staggering about, tripping over chairs and tables, which their bleary eyes could not focus upon. Gibberish speech combined with their Dorset drawl, which at best was itself difficult to unravel, resulted in a strange, garbled language. Their earlier animosity ceased, and we were offered many hands in friendship. Beth and I concluded that this entertaining tragicomedy was the best ever performed upon a stage. However, this was not beneficial for us, as not one of the actors in this scene was capable of sitting still, let alone being foretold their kismet. We decided the best course of action now would be to swill a pint or two of this devil's piss and join in the merriment. After a long drunken evening, we stumbled across our room, with more luck than judgement, collapsing on the bed fully dressed and knowing nothing more until morning.

Our day started late, Beth and I languishing in bed, our heads as heavy as lead and with such a pounding therein we could scarce lift them from the soft pillows. Eventually, the necessity of pissing forced us to rise. Because of the lateness of the morning, we missed the knock of the maid bringing fresh water to wash, obliging us to cleanse face, hands and feet in soiled water from the night before. Beth attended to my ulcerated neck, applying a fresh cerecloth and observing that it was healing a little. I knew this to be the case, for the searing pain had ceased only to be replaced by an annoyingly irritating itch. Ready to face the day, and now wanting for food, we went downstairs to break our fast. At table, we sat quietly, the drums in our heads not favouring conversation, when we spied a man walking towards us.

"Good morning to you." he bellowed, "I gather that you slept like the dead, given the lateness of the hour, and if I am not mistaken now suffering the demons of the cider's might."

"Good morning, Woodcock. Do join us. Have you eaten yet?"

"Many hours since, Hellawaits. I have always risen before dawn, even after a heavy night in the Giant."

Beth, looking very pale, excused herself saying that she needed to lie down for a little while longer as she was not altogether well.

"Tell me, Hellawaits, and if I appear presumptuous I apologize for it…" started Woodcock.

"Presumptuous, Woodcock?" I interrupted.

He continued, "I am told I am a man of many mysteries and have gifts similar to you, and I perceive all is not well."

"Go on," I said.

"I judge an illness that ails you has caused you grave suffering, and concerns others close to your heart. Am I right that your condition is desperate and far beyond any medical cure?"

"How you could know this mystifies me, Woodcock, but sadly you read true in every detail."

This sage had crossed the threshold of my soul.

I told him of our desire to have a child, but that I was fearful it would bring ill tidings upon the infant.

Woodcock, smiling said, "I could, if you are willing, help you overcome your uncertainties."

"Woodcock, I would be prepared to do anything for Bethaven and me to have a healthy child."

"Are you not curious of the name of this inn?" said Woodcock.

"Only that it is rather small to have such a large title," I said, grinning.

"The mystery of Cerne is unknown to you is it not, Hellawaits?"

"Yes. It is the first time I have ventured in this neck of the woods."

"The inn is so named because less than a mile from this very spot, directly due north, on a large hillside, lies the Giant of Cerne Abbas," Woodcock explained.

"A giant? Lying on a hill, Woodcock?"

"Yes, Hellawaits. Just lying there."

"But what does he look like, this giant?" I asked, intrigued.

"Nobody knows how or from where he came, but it is believed that *The Old Man of Cerne* has lain there for many thousands of years. His whole form had been carefully etched out upon the hill to reveal a clear white outline of the chalk rock that lies not far beneath the grass. For many centuries, this giant has held mysteries for man, and his powers have helped many a tormented, ill soul when despairing of life. Do you have belief in your heart, Hellawaits?"

"I do, Woodcock. I do not know why or how, but I believe that you are one of the truest and most honest men I have ever chanced to meet."

Woodcock then proceeded to tell in detail the course of action we should take in the begetting of a child. He told how Bethaven and I, at dusk that night, must make our way through the village towards the Abbey ruins and onward up a steep hill where, after a short time, the giant would be revealed to us.

"You must continue towards the giant, at which point his phallus will come into view. Then, as darkness descends, you both must lay upon his member and there, in the natural course of things, employ yourselves in the conceiving of a child," Skeleton imparted this with great conviction and added, "at which time *Cerne's Old Man* will sheath you, and in so doing protect Bethaven's body from the evil disease that dwells within you."

I sighed, and told Woodcock that I was more than prepared to go through with this curious ritual. He smiled, placing a firm hand upon my shoulder and then left the tavern without uttering another word.

I went upstairs and found Beth asleep. On waking her, I spoke of the wondrous giant upon a hill, as told to me by Woodcock.

"*The Old Man of Cerne*, for that is his name, Beth, is believed to hold magical, curative powers and to make barren wombs fertile."

She believed, as did I, that Woodcock was telling the truth. Why would he lie? What would he gain from it? Trusting him, we made ready for the hill.

As dusk fell, we donned our cloaks over our naked bodies and walked towards the Abbey ruins, then up the steep hill. In the distance could be clearly seen the white outline of a man whose immense scale was beyond belief. Darkness now enveloped us, and there, standing upon the *Old Man's* phallus, Venus and Cupid entered our hearts.

We were charged with a frenzy of eroticism and, lying upon our discarded cloaks, soon yielded to abandoned passion. Afterwards, we lay breathless and spent, on the dew-covered ground. Anon, a cool mist swirled about us and then mysteriously rose heavenwards. Under a starlit sky, we shivered and so made haste to cloak ourselves. Silently, we descended the hillside towards the inn and once there, being most weary, we again cast off our cloaks and held each other close under the warm coverlet of our bed.

CHAPTER SEVENTEEN

The Debauched Mistress

Back in London, Beth's loving disposition towards me had much cooled. She seemed bored and agitated in my presence. She was inclined towards other friendships, both male and female, and to discard my company entirely, and despite the warmth of spring, there was a chill in the air at Wych Street. The true cause of her abrupt coldness I never did fathom. Perhaps she had some inkling of my dishonourable intention to keep her merely as a mistress, she perceiving that her notions of grandeur would in truth never be fulfilled.

We drifted apart and, on the rare occasions we chanced upon one another, we were as complete strangers. I had lost my heart to a woman who no longer wanted the love and affection I could offer. If a healthy child were conceived upon the old man's pintle, the chances of my acquaintance with the infant were now slim.

❧

With the theatres closed for the summer, and with an angry letter from my mother demanding my immediate return to Elizabeth and the children at Adderbury, I left London, now glad to be away from Mrs. Barry, and made my way to Oxfordshire. Arriving there, I found Elizabeth and the children well, and though the weather was pleasingly warm, it being early May, I suffered the usual indifference from my wife, for which I did not chide her; after all, I had been absent from Adderbury for far too long.

My beautiful Charles seemed in remarkable good health and,

now six years old, displayed the presence and intelligence of a boy twice his age. One of our servants, Benjamin Pickerel, being a keen angler had been teaching him the art of fishing. Charles showed a natural ability as an angler, and on several occasions caught good-sized carp in our lake. Indeed, this very day he had caught one such and presented it to his mother with great excitement, to be cooked for dinner.

Fate now dictated that I spend time at Adderbury, and in its relative peace and tranquillity I vented my spleen in the writing of satires based on those courtiers I despised the most. I also spared neither their wives nor mistresses, reflecting in truth the sad state of a debauched Royal Court. These satires I kept under lock and key, so that my wife or mother should not read such sinister, debasing and malicious works.

In the heat of summer, in mid-July, I became much alarmed when Elizabeth fell ill to a fever. Her symptoms showed themselves in a rash on her chest, upper arms and face. The physician, who was summoned urgently to the house, assured us there was no cause for alarm, for it was not the smallpox, despite our first fears. He ordered her to rest for seven days and to diet on fresh fruit and on warmed milk infused with sage and lovage to cool the blood, so as to favour a swift recovery. I consoled myself that her malady was not the smallpox, but was concerned over the likeness of Elizabeth's symptoms to those of Charles in his periodic illnesses. It also reminded me all too much of the sickness I had myself so often suffered during the past few years. To my relief, the physician's prognosis held true. Within a week, Elizabeth was completely recovered and once again the demanding and irritating wife that I had come to expect.

Elizabeth's condition had delayed my returning to High Lodge but, soon after my wife was restored to health, I relinquished Adderbury to attend my duties as Ranger. On my arrival, there was a letter from George, Duke of Buckingham, awaiting a reply. He had written saying he wished to join me at High Lodge on the First of August, for two weeks' sport, on and off the field. I replied saying that he would be most welcome and that I would delight in his company.

Before his arrival, my servants there were to make the house clean, comfortable and warm and to ensure that the very best of the linen be placed on the beds. I ordered that the cellar be supplied with the finest wines and a barrel of good brandy and for the stocking of vittles in good time for the Duke's stay.

George is a handsome and charismatic man, holding a great power and influence with the King for he, like me, has family connections with the seductive and handsomely rich Castlemaine. His stature is gracious and he possesses great intelligence and wit with an unrivalled geniality but, when provoked, he can reveal an uncompromising and lethal temper. His partiality for good food and drink and for the ugliest insalubrious whores in London is renowned.

The Duke's poor long-suffering wife is Lady Mary Fairfax, the daughter of Baron Thomas Fairfax, the most famed of Cromwell's generals. This woman's virtuous nature, infused with a steely realism, equipped her well indeed for marriage to the Duke. George's fondness for life at Charles's Court keeps him often away from his estate at Helmsley, so that visits to his wife are few and, on those rare occasions, more to view his fillies at stud than his lady.

By mid-August, the Duke had left for London. He had enjoyed good sport at Woodstock, and although his health and stamina were far superior to mine, I was still his equal in the drinking of liquor. In fact, I believe I surpassed him on every occasion.

During those two pleasurable weeks, I received a letter from dear Henry enquiring of my health. He had heard reports that Mrs. Barry was no longer my mistress, and he wrote with regret that he had learned her conduct had been most debased since I had departed for Oxfordshire. Apparently, she was now drinking heavily, and invariably was to be found in the company of rakes and whores of the lowest order. Henry declared that he was saddened to write of her in such terms, but that, as a true friend, he felt I should know the facts.

This news came as no surprise, but I still felt a certain love and affection for my dear Beth, yet in truth knew she had forsaken me.

Henry concluded he was longing of my company and urged my return to London when I felt able.

ঔ⁖ও

At the end of August, remorseful and ill humoured, I returned to Adderbury, my wife protesting bitterly that I had declined yet again for her to join me at High Lodge. This feeble argument had persisted for many a year and was wearing most thin. Angry, I fell into a rage shouting that High Lodge was *my* business and my business alone. I was master there and as such, my wife was not welcome.

"I see, John." said Elizabeth, "It is fine for you to enter the world of Enmore, where I am sole mistress and where you have always been welcomed, but alas I am ever prohibited from visiting your Woodstock universe."

"Is the law of the land a complete mystery to you, Elizabeth?" I retorted angrily, "Your betrothal to me gave me rights to do as I wish. I am your lord and master and you will obey me in all things. I have been indulgent to your moods, but I have gone beyond leniency and you will do as I ask."

This belittling was too much for her to bear and so she left my presence, running to her private sitting room, where she remained for many hours. I retreated to the sanctuary of the parlour, with only liquor for comfort.

ঔ⁖ও

157

A servant brought a letter to me. It was addressed from the High Sheriff of Taunton and Somerset who informed me that, through my marriage to Elizabeth, I was to be elected Alderman of the county. A formal dinner was to be held in my honour, to which I was invited. I replied, thanking him for this honourable duty, and confirmed that Lady Rochester and I would be only too pleased to be there.

To my great contentment, I found Elizabeth congenial and attentive in the morning, we having slept apart that night. I informed her of my forthcoming election as Alderman and she responded with great excitement. I suggested she must accompany me to Somerset, and she accepted willingly. We would be absent from Adderbury for three weeks, our children being left at home in the trusted care of our servants.

᷈᷉

At length, after a laborious journey over several days, we arrived at Enmore Castle, where Old Shepherd greeted us. Servants hauled our two laden trunks laboriously to the large bedchamber and a housemaid then attended to the unpacking of our apparel. This luxurious room afforded ample comfort. Rich velvet curtains hung against the five-panelled oriel window. Crisp linen sheets, topped with soft pillows, adorned the carved oak tester, which abutted a wall of rare linenfold beech wood panelling. The other three walls were draped with lavish tapestries, a gift to Unton from Sir John Warre on their marriage. Woven rush matting upon the floor gave warmth, comfort and quietness underfoot; far better than the bare wooden boards at Adderbury, upon which clattering footsteps would resound.

On the appointed day of my election to office, Elizabeth and I travelled to the large town of Bridgwater, but a short distance of two miles from Enmore. The ceremonial dinner held in my honour was at mid-day, in the newly furbished Aldermen's Chamber in the old Town Hall. The original medieval building had been much extended since the restoration and was now most airy and spacious.

During our late wars, the people of Bridgwater had built sturdy fortifications around the town's perimeter. They had paid particular attention to the points where the River Parrett flowed into and out of the town, these positions being exceedingly vulnerable to attack. However, the defences had been torn down once hostilities had ceased, and Bridgwater was once again a prosperous and fashionable town. Its townsfolk though, to the casual observer, seemed more than usually decorous for town dwellers.

In the Chamber there were several Aldermen gathered and William Petherton, by far the oldest, gave a speech, firstly to welcome Elizabeth and me to the town, and secondly to honour my election as Alderman. He was now in his eightieth year and, having served the town admirably for thirty of those years, he was relieved to relinquish his authority, so allowing a younger man to take on his now burdensome duties.

After the celebratory dinner and excellent fine wines, Elizabeth and I discoursed with many wealthy citizens of the town. Their prosperity was due not only to the rich and fertile farmland, but also in particular to Bridgwater's close proximity to the Bristol Channel and the shipping port of Bristol itself. Here, the Bridgwater merchants had traded for many years in goods from the Americas and the Caribbean Islands and from continents to the east producing spices and that most expensive commodity, tea. The merchants' shrewd dealings at the docks in these exotic goods earned them a handsome profit from the London traders.

As the formalities drew to a close, we prepared to travel back to Enmore. William had presented me with a badge of office, beautifully wrought in silver and inlaid with gold. This official emblem was to be worn as and when I commenced my duties. I bade farewell to my fellow Aldermen and townspeople, and we boarded the coach.

At Enmore, we rested for a while in the large parlour before contemplating retiring to bed.

"I was very proud of you today, Elizabeth. You conducted yourself well and made a good impression on the Aldermen. They seem to be content in the presence of such a sober and pious woman."

"Thank you, my Lord. I believe you too gave a good account of a man fit for his duties as Alderman, but I fear that you struggle indeed to match me for sobriety and piety."

"Why, madam, do you ever persist on the immorality of my drinking and my debased life as I choose it?" I scowled, adding, "I shall drink whenever I feel the need, and if the company of a whore is my want, that will be my choosing."

Elizabeth responded angrily, "I am only concerned for you, John. You know as well as I that your health has suffered irreparable damage through your drinking and whoring, and now it deteriorates daily. I know the love you now feel for me is but shallow and all too transparent, but the true love you hold for your children can never be denied. So for their sakes alone, can you not curb your ways and prolong what little life you have left? Can you not be content to forego your over-indulgences and so be a more sober father to your children?"

Elizabeth's anger was all too evident and she, too tired to argue more, begged leave and retired to bed.

Our stay in Enmore at an end, Elizabeth and I returned to Adderbury with very little in the way of conversation on the journey home.

Impatiently, I soon took my leave of Elizabeth and announced that I would not return to Adderbury until Christmas. My wife, in her usual nonchalant manner, said little regarding my plan, only wishing me a safe journey and hopeful return.

෨᳟ᢩᡈ

I travelled to London and made straightway for my lodgings at Whitehall. The King returned that very day from Winchester with Nelly and Wren. He was planning the building of a new grandiose palace there, thus adding to the concerns of his treasurer over continually depleting finances.

On my way to the Duke's, I first had need of an inn, which caused me great delay in arriving at the theatre, so that once there I found the day's performance long since concluded. On leaving, I spied a group of people, none familiar to me but one. I recognized Mrs. Barry in an instant, in the midst of this uncouth rabble. She was wearing a fine cloak lined with red silk and had masked her tired, gaunt face under a heavily painted exterior. She was clearly under the influence of much drink, and steadied her balance by the linking of her arm to a *gentleman*, who was well dressed yet an obvious rogue. I looked again to her for signs of a swollen belly, but as she was all but hidden from view by her entourage of scoundrels and whores, such detection was impossible. I had now witnessed with my own eyes her blatant immorality as was alluded to in Henry's letter. I could now only hope that our encounter upon *that* hill had met with a barren womb. I turned swiftly away from this ugly scene and returned dejectedly to my lodgings. Henry, having heard of my return to London, was waiting on a chance meeting there. As I approached, he greeted me at a distance with an enthusiastic wave, but as I drew closer, his smile gave way to a look of shock. He clearly detected the deterioration that had occurred in my health since the last time we met.

"John, it's good to see you!"

"And you likewise, Henry."

We entered my lodgings and presently drank each other's health. We then talked at length, not having spoken for far too long. Several glasses later, there was mention of Mrs. Barry, and I told Henry of my sighting of her earlier that day and of the debased company she now kept. If that damned woman was bearing my child, she was disguising it well, for there was no talk of a swollen belly from Henry and I, for my part, said naught to him on the matter.

"I still hold a great passion for that damned woman you know, Henry."

"You must follow your reasoning, John, as you have in all things, but I deem your lot should be with your wife and children."

"That, Henry, is the truth of the matter and the reason I shall be travelling back to my home.

"Take care, John."

Henry embraced me and then we parted company.

My wife's astonishment at my premature return to Adderbury caused much tension between us, she ever suspicious of the motives for my comings and goings.

Anon, the season of peace on earth and goodwill to all men was fast approaching, and I hoped then to rekindle the love and esteem my wife once held for me. But alas, I sensed that Elizabeth was no longer willing or able to offer me even that charity.

CHAPTER EIGHTEEN

A Wife's Comforting and Loyalty

At Adderbury, with Christmas now passed, and to my great relief it was spent in surprising harmony, a new year began.

I received a letter from Henry informing me to my astonishment, and apparently to his, that Mrs. Barry had given birth to a girl in late December. I wrote to her immediately, saying I was pleased and relieved to hear of the safe delivery of the child. I felt compelled to visit them, but my health had unfortunately spiralled downwards and, with the weakness in my body and limbs, travelling any distance would I fear have proved fatal. Simply walking across a room was difficult enough.

At thirty years of age, I was a decrepit specimen of human kind. I suffered repeated outbursts of the ulcer on my neck. I now too endured a weeping sore on the inside of my right thigh, which made riding impractical. At times my bladder felt as though it was on fire and, when I *was* able to piss freely, the agony of relieving myself was unbearable. Decaying teeth and reddened gums were a constant source of nagging irritation to me.

❧

On All Fools' Day 1678, by sheer doggedness I reached the age of thirty-one. Some thought it a miracle, but I knew no divine intervention was helping this poor wretch. I had been confined to my bed for four days and I reluctantly permitted a physician's attendance upon me. He was also administering to Charles, for the boy had become ill once more of the fevers; at seven years old, my darling boy had suffered more than many a man three times his age.

My poor despairing wife was worn out from worry and the constant attendance upon us both. In the evening quiet of Adderbury, accompanied only by the loathsome ticking of time from our hall clock, I could hear Elizabeth praying for God's help in the healing of her child and husband.

The physician had, over many days, attempted to alleviate my pain with his medicines and barbaric tools of his art. He expressed concern to Elizabeth over his inability to cure me of the constantly weeping, spreading sore on my thigh, which he was afeared would become gangrenous, and so unbeknown to me a drastic decision was made. He arrived early one morning with two men. Elizabeth, who had been at my bedside, was asked to leave the room. With the sight in my right eye long since impaired, and with the other eye partially closed with a stickiness oozing from it, the physician's strong assistants soon held me fast. I could hear the sound of metal against the fire grate. The bandages were removed from my thigh and the stench of festering flesh rose in my nostrils. I could just detect the physician striding towards me holding in his hand an iron rod, the end of which glowed fiercely, he having just raised it from the fire. He apologized, but said it was the only course of action now open. With a searing pain and the smell of burning flesh, I screamed out in the most deplorable agony and fell unconscious. I awoke several minutes later, my thigh tightly bound, with the fires of hell burning under the fresh bandage. Elizabeth came into the room and sat at my bedside. Weeping, she cupped her gentle hands around my pale, gaunt face and cried out for my forgiveness, she having consented to this barbarous remedy. I lifted my trembling hand and placed it lovingly upon her bowed head. Whispering, I said, "No, Elizabeth. It is I who must crave forgiveness. Is there room in your heart to pardon such a wretched soul?"

During this recent sickness, my mortified mother had graced us with but one anxious visit. She spoke to me in the privacy of my bedchamber of her utter disgust at hearing of the illegitimate brat born to Mrs. Barry, and the certainty as to its father's identity. In like mood, she enlightened Elizabeth of this scandalous news, and to my wife's credit, she uttered not a single word on the subject, giving my mother no satisfaction as to the telling of it. Elizabeth, who had not only shown great courage and fortitude throughout these past weeks had in addition, poor wretch, to contend with the heartless comments of the Countess. I, for my part, held silent too upon the matter.

Our dear Charles was recovering steadily, more by luck than by the abusive judgement of the physician and in time I too took a turn for the better. The boy was permitted to visit me in my bedchamber on two occasions a day, when he sat on my bed and played happily with his toys, begging for his father to be well again. He was eager for us to venture outside to fish the lake, and for his father to witness him climbing trees.

Little by little, my weakened constitution was regaining strength, when at last I was able to leave the confines of my bed. On days when the warm spring sunshine allowed, I strolled out of doors and down to the lake to sit awhile and watch Charles fishing, he now restored to health. On occasion, he would run to me, proudly holding his catch. We would also wander in the garden, where in an instance he would scamper up a sturdy oak with ease, sparking happy memories of my own boyish days at Ditchley.

Sometimes, Elizabeth and I would discuss with our gardeners the planting of additional apple and pear trees and fruit bushes or perhaps the year's planning for the growing of vegetables in our kitchen garden, hoping for a plentiful supply for the lean winter months.

Elizabeth's herbs were harvested daily, and provided a good supply for culinary and for medicinal purposes. Some were used for their freshness of flavour to garnish and add palatability to our food. Others would be placed in the herb drier; a closet, whose opened south facing window allowed warm air to circulate around the variety of posies hanging from hooks in the ceiling.

The month of April was unusually mild and surprisingly dry for Oxfordshire, proving most beneficial to both Charles and me. The boy spent many hours outdoors, the warm sunlight adding a healthy, rosy hue to his all too often pale features.

As the month of May approached, the weather turned without warning and although still warm, it rained incessantly for days on end. Dank air crept through the large house and necessitated the burning of coal fires in all the hearths to alleviate the pervasive damp.

Alarmingly, heavy downpours flooded the kitchen garden frequently, and so the gardeners had dug channels, thus draining the rising waters directly into the lake. When the rain occasionally relented, giving a few hours respite, Charles and I would stand by a channel and observe the waters running by. We sailed small boats that we made together from old parchment folded firmly, and we raced them in the turbulent waters. On two days, we sailed our vessels along the main channel, but on the third day, after stormy seas, our little boats were hindered by flotsam of leaves, twigs and blossom wrenched from the fruiting bushes. The debris soon choked the passage of water, so consigning our boats to the dry dock of the hall floor.

❧❧

By June, the weather was fair once again. Leaving Lizbet and Mallet with our servants at Adderbury, Elizabeth and I, with our servant Pickerel, travelled with Anne and Charles to the annual Stow Fair, breaking our journey for a night's rest at Chipping. The fair was usually held in May, but this year the earlier inclement weather had dictated that it be held late. The venue too was changed due to waterlogged ground, thus breaking with the tradition of centuries.

The new site was set upon a plateau atop a hill, with a large lake at its foot, enabling for the first time a grand fishing match to be held. News sheets had been circulated advertising a guinea prize to the victor, inviting all those who wished to take part in the contest. Charles's enthusiasm for this sport made him the youngest angler there. Pickerel helped him set up his rod, and he also carefully placed the bait on the hook, whereupon Charles sat patiently in deep concentration with a steady line. There were as many as twenty anglers sporting for the prize, and Charles was the only child. We left him under the eagle eye of Pickerel and we, with Anne, walked to the heart of the fair.

There were the customary booths selling roast beef, ham, pies, bread and cheeses. The sellers of beer and wine were making their usual handsome profit, and for the more discerning customers, port stored in oak casks was available by the measure, at a price. There were acrobatic entertainers to dazzle the eye, leaving their bewildered audiences transfixed by their somersaults and precarious balancing acts. Twenty feet above the people's heads ropewalkers performed, traversing with courage and dexterity the narrow line of rope, aided only by a pole for balance.

Each year, a modest horse fair is also to be seen, where horses and ponies of good quality and bad, young and old, fit and knackered are bought and sold with enthusiastic bartering. Often they are purchased by the unwary, but nonetheless these transactions are binding, for tradition has it that once money is handed over to the seller, the new owner, if not pleased with his purchase, can neither return nor exchange the animal or expect his money returned. The wily horse dealers and their families live under rough canvas and spend the summer months journeying through the south of England, trading at the fairs. During the winter months, they encamp on the north facing sheltered slopes of the Sussex Downs. They not only buy and sell horses and ponies but also trade in good luck charms and trinkets, the gullible purchasers believing these wares will bring them riches beyond their dreams. The travellers' dress, characteristic language and sun-kissed skin appear foreign and, as with the Latinos, they are blessed with good, white teeth and alluring dark eyes. They seem to be friendly and jovial when bartering, but immediately the deal is struck, they will become aloof, once more joining their kind.

Anon, Elizabeth, Anne and I made to join Charles at the lakeside. On our way, we bought a large hare pie and a jug of Stow beer. At the lake, we found Charles, Pickerel and four other gentlemen deep in fishy conversation. The contest at an end, Charles had netted the fourth largest fish, a noteworthy feat for a boy of only seven. His prize was a small medal, crafted by a silversmith in Stow and struck especially for the competition.

This was indeed a joyous occasion, and to celebrate, Elizabeth proudly handed Charles a generous portion of our pie, the remainder shared between Pickerel, Anne, Elizabeth and me.

As dusk descended, lanthorns were lit for late night revellers. Anne and Charles, weary, were carried to our coach, and slept soundly until we had need to awaken them on our arrival at the Norton's Falcon. In our room there, with our children between us, Elizabeth and I slept contentedly in one of the inn's comfortable beds, whilst poor Pickerel made do in one of the servants' cramped attic rooms.

かくら

Journeying home, we discussed the prospects for Charles's tuition. Owing to the boy's frailty and his vulnerability to ill heath, we agreed that for the next three years he would be taught privately at Adderbury. This was to be under the tutelage of an exceptional Oxford graduate, Godfrey Wrightwell, who had been recommended by the King. This young man of eighteen had been most keen to oblige in our son's education and accepted the post of private tutor without hesitation. Master Wrightwell was tall and slender with fair hair, blue eyes and angelic features. He possessed a soft, melodic voice and a sharp wit, and Charles warmed instantly to this personable man on their first meeting. The small library on the ground floor was designated as their classroom. Godfrey was an inspired tutor, with a passionate pursuit of botany. He was already renowned as an accomplished artist of the botanical, and brought with him to Adderbury many of his fine drawings of flora to be found in the English garden. This pleased Elizabeth, whose interest in herbs gave occasion for lengthy discourse with him. She had looked forward eagerly to his return after his summer recess, when he presented Elizabeth with a variety of seeds and seedlings, in which he knew she would take pleasure.

With the question of Charles's education satisfactorily resolved, I was now to spend a few weeks at High Lodge, for during my recent bout of illness I had, of necessity, neglected my duties there.

My unannounced arrival at the lodge caused great alarm among the servants. They had clearly heard news of my illness, and had assumed wrongly that my return would be a long time delayed. The house was cold, dusty, unkempt and unlit. There was not one fire burning in any grate. The kitchen, larder and cellar were deficient of vittles and wine and the servants themselves were unwashed, their clothes stained and filthy.

I chided them in the strongest of terms for their sloth and their slovenly state. I said I would return in two days to a house suitable managed, adequate stocked and with a welcoming fire in every room. I left them in no doubt that if these duties had not been executed by the time I returned, they would all be dismissed without pay, and that I would personally ensure that they would not find employment elsewhere in the shire.

On my direct return to Adderbury later in the day, I was alarmed to find clouds of black smoke billowing from a small attic window. I rushed into the house to find Elizabeth and all the servants running around in chaos carrying vessels of all shapes and sizes filled from our well. They were running up the stairs to the fire in an endeavour to quench the growing flames, and down again for more water, and I joined them immediately in their attempts. A lit candle that was thought snuffed had apparently started the fire, which then set alight the mattress of a nearby trundle-bed.

We were fortunate that the fire had been observed quickly and brought under control and so confined did not spread through the entire room, or worse. I praised Elizabeth and the servants for their diligence and bravery in dealing with this frightful incident.

I added sarcastically, "If this unfortunate mishap had occurred at High Lodge, the entire building would have been burned to the ground before any servant there had sense enough to do a thing about it."

On the day following the blaze, the servants made haste clearing and replacing the burned and scorched items in the attic room. Elizabeth and I agreed to reward them with a small payment, to be added to that week's wage. They were also invited into our hall where each was given a glass of wine as a token of our appreciation.

☙❧

I returned to Woodstock and High Lodge, which to my great contentment I found now to be in order. That same evening, my nearby circle of friends having heard of my homecoming, honoured me with a visit to the lodge to welcome my unexpected return. They had heard rumours that I was either bed ridden, in the course of dying or actually dead.

"Well, ladies and gentlemen, as you can see with your own eyes, I am neither ridden nor rotting in my bed, neither dying nor in fact dead. Although the body you see before you is emaciated and in the poorest condition, I possess a little life yet, to enjoy your company and the pleasures that brings."

Although weary, I sat amongst them playing at the cards and drinking to excess. The whores of that company made their usual advances to me, but I had not strength enough to rise to the occasion to satisfy their needs. They were, in the circumstances, content to be satisfied with my wit alone.

I sent word to Henry that I would be pleased for him to join me at Woodstock, and he replied in the affirmative. The anticipation of his arrival filled me with contentment. We spent every waking hour in each other's company, taking long walks through the estate and down to the small lake near the lower wood.

"I suppose this is the famous lake, John, in which you and others of your company swam to cool down in the heat of summer and afterwards, naked ran amok startling the Woodstock residents?"

"Yes, Henry, the very same. We were but drying our bodies before dressing," I said with a wry smile.

Grudgingly, I enquired of Henry as to the welfare of my baby daughter in London under the care of her hussy of a mother.

"John, Mrs. Barry returned to the stage, out of necessity, only a month after the child was born. I hear from gossip that the baby is a fine healthy child, so there is no need for despair on your part. You see, she has engaged the services of a wet-nurse, seeming now to have the means and by all accounts the nurse, though of dubious reputation, has suckled and nurtured the child well. As far as I know, since the theatre closed for the summer, Mrs. Barry has looked after the child herself to the best of her ability, though she *is* seen most evenings in the lowest of company."

"My poor darling daughter, Henry. Despite your assurances, I have grave concerns for her wellbeing."

"Well, John, I did chance to meet Mrs. Barry just four weeks ago, but during our short conversation she never once enquired of you. You are far from her thoughts. She did however remark that she had now become well acquainted with George Etherege, she having played the leading female rôle in his successful play, *The Man of Mode*. Perhaps there lies the source of her means."

We returned to the lodge for dinner, and there upon the table awaiting us, a fine spread of cooked meats, pies, a rarity of green leafed salad and of course four bottles of my finest claret; a fitting dinner for our last evening together.

ॐॐ

In early April 1679, my wife and children journeyed to Enmore for the summer months, there the prevailing winds carrying clean air from the coast benefiting Charles's health once more. Wrightwell accompanied them, to continue the boy's education until the end of June, Godfrey as usual looking to spend July and August touring Europe in his quest for botanical rarities.

ॐॐ

In May, I returned to London and resumed my bedchamber duties. His Majesty welcomed my return once more, saying he hoped my sharp satirical wit had not been marred by my latest illness.

Cynically I answered him, "As long as the frailty of my body is surpassed by the sharpness of my wit, so as to divert you and your Court, what more could a man in the throes of death wish but to thus entertain His Gracious Majesty?" Bowing gracefully, I then added, "To be the bringer of pleasure and jollity to the most deserving of enthroned Monarchs is all I could desire."

The King, smiling, invited me to walk with him and his yapping dogs in the privy garden. He was eager to show me his new collection of shrubs and plants, indigenous to the Americas, which had been brought to England specifically for planting in the garden at Whitehall.

"How is your beautiful wife, John? And dear Charles? I do hope they are in good health," His Majesty enquired.

He had a particular fondness for his namesake, having been dazzled by the child's beauty and grace when the boy was just six years of age.

"My wife is fine, and residing at Enmore for the summer, and my dear son is now well again, Your Majesty, after his falling desperately ill several months ago."

The King remarked on my excellent choice of tutor in Godfrey. This exceptional young man had been invited to make fine drawings of His Majesty's rare collection of plant species in the Whitehall garden and the King's most knowledgeable gardener, Mr. Rose, had accompanied Godfrey in this unceasing work. They had completed the painstaking task in just four weeks.

"And your daughters, John, all *four* of them? Are they well too?"

"Three I can answer for, and they are in good health. But as to the fourth, I can only hope she is thriving, given the sparse attention she receives from her infamous mother."

"She could fair far better, even with a rogue such as you. Think on it, John."

The social necessities at an end, the King retired to his private apartments. Returning to my meagre lodgings through Whitehall's many corridors, I passed along the matted gallery and there chanced upon the eminent Etherege, he strutting towards me with three young gallants. I had not seen George for many months, and now found his air and manner quite different from that prior to his new-found fame as an admired playwright.

"John, my Lord Rochester! How good it is to see you. I had no word that you were in town. Henry told me that you were hidden away in deepest Oxfordshire, and were unlikely to be returning for some considerable time."

"Yes, that is not far from true, George. I have been residing at

Adderbury for many months, though Henry has kept me abreast of your successes at the theatre."

"Well, John, I am most heartily pleased to see your return. Have you by chance honoured Mrs. Barry with your presence?"

"I have no intention of either honouring or being remotely re-acquainted with that woman. I believe, George, from what I hear, that you yourself are honouring her on a regular basis."

"What Mrs. Barry does and who she sees are her own affair," said George.

"Affairs indeed. The lady certainly sees to her affairs which, no doubt, will not only swell her belly, but her purse too," I suggested.

"Well, it is no business of yours." George countered, "But I have met with her from time to time, mostly on theatre business and I must admit, John, I find the lady a most eloquent and captivating companion."

"And her young child, George? Do you find her eloquent and captivating too?"

"In truth, John, I am afraid that Mrs. Barry considers your brat an inconvenience. She finds the child interferes with the social life to which she has now become accustomed, and so has little time for her. But, I might add, the lady sees to it that the child wants for little. Mrs. Barry has friends in Bath and visits them often, and at such times, her daughter is in the care of a good, honest maid. In fact, she is away there at this very moment for a month's stay."

At this, I promptly begged leave and returned to my lodgings. It was at that moment that I vowed to take personal care of the child, and so devised my plan of action.

I wrote immediately to William, my trusted steward at Enmore, asking for his urgent assistance in London regarding a very private and pressing matter of mine. I told him in my letter to inform my wife as to the action I was undertaking, so she would be fully aware of the circumstances. I received word straightway that he would arrive at the end of the week following. With the enlistment of their help, the plan to secure my child was now complete.

With Mrs. Barry out of town, my planned abduction of the child proved trouble-free, without interference or protestation.

Anon, the child, together with William and a female companion, was put upon a coach and all three arrived at Enmore without harm or delay. My wife, although not entirely at ease with this situation, had been willing to concur with my plan. Although compromised, she was in agreement that the poor unwanted child deserved the love and care of a family home; something which the uncaring selfish mother was incapable of offering.

I soon departed London for Enmore, long before Mrs. Barry received news of the kidnap. She herself returned immediately to London from Bath, distraught and in the utmost shock, constantly bewailing her loss for several days. Her friend and confidante, Nelly, tried in vain to console the poor woman, and Nelly's anger at me now grew ever more intense.

I had counselled Mrs. Barry time and again regarding her lack of care for my child. She had blatantly refused the advice I was offering, despite being made fully aware of my continuing concerns. Unfortunately, in these unhappy circumstances, my only option had been to take this seemingly cruel action.

Since she, I believed, had not formally named her only daughter, I took it upon myself to name the child Elizabeth Clerke, this surname being that of a most trusted friend and associate. Yet I would always call her my sweet Betty. I hoped that in time the child would, if circumstances allowed, be returned to Mrs. Barry and I wrote to her the following letter...

❧

Madam,

I am far from *delighting* in the *Grief* I have given you, by taking away the *Child*; and you, who made it so absolutely *necessary* for me to do so, must take that *Excuse* from me, for all the *ill Nature* of it: On the other side, pray be *assur'd*, I love *Betty* so well, that you need not *apprehend* any *Neglect* from those I employ; and I hope very shortly to *restore* her to you a *finer Girl* than ever. In the mean time you wou'd do well to think of the *Advice* I gave you, for how little *shew* soever my *Prudence* makes in my own *Affairs*, in yours it will prove very *successful*, if you please to follow it; and since *Discretion* is the thing alone you are like to *want*, pray study to *get* it.

એ᠊ન૭

At only nineteen months, Betty missed her mother greatly, despite Mrs. Barry's earlier infrequent attention, and naturally all seemed unfamiliar at Enmore initially. However, she soon settled in well with Elizabeth and the children and became part of our family.

She was a beautiful child, with bright blue eyes and light brown hair. She held a surprisingly robust constitution, despite her mother's dearth of care, and my deplorable condition at the time of her conception. But I felt sure all would now be well with her, she receiving the constant love and care of Elizabeth and our good Enmore servants.

Betty suffered the usual infant teething, and a particularly serious fever, from which we all feared she would not recover, but blessed with that stubborn determination so often displayed by her mother, she survived the illness. Her recovery had been due in no small part to Elizabeth's admirable patience and care. Our youngest daughter Mallet, just two years older than Betty, was particularly fond of her young half-sister and spent many happy hours helping Elizabeth and the servants to look after her, in her childlike way.

Even at this tender age, Betty had already grown into a lively young child, soon displaying her mother's tendency to wilful stubbornness. She was chided most severely for such haughtiness, but in the fullness of time, surrendered these annoying traits, much to my wife's relief.

Elizabeth and I agreed that Betty would be best remaining at Enmore when my wife and the other children eventually returned to Adderbury, whilst I myself planned to leave some time before them. We both thought this decision rather harsh, but felt it was the wisest course, so as not to uproot sweet Betty again in her young life, until such time as she might be returned to her mother. Betty seemed happy and content with her adoptive family at Enmore, and became very close to our maid Jane, a kind, honest and jovial woman who had been in the service of the Malets since she was ten years old. Jane had been orphaned at the age of six, both her parents succumbing to a mysterious illness, and had miraculously survived due to a neighbour's kindness in taking her away from peril whilst her parents lay a dying. So Betty and Jane now shared a kinship owing much to their similar woeful circumstances.

I left Betty and my family in Somerset, and travelled back to Adderbury. On my return there, I had word from Henry that Betty's abduction had become common knowledge and that I was depicted as the evil perpetrator of a callous, malicious act committed upon the girl's mother. I felt wretched and alone. Even Henry hinted that my actions were rash, but he added that the King, on hearing of the abduction, had surprisingly made no comment on the matter. I was in total disarray, with moods of melancholy haunting me for hours on end. These times were accompanied by pangs of guilt over the years of deception, degradation and blatant foolhardiness, maliciously aimed at those poor souls whose only crime had been to make my acquaintance. The most heartrending circumstance of all was the frequent indifference I had shown to my poor wife during those wasted years.

My servants, although aware of my frailty in health and mind, were in ignorance of the true depths to which I now was sinking. They continued diligently with their duties in the house, despite Elizabeth's absence and my reclusive presence. I stayed in my bedchamber for days on end without venturing out. They left food and drink outside my room and, whether eaten or not, the remains were cleared away and fresh food brought again each day.

During my confinement, an anonymous donor sent to me a copy of Gilbert Burnet's *History of the Reformation of the Church of England*. The author's apotropaic beliefs, together with his clear and precise understanding of the subject, awakened thoughts and complexities hidden deep within me.

After concluding my reading of the volume, I had a mind to meet with this extraordinary servant of God. Our King however, suspicious of Burnet's allegiances, had dismissed him from his post as Royal Chaplain and banished him from his Court. This abrupt turnabout had not deterred Burnet, he continuing with his writings and studies. He was given over to ministering to the sick and dying, favouring those wretched souls whose imminent deaths would be the result of debauched living.

Intrigued by this man, I wrote to him requesting his company at Adderbury for a week or two. He graciously replied, saying he would be only too pleased to be a guest in my home.

His letter prompted me to relinquish my reclusive condition, and so make arrangements for his arrival. I informed the servants of his impending visit, and a bedchamber was prepared for my guest, with fresh clean linen and all the usual comforts. He arrived mid-morning on the subsequent Monday, and I ordered a servant to collect his two bags of belongings from the coach and to escort him into our parlour.

"My Lord Rochester. I am most honoured to be invited to your country seat," he announced.

Standing, I welcomed him and offered him a chair. Burnet, just four years my senior, was a softly spoken Scot, a man of average height and with rounded, gentle features and kind all-knowing eyes.

"You are most welcome, Gilbert. I have been looking forward to these days in your company, for I wish to debate views on your devout loyalty to your God, though I fully intend to counter with my scepticism of that divine being."

For two weeks, we discoursed at great length, debating the need for religious study, God's potency over the human soul and the consequences in damnation aimed at the pessimistic atheists among us. Gilbert is an exceptional being, whose life has been governed by God's spiritual force. By the end of his stay, I had grown to love and respect this learned man. His forbearance in the face of my irritating counter-attacks upon his beliefs was evidenced in his calm countenance and patience, and by the time of his departure, a close friendship had developed between us. When he left, an unexplained emptiness rose in my heart. I greatly missed that most compassionate of men.

CHAPTER NINETEEN

The Wells and Woodstock

At the beginning of August, with my health a little more in balance, and with the good fortune of a payment to me from an indebted gentleman in Adderbury, I decided to travel to Tunbridge with my trusty servant Tom, once there, I to imbibe the waters of its famous wells, in the desperate hope of delaying a little my certain decline.

We arrived in Tunbridge on a warm sunlit afternoon, renting a room close by the Queen's Wells, we then taking the air along the Walks. At two of the clock, we entered a tavern and there ate a fine dinner accompanied by excellent wine, and afterwards to our lodgings where, feeling frail, I rested for a while. Tom had made ready my evening clothes and on awakening, I refreshed myself with the washing of face and hands, he assisting in my dressing. In the early evening, we up to the Walks again and sat awhile in the warm air, delighting in one of the fine concerts of music.

I returned to our lodgings alone, a little before midnight, leaving Tom discoursing with a young servant wench to whom he had taken a fancy. He had laid out my loose-fitting garments for the morning, for such attire is the fashion when drinking at the Wells.

We rose at five of the clock on the morning of our first visit to the waters. On our arrival, we found many gentlemen and ladies already present, drinking great quantities from the curative wells. I sat in a small arbour, whereupon Tom fetched a jug of the water and on the jug's handle was fixed a length of chain at the end of which was attached a small metal cup. Upon quaffing the liquid, I found it to be surprisingly refreshing and cool yet with a somewhat earthy taste.

I stayed until nine of the clock that morning when everyone, having had their fill of the waters, returned to their lodgings and changed into their day clothes. By ten of the clock they, in their fine attire, paraded the Walks. Many of the ladies were to be found at *Hazard* or the drinking of tea. Meanwhile, the men visited the coffee houses, conversing on the general news of the day, whilst some enjoyed the playing of *Pall Mall*. At two of the clock, everyone departed for dinner.

Visitors to the Wells were varied indeed, some young and some old. Among the ill and infirm there were cripples who could not walk but for the aid of crutches or who were placed in special chairs for their conveyance. Some poor deformed wretches sported twisted bodies and limbs, whilst others displayed horrific facial deformities; if the waters could cure and make straight again these poor woeful specimens, then the waters held powers beyond any understanding. Yet there were also those in the most robust of health. The young rakes of the town paraded themselves in plenty, dressed in the latest fashions and preened to perfection. These gallants flaunted themselves in the hope of a favourable marriage to a wealthy heiress, whilst eagle-eyed parents would scrutinize these ambitious suitors. For those who failed in this pursuit, there were many painted whores ready to offer their pleasures and relieve the gallants of their heavy purses.

After taking the waters for three days, and now in need of rest, I confined myself to my lodgings and had my vittles brought to me by Tom, whose own amorous adventure, he confided, was giving him the greatest of pleasure. Alone in my room, I pondered on the intrigues at Tunbridge, and with quill to hand, a clear vision was decanted…

෯෨

Tunbridge Wells

෯෨

At five this morn when Phoebus raised his head
From Thetis' lap, I raised myself from bed
And mounting steed, I trotted to the waters,
The rendezvous of feigned or sickly praters,
Cuckolds, whores, citizens, their wives and daughters.
My squeamish stomach I with wine had bribed
To undertake the dose it was prescribed,
But turning head, a sudden noisome view
That innocent provision overthrew
And without drinking made me purge and spew.
Looking on t'other side, a thing I saw
Who some men said could handle sword and law.
It stalked, it stared, and up and down did strut,
And seemed as furious as a stag at rut.
As wise as calf it looked, as big as bully,
But handled, proved a mere Sir Nicholas Cully,
A bawling fop, a natural Nokes, and yet
He dared to censure as if he had wit.
To make him more ridiculous, in spite
Nature contrived the fool should be a knight.
Grant ye lucky stars this o'ergrown boy
To purchase some inspiring pretty toy
That may his want of sense and wit supply,
As buxom crab-fish do his lechery.
Though he alone were dismal sight enough,
His train contributed to set him off,
All of his shape, all of the self-same stuff.

In short, no malice need on him be thrown,
Nature has done the business of lampoon,
And in his looks his character hath shown.
Endeavouring this irksome sight to balk,
And a more irksome noise, his silly talk,
I silently slunk down to th' Lower Walk.
But often when one would Charybdis shun,
Down upon Scylla 'tis one's fate to run;
So here it was my cursèd fate to find
As great a fop, though of another kind,
A tall, stiff fool who walked in Spanish guise;
The buckram puppet never stirred its eyes,
But grave as owl it looked, as woodcock wise.
He scorned the empty talking of this mad age
And spoke all proverbs, sentences, and adage,
Can with as much solemnity buy eggs
As a cabal can talk of their intrigues,
A man of parts, and yet he can dispense
With the formality of speaking sense.

From hence into the upper end I ran,
Where a new scene of foppery began
Among the serious and fanatic elves,
Fit company for none besides themselves.
Assembled thus, each his distemper told:
Scurvy, stone, strangury. Some were so bold
To charge the spleen to be their misery,
And on the wise disease bring infamy.
But none were half so modest to complain
Their want of learning, honesty, and brain,
The general diseases of that train.
These call themselves ambassadors of Heaven
And saucily pretend commissions given,

But should an Indian king, whose small command
Seldom extends above ten miles of land,
Send forth such wretched fools in an embassage,
He'd find but small effects of such a message.
Listening, I found the cob of all this rabble,
Pert Bayes, with his importance comfortable.
He, being raised to an archdeaconry
By trampling on religious liberty,
Was grown too great and looked too fat and jolly
To be disturbed with care of melancholy,
Though Marvell has enough exposed his folly.
He drank to carry off some old remains
His lazy dull distemper left in's veins.
Let him drink on, but 'tis not a whole flood
Can give sufficient sweetness to his blood
To make his nature or his manners good.
Importance drank too, though she'd been no sinner,
To wash away some dregs he had spewed in her.

Next after these a foolish whining crew
Of sisters frail were offered to my view.
The things did talk, but th' hearing what they said
I did myself the kindness to evade.
Looking about, I saw some gypsies too
(Faith, brethren, they can cant as well as you).
Nature hath placed these wretches beneath scorn;
They can't be called so vile as they are born.

Amidst the crowd next I myself conveyed,
For now were come, whitewash and paint being laid,
Mother and daughters, mistress and the maid,
And squire with wig and pantaloons displayed.
But ne'er could conventicle, play, or fair

184

For a true medley with this herd compare.
Here squires, ladies and some say countesses,
Chandlers, egg-wives, bacon-women, seamstresses
Were mixed together, nor did they agree
More in their humours than their quality.
Here waiting for gallant, young damsel stood,
Leaning on cane and muffled up in hood.
The would-be-wit, whose business was to woo,
With hat removed and solemn scrape of shoe
Advanceth bowing, then genteelly shrugs
And ruffled foretop into order tugs,
And thus accosts her, 'Madam, methinks the weather
Is grown much more serene since you came hither.
You influence the heavens and should the sun
Withdraw himself to see his rays outdone,
Your brighter eyes could then supply the morn
And make a day before a day be born.'

With mouth screwed up, conceited winking eyes,
And breasts thrust forwards, 'Lord, sir,' she replies,
'It is your goodness, and not my deserts,
Which makes you show this learning, wit, and parts.'
He, puzzled, bites his nail, both to display
The sparkling ring and think what next to say,
And thus breaks forth afresh, 'Madam, egad,
Your luck at cards last night was very bad.
At cribbage fifty-nine, and the next show
To make the game, and yet to want those two.
God damn me, madam, I'm the son of a whore
If in my life I saw the like before.'
To pedlar's stall he drags her, and her breast
With hearts and such-like foolish toys he dressed;
And then more smartly to expound the riddle

Of all his prattle, gives her a Scotch fiddle.

Tired with this dismal stuff, away I ran
Where were two wives with girl just fit for man,
Short-breathed, with pallid lips, and visage wan.
Some curtsies passed, and the old compliment
Of being glad to see each other, spent,
With hand in hand they lovingly did walk,
And one began thus to renew the talk.
'I pray, good madam, if it may be thought
No rudeness, what cause was it hither brought
Your ladyship?, She soon replying, smiled,
'We have a good estate, but have no child,
And I'm informed these wells will make a barren
Woman as fruitful as a cony warren.'
The first returned, 'For this cause I am come,
For I can have no quietness at home.
My husband grumbles, though we have got one,
This poor girl, and mutters for a son.
And this is grieved with headache pangs and throes,
Is full sixteen and never yet had those.'
She soon replied, 'Get her a husband, madam.
I married at that age and ne'er had had 'em,
Was just like her. Steel waters let alone,
A back of steel will bring 'em better down.'
And ten to one but they themselves will try
The same means to increase their family.
Poor foolish fribbles, who by subtlety
Of midwife, truest friend to lechery,
Persuaded are to be at pains and charge
To give their wives occasion to enlarge
Their silly heads. For here walk Cuff and Kick
With brawny back and legs and potent prick,

Who more substantially will cure thy wife,
And on her half-dead womb bestow new life.
From these the waters got the reputation
Of good assistants unto generation.

Now warlike men were got into the throng,
With hair tied back, singing a bawdy song.
Not much afraid, I got a nearer view,
And 'twas my chance to know the dreadful crew.
They were cadets, that seldom can appear,
Damned to the stint of thirty pound a year.
With hawk on fist or greyhound led in hand,
The dogs and footboys sometimes they command.
And having trimmed a cast-off spavined horse,
With three hard-pinched-for guineas in the purse,
Two rusty pistols, scarf about the arse,
Coat lined with red, they here presume to swell;
This goes for captain, that for colonel.
So the Bear Garden ape on his steed mounted,
No longer is a jackanapes accounted,
But is by virtue of his trumpery then
Called by the name of the young gentleman.

Bless me, thought I, what thing is man, that thus
In all his shapes he is ridiculous?
Ourselves with noise of reason we do please
In vain: humanity's our worst disease.
Thrice happy beasts are, who, because they be
Of reason void, are so of foppery.
Troth, I was so ashamed that with remorse
I used the insolence to mount my horse;
For he, doing only things fit for his nature,
Did seem to me (by much) the wiser creature.

ఇం‍‍‍‍‍‍ఈ

With the wells' tonic seeped into my veins, Tom and I departed Tunbridge bound for Oxfordshire. As the coach pulled away, I thrust my head out of the window with a sombre gaze and knew for certain that was the last time I would cast my eyes upon Tunbridge.

ఇం‍‍‍‍‍‍ఈ

On my return to Adderbury, I was pleased to see my wife and children, recently returned from Enmore. Elizabeth remarked that I looked a little better in health and was sure the wells had benefited me.

My children themselves, and particularly Charles, looked in the best of health. The pure Somerset air had treated them kindly. Godfrey was taken with my son's aptitude for learning and observed that he was exceptional for one so young, proving highly intelligent and quick of wit. His written work was neat, clear and precise. He was unmistakably my son. He also had a good eye for detail, shown in his drawings of flowers and foliage growing in profusion on the estate. One fine day away from Enmore, Elizabeth and Charles, accompanied by Godfrey, had sat upon a small hillside overlooking Bridgwater Bay, where Charles sketched ships both a-sail and at anchor. Godfrey had marvelled at the boy's impressive drawings of these majestic sailing vessels.

Our three beautiful daughters, Anne, Lizbet and Mallet aged ten, five and three respectively, were each growing into fine young girls.

Anne, the eldest, was beautiful and intelligent, nurtured by her mother's tuition. They had become very close, and she had been of great help and consolation to Elizabeth in my frequent absences from Adderbury. Anne was accomplished in sewing and reading. She danced like an angel, although her singing voice was not quite so angelic, but tuneful enough.

Graceful, slender Lizbet often accompanied Elizabeth and her beloved older sister during their daily duties. Lizbet's nature was bright and breezy, and she was seldom seen without a happy, smiling face.

Mallet was a sweet child, although more delicate in health than her two sisters. But, at the age of only three, she was determined to mimic her siblings, which resulted in many falls, her balance not yet fully secure.

৵৽৽

In September, I left Adderbury to attend the Woodstock Races and Tom accompanied me on my short journey to High Lodge. The servants there had for weeks been working tirelessly, preparing for the annual event, when the walls of the lodge would echo once again with my guests' joys and disappointments of the race.

Lord Lovelace's invitations to the races had been sent as usual to the pompous aristocratic misfits of Oxfordshire, whom anyone with a modicum of sanity would have great misfortune to meet. The worst of their kind, the young sparks, with their gloomy painted ladies shackled to their arm, wagered more on those race days than they would allow those poor wretches in a year. Their attendance, though intolerable at times, was nevertheless profitable for the inns and alehouses of Woodstock.

For the duration of the meeting, my rakish friends enjoyed all the comforts High Lodge could offer. They consumed vast quantities of food and the best of wines supplied by an eager Oxfordshire merchant, for his profit was not to be missed by neglecting to furnish some of the most celebrated drinkers in the land.

The significant race that the spectators came to view was held on the last but one day. To the winner would be awarded the valuable Woodstock Plate; a large silver salver engraved with a horse in full stretch at the gallop and, every year since the race was first held, the winning rider's name also 'graved upon it. The heats to decide the finalists were held at midday on the first three race days, when large wagers were occasionally won, but more often as not were lost.

To my friends' utter amazement I announced that I was to ride in the heats on a beautiful grey stallion, *Satire's Folly! 'a most appropriate name'*, I thought. The grey, I had borrowed for the occasion from a generous lender in gratitude of services rendered. I was sworn to secrecy that the identity of the owner was on no account to be revealed. I felt prepared for the challenge of the race, stronger in body and soul than I had been for some time. Though still presenting a frail exterior, this belied my new-found strength.

Rumour of my race riding was soon on everyone's lips, and my odds were favouring a win. Though my rakish friends were convinced my chances were slim, this did not in any way deter them from laying out considerable sums on the spirited grey in the hands of its emaciated but headstrong rider. To the astonishment of all, I won my heat, more by luck than judgement, and gained a place in the final.

On the morning of the plate, the Sixteenth of September 1679, I awoke in a haze from a night's debauch. With a bright blue sky, the day promised sunny and warm, boding a good day's racing for one and all.

At midday, I was cheered loudly by friends and onlookers as I walked towards the young lad who held *Satire's Folly*. I thanked him for his care of the horse and, before climbing into the saddle, gave him an Angel for his trouble. All eight horses and riders were lined up at the start for the four-mile chase. The riders made for a colourful spectacle, dressed in rich embroidered velvet coats. I wore vivid red and silver, which complimented the silvery hues in Satire's flowing mane and tail. The other riders variously donned coats of green, dark blue, yellow, gold, pastel blue and crimson. One rider surpassed all, majestic in black velvet adorned with gold and silver, he upon a black stallion; both horse and rider presented a formidable air.

"Away you go!" hollered the steward.

We sped off at a frantic gallop up a slight incline into the distance. I was lying fourth after the first mile, with the black clearly in the lead. As we descended the valley, I overtook at a swift pace, a rider in blue at Wootton Gate. The course two mile on led to flat level ground where Satire showed a good turn of foot and we were neck and neck with the second placed rider when his horse stumbled in a shallow dip and they dropped back, clearly out of the race. Satire, going a good pace, was now gaining upon the black. At the three-mile marker the course ran gently downhill towards the finishing post, I now ever closer on his tail. Satire knew instinctively what he must do, and as the onlookers cheered and shouted, urging us to win, he carried me swiftly by the leader and flew to the finish by the judge's seat, with the unfortunate black beaten into second place.

Crowds gathered around Satire and me, cheering and waving us on to where Lovelace was waiting to present the plate. Tom did cheer the loudest, he having pocketed a good deal on the day.

"Well done, Rochester! As fine a show of horsemanship as ever I saw," Lovelace pronounced.

"I thank you for your compliment, Lovelace, but it was won by the best bred and most honest grey in the country."

⊱⊰

I remained content at Adderbury until the following March, when I received an invitation to attend the King for the races at Newmarket, where also would be his staid brother James, his bastard son Monmouth, his whore French Louise and our *dear* Nelly, along with the rest of his entourage.

On the first day of the races the King, splendidly attired, sat astride his favourite *Old Rowley*, but merely as a bystander. He, lately recovering from a short illness and on the advice of his physician, would not attempt to race. And so it was left to others, including the dashing Monmouth and several young Gentleman of the Court, to display their expert horsemanship. Monmouth was favoured to win, and many bets were placed upon his head. He ultimately won his race by almost three lengths, pleasing those who gained by it.

The day's racing over, the King, James, Monmouth, Nelly and Louise retired to His Majesty's newly built house close by, whilst my friends and I made our way to the King's stables. There we looked over his horses and watched the stable boys busy with hay wisps drying the sweating animals, following which each horse was fed bran, mixed with a little warm water for ease of digestion. Hooves were picked out meticulously and inspected for any foreign bodies or the dangerous hazard of a loose shoe. Their legs were washed down with cool water cloths and checked carefully for any heat in the tendons or feet. Lastly, the horses' backs were inspected for any sores or abrasions made by the saddles and ointment applied to any found.

The mounts would then be bedded down for the night on deep, clean, golden straw and were given plentiful water and sweet smelling, long cut hay piled loose in one corner. The King's stable boys also bedded down in the stables, with blankets for warmth and with straw filled pillows. Their night vigil ensured that no malicious harm might befall his valuable stock, and should any of the horses become ill or distressed, they were on hand to attend to this too.

With the stable boys at their rest, His Majesty's and other grooms grouped together in the tack room. Each was charged with looking after the tack of their owner's horses. By regular cleaning and oiling, the saddles and bridles were kept in the very best of condition. Meticulous checking of the stitching for any wear, tear or fraying was undertaken for the safety of horse and rider. Although a long, laborious task, these grooms were privileged, for the Lords, Ladies and Gentlemen who were the proud owners of their charges would ensure wine and good vittles were brought to them. The lot of the poor stable boys was less generous, for their meagre rations comprised only bread, cheese and small beer.

We later made our way to the inn, some drinking to their gains and others drowning their losses to this sport of kings.

I had hoped to stay at Newmarket for the week, but my luck with both horse and health was naught but bad, so I left reluctantly the next day for Adderbury.

After three days at home, I felt altogether better, due once again to Elizabeth's patient care. I spent precious time with my son, when he was not at his lessons, we walking in the garden and fishing the lake for hours together.

In the middle of May, Elizabeth received a letter from Enmore regarding some pressing business on the estate. I offered to travel there and to attend to matters personally in her stead, so as to spare her unnecessary grief at being parted from our children. Recklessly, I rode post for Enmore.

CHAPTER TWENTY

Spelsbury, A Finite Journey

I set out at a good brisk pace, accompanied by two of my servants. We had travelled but ten miles when I was obliged to pull up my horse, experiencing a sudden onslaught of excruciating pain in my lower bowel. I collapsed forwards, slumped upon the horse's neck. With great alarm, the servants rushed to my aid and, lifting me out of the saddle, gently laid me upon the ground. One remained by my side, whilst the other rode post-haste to the nearest town to convene transport for my urgent journey home.

After an agonizing wait, at last I was placed inside a small, rickety old coach, my two attendants wrapping me securely in a warm blanket. The coachman, aware of my dire situation, drove his two horses fast and hard, my servants riding at the gallop behind, whilst my own horse was ridden by a friend of the coachman. I screamed out in pain from the incessant jolts and swerves of the rigid, unyielding vehicle. The fires of hell were burning in my bladder, and on the necessity of pissing, the pain was unbearable; the small amount I could manage was of bloody hue, accompanied by foul smelling matter secreted from my inflamed ulcer. We made for High Lodge, being the nearer of my residences and, with the pain rendering me unconscious several times during the journey, my arrival there, to my relief, was sooner than I anticipated.

My outer garments removed, I was placed upon my canopied four-poster, its woven woollen hangings of deep mustard yellow draped oppressively around me, as I lay very ill and very repentant in the very bed that had repeatedly borne witness to my debauched conduct.

*'Sarah! Sarah! You alone are the very reason for my misery. I despise
you with a passion, fearing the devil paid you favourably to secure
my delivery.'*

My wife and mother were notified of my bed-ridden state, and each
travelled immediately to High Lodge where, during my rangership,
neither had ever had a welcome invitation. Once there, on entering
this house of ill repute, they each were shocked to the core, for on
the walls were displayed many deplorable pornographic pictures and
scattered around were numerous filthy verses. Elizabeth rendered
speechless, my mother right away commanded the servants to take
down this disgusting filth and to search thoroughly the drawers of
furniture for any more images or writings of such unsavoury and
despicable nature, and to burn the lot.

News soon reached London of the seriousness of my condition.
My mother, having removed all traces of sordid material, gave her
consent to anyone wishing to visit the sick and dying Rochester to
do so.

A few came. Some I hardly recognized, for I was heavily drugged
and asleep for much of their stay. Others, who I longed to call, were
either out of the country or selfishly indifferent. Yet others, I
suspected, preferred to remember Rochester as the sane man of
pleasure rather than the insane repentant, for repentant I was; news
of this soon reached the ears of my alleged friends and the majority,
disbelieving the rumour, concluded that my poxed body and
disturbed mind were the causes of such uncharacteristic madness.

Several physicians were attending upon me, including a personal
favourite of the King's, but all, on examining me, came to the same
sad conclusion; that there was nothing to be done other than to
alleviate my painful agonies with laudanum and other unpalatable
concoctions.

Elizabeth's herbal remedies gave me more relief than any of
those quacks' mixtures apart from the laudanum, which, thank God,

aided me to welcome, oblivious sleep. My devoted wife sat at my bedside for many hours during the day and night and left only when forced to, through dire need of sleep. I begged her to allow our children to the lodge and to this, she readily agreed. They arrived accompanied by two servants from Adderbury and were brought to my room by their mother. They were clearly distressed at seeing their father so ill. And all, including four year old Mallet, wept uncontrollably at my bedside.

My mother's pious, stubborn nature took an unexpected turn, she displaying a genuine warmth and compassion towards her dying son. Her heartfelt empathy had no doubt been prompted by the arrival of Gilbert Burnet, he having learned of my grave situation and without a moment's hesitation having journeyed to Woodstock.

I was at last resolved to allow this tender man of God to guide me, this sinner, down my new chosen path. With Gilbert's prayers, Elizabeth's selfless devotion and a mother's love for her son, although desperately ill, I felt a contentment that I had only known as a young boy.

☞⸙☜

'I have lain in this damnable bed for nine weeks, enshrined as a living corpse. The pain I now suffer is so utterly severe that I feel I have entered the realm of damnation itself. My wretched, diseased and stinking body lies in its own sweat, blood and puss, which it extrudes at will. This deathbed, in which I now lie praying and welcoming an end to my suffering, is the very bed in which I have pleasured many a filthy and wayward whore who afterwards I reviled with such intensity. My body is now but a skeleton, with skin so thin it is all but transparent, yet only God's eyes can see through to my very soul. My toes and fingers are black, as no living blood can reach to feed them. The only breaths I take are through my distorted mouth, whose toothless interior cries out the agonies of my sin. My nose,

which has been eaten away with disease, has not smelled the air of this world for weeks. The eyes that God bequeathed me are now blind spheres lying deep in hollow sockets. At night, I fall into deep yet agonising sleep, where I am tormented by the sight of hideous creatures imagined in my black, unseeing eyes and on awaking into the darkness of morning, I pray for God to make it my last.'

∂∾∽

Whilst I was sleeping one Sunday, Gilbert was called away on an urgent family matter in the early hours. He'd had no wish to disturb my rest and had told Elizabeth he would swiftly return to be by my side. His absence was of great sadness to me, and I knew I would die before his promised return.

My end approaching, Elizabeth tearfully but silently clutched my hand in hers and gently placed therein her most treasured keepsake; the button with entwined hearts, my first gift of love to her.

∂∾∽

On the morning of Monday the Twenty-sixth of July 1680, at the cold dark hour of two, with wife, children, mother and dutiful servants present, John Wilmot, after only thirty-three years, exhaled his last breath, the button he had clasped falling silently from his palm. In a tearful embrace, wife and mother praised God for his mercy and Rochester's atonement.

∂∾∽

I lay undisturbed for thirteen days, entombed in wool and oak in the cool, dark, dank cellar of Adderbury. On the fourteenth day, my coffin, draped in a velvet pall, was placed in a mourning coach and pulled at a slow pace by two black horses to the church in the hamlet of Spelsbury. Following, were two mourners' coaches and in the first sat my wife, children and mother and in the second were my good servant Tom and but few friends.

As daylight gave way to dusk, my coffin was carried into the flickering candlelight of the small church and placed at the foot of the altar. In great solemnity, Elizabeth and my children, followed by my mother, entered the church led by the chaplain, Dr. Robert Parsons, who ushered them to their seats. The other mourners entered the church and took their places.

Dr. Parsons, who during the last weeks of my life had visited me on many occasions, made great play in his long funeral sermon of God's mercy for this sinful penitent and, on the conclusion of his reading, my coffin was carefully taken and placed in the Lee family vault, whilst the mourners left the church silently.

CHAPTER TWENTY ONE

A Year On and Further Devastation

Tragically, soon after the first anniversary of my own demise, a further coffin was carried down into the vault and placed carefully next to mine. The body lying therein was that of my beloved wife. She had succumbed to a distressing short illness, and her death had left our children devastated and overcome with grief. My poor mother once again found herself the guardian of orphaned grandchildren.

৵৽

A few months later, on the Twelfth of November, Charles, the ten-year-old Third Earl of Rochester, died. He was placed in a small oak coffin between us. Although our two hearts had long ceased beating, they shattered into many sad fragments and in the darkness rained upon that small coffin.

Epilogue

How did he conclude his story from the grave? You may ask.

Well, the truth is he did not. Poor father could not have put quill pen to paper during the last throes of his crippling illness. This dying Lord could barely lift a finger to summon water to quench his parched mouth.

Such wretched times were the summer months of 1680 and 1681, for first came the tragic death of my dear father and then my beloved mother was to follow. As if God had not punished our family enough, a further death was called for. Charles, the Third Earl of Rochester, my beautiful, handsome but delicate brother died at the tender age of ten, so very soon after our dear devoted mother.

But to dwell on the past in such a melancholic way does not bode well, so away from these sad accounts. If you are willing, I will indulge you in a little of my own story, so as to tell a tale of enlightenment.

≫◦≪

Following that tragic time, my grandmother, the formidable Anne, Dowager Countess of Rochester found herself in the unfortunate and moreover unenviable position of caring for her three orphaned granddaughters; Anne, Mallet and me.

All too soon, we orphans were removed from Adderbury House with little by way of possessions; just our clothes, a few loved toys and our brother's beloved Omah. We were to reside at Ditchley, our grandmother's beautiful but quaint medieval Cotswold estate. Ditchley House became our home for many years, and its ancient walls would witness our growing into fine young and available women, well-educated and groomed in readiness for a good marriage. An advantageous marriage was a crucial requisite, which the Dowager was determined to procure for each of us at any cost, for our guardian was used to having her way. At the time of the Civil War, she was married to our heroic grandfather Henry Wilmot, a charismatic, handsome and brave royalist soldier. Even though Henry was exiled, the mighty sequester Cromwell found he had not the power to seize her beloved Ditchley. The Lee stronghold was hers, and hers alone and woe betide anyone who strove to take that from her grasp.

Our grandmother was resolute that her beloved charges would be shielded from the truth of their father's wild escapades and numerous infidelities. This must have seemed an impossible task, we being the daughters of such an infamous father. But grandmother was steadfast, and we quickly learned that any indiscretions of an unsavoury nature that we might accidentally hear about must fall upon deaf ears. She was adamant that her son had always been a good and doting father whose somewhat dubious reputation had been the work of jealous bigots at Court; they detested his intimate friendship with the King and so looked upon Rochester as their hated rival, she insisted. As a consequence, as young girls, we were distrustful of anyone who spoke ill of our father. But in later years, we heard such fantastical accounts of Lord Rochester's daring that, unbeknown to grandmother, we longed for those tales to be true.

Our cosseted years at Ditchley passed all too quickly and the reality of our marriages was soon upon us.

Anne, at sixteen, was the first to be wed. A good man, Henry Bayntun, was chosen for her and they were joined in matrimony in the beautiful church at Adderbury on the First of September 1685.

As for my own marriage? Things were rather more fraught, with lengthy wrangles between the gritty Dowager and my prospective father-in-law. At last, at the age of sixteen myself, I married Edward

Montagu, Third Earl of Sandwich on the Eighth of July 1689 and thus acquired the much envied title of Countess. The sudden death of his father, the Second Earl, had put an end to the bickering and enabled the marriage to take place without further hindrance.

In 1692, the youngest of us, Mallet, took her marriage vows with her husband John Vaughan, later Viscount Lisburne of Antrim, at St. Giles in the Fields on the Eighteenth of August.

❧

How lucky my sisters were, to be blessed with harmonious, happy marriages in complete contrast to my own. My marriage was one of convenience; discordant and predictably not a happy one, as is often the case where wealth and greed hold more merit than true love. However, a measure of tolerance was attained between my husband and me, and when out in society we appeared congenial, a charade so perfected it was as natural to us as breathing.

We resided in London and also at Hinchingbrooke, my Lord's seat in Huntingdonshire, but often lived quite apart in those large, spacious abodes.

Our first child, Elizabeth, tragically died when an infant. Her loss was so great to me, I plummeted into a melancholic condition. Astonishingly though, Edward, who I supposed incapable of showing any true affection, helped me to overcome my despondency. Such tenderness I had not thought possible from a man whose indifference towards me had been evident from the day of our marriage.

In due course however, as are all good wives duty bound, I gave birth to the obligatory son and heir. Edward Richard Montagu, Viscount Hinchingbrooke was born on the Seventh of July 1692.

But let not my hapless marriage taint your curiosity to read on, for there is much of intrigue to tell.

I know that Rochester's spirit lives in me like no other, and I am truly my father's daughter being, I am told, highly intelligent and possessing, I feel, an admirable wit. I am well read in English, Latin and French and have inherited Rochester's passion for music and theatre. I love to dance, but believe father was never too fond of this gaiety, though he did on occasion show a good turn of foot to impress my mother. There our similarities cease, for I have never once given way to infidelity, not for the want of many a libertine's desires I might add. There is no doubt that this moral trait of mine is a legacy from my long-suffering mother.

In the middle of April 1707, my Lord and I travelled to the county of Suffolk on the occasion of our son Dicky's marriage to Elizabeth, daughter of Alexander Popham of Littlecote in Wiltshire. Dicky was fifteen and his bride two years younger. The day was most agreeable, with warm spring sunshine, and the occasion was attended by a small number of relatives on either side of the family. The nuptials took place at Leiston, a village just three miles from the Suffolk coast. This remote place was Dicky's choice, albeit prompted by an invitation from his close friend Immanuel Munnings. Immanuel, who Dicky knew affectionately as Immy, was four years the older. They had been scholars at Westminster School together and had remained good friends thereafter, corresponding regularly for many years.

The Munnings are minor Suffolk gentry who own land in and around Leiston. After leaving Westminster School, Immy, being the younger of two sons, was forced to make his own way in the world. Eventually he studied for the cloth, since a military career was no option for this gentle man who abhorred any form of physical violence. Despite Immy's loathing of war, he greatly admired Dicky, who had been earmarked from an early age for a career in the military. This was an obvious choice, he being the grandson of the renowned naval commander, Vice Admiral Edward Montagu, First Earl of Sandwich. The Admiral's demise was dreadful. He was killed fighting the Dutch in the formidable battle of Sole Bay in 1672, when disastrously his flagship, *The Royal James*, was set afire and sank. Two weeks after the skirmish, his rotting corpse was washed up onto the Suffolk shore amid the lapping waters. His blackened and charred body could only be identified from fragments of unburned clothing fused to his blistered skin, these showing clearly the rank of the man.

The Reverend Immanuel Munnings, as he was now titled, had at the young age of eighteen and a half years attained the appointment of rector at Leiston. This position had given him a good living and a substantial manor house close to the church. Immy had been married for a year to Caroline, a rather plain young woman, but of a happy and friendly disposition. She was the only daughter of James and Caroline Parham. The Parhams resided in a fine house in the coastal town of Southwold. Mr. Parham was a retired naval officer whose father had at one time proudly fought alongside the Admiral. Their two sons, James and William, had both followed their father and grandfather into naval careers and were well-respected officers of the fleet.

Reverend and Mrs. Mullings had been most generous to Dicky and Elizabeth and to their immediate family, they having offered their home for the wedding feast and comfortable accommodation for three days. Other guests were required to make their own arrangements at the nearby market town of Saxmundham.

The day after the wedding, the child bride had travelled with her parents to their Wiltshire home, for she was to live there until after her fifteenth birthday.

In April 1708, Dicky left Hinchingbrooke for the continent. He was away for nigh on two years, and on his return in December 1709 went to reside in his substantial manor, six miles south of Hinchingbrooke. Before long, his wife, accompanied by her three servants, travelled the long arduous winter journey from Wiltshire to this her new home in Huntingdonshire, where finally the young couple lived together as man and wife. But all too soon, Dicky was given command of a troop in Sir Richard Temple's Regiment of Horse, and left Elizabeth and England for Flanders and war.

Our earlier joy at Dicky's return from the continent was now somewhat overshadowed, not only on his leaving again for war and the continent but also with the unexpected death of my dear sister Mallet, aged just thirty-three, on the Thirteenth of January that following year. My elder sister, Anne, had tragically also died early. Was there a Wilmot curse that decreed we should all die so young? At thirty-five I was alone, my close family all deceased and I only too well aware of the vulnerability of my age. Whether cursed or not, it gave me great concern as to my own mortality.

With my son having left for Flanders, and with his young wife's despondency at his departure, she had returned immediately to her family in Wiltshire. And so I could no longer bear the dreary isolation of our Fenland home as, unhappily for me, friends were ever reluctant to visit during the winter months. The chilling east wind and featureless landscape signified my husband's frigid indifference to me. His only interests were horses, gambling, drinking, hunting and eating his quarry, his intelligence only marginally superior to the dumb animals he hunted. His companions on his pursuits were ill mannered and poorly educated, with a visible lack of refinement. His great passion in life was the breeding and racing of horses. With Newmarket just a few miles from Hinchingbrooke, he was better placed than most to keep a good eye on the competition.

And so I informed his Lordship that I was to remove to Barnes Carlton, our Northamptonshire estate, excusing myself as to overseeing of the building works we had commissioned there. To be in the company of masons, joiners and general labourers was far more amenable than that to which I was subjected at Hinchingbrooke.

Barnes Carlton is a strikingly beautiful house but, built in the latter years of Elizabeth's reign, the rooms were somewhat sombre.

Its dark oak panelling was unfashionable for an elegant country house and so Barnes was at that time undergoing refurbishment and extension. On a warm April day, I arrived there and found the building works in order and well progressed, despite the freezing cold of January. Plans had been drawn up to accommodate four large bedchambers to be built at the rear of the house. Each room would have a magnificent view over the picturesque landscaped garden and parkland beyond. The two largest of the rooms, one for each of us, were to be luxuriously furnished. The other two were intended for guests and, although a little smaller, would be very comfortable, with fine decoration. Work continued to progress well and John Thoroughgood, the Clerk of the Works, confirmed that all would be completed, as had been hoped, by the end of June, at which time the last instalment for the work would be due. In course of time, I wrote to my Lord to inform him of this, knowing he would join me at Barnes for the summer months once hunting at Hinchingbrooke was at an end. His reply, as usual, was short and to the point, stating that he would travel to Barnes a week before completion of the works, so as to satisfy himself that all had been adequately accomplished before parting with his money.

I give the impression that my Lord was miserly, but he was never that. Quite the opposite, for he was generous to a fault. I myself have never wanted for funds, yet neither had his alleged friends. If they were ever in need of money, my Lord obliged, but the promissory notes he received were never honoured and just conveniently forgotten.

Two weeks after my husband's arrival at Barnes, I fell ill of a fever. The hot June weather did not help my condition. The humidity was unbearable and terrifying, violent thunderstorms around midday had been a regular occurrence later in the month.

Our servants took good care of me and nursed me throughout the height of the illness. Herbal compounds that I drank, that were rubbed upon me or that I breathed through a steaming-pan were given, applied or smothered. Those wonderful remedies, that clearly improve one's health, were gleaned from my mother's medicinal herb book; recipes she had written down meticulously over many years. All her life she'd had an avid interest in the cultivation of many species of herbs. The garden at Adderbury had been renowned as the best-stocked herb garden in Oxfordshire and was the very envy of our neighbours. I inherited the book on her death, and it is by far the most treasured book in my entire library.

∾∾

By the middle of July I was once again, thank goodness, in good health although at times a little tired and pallid. My Lord had insisted that I travel to Bath to take the waters. I had done so every year during the month of July, and never needed much persuasion to visit there, for it is a most wonderful tonic, not only for its curative waters but also for the whole city's lively and most congenial atmosphere. Visitors to Bath take great pleasure in the theatre, dancing or, as is the fashion, simply promenading its streets or its peaceful riverbanks. The inns and taverns turn a fine trade in good beer and wine, and the drinking of coffee or tea is highly recommended.

I was in desperate need of the many diversions that Bath offered. Alas, such genteel recreations held little or no interest for my husband, and so I left Barnes without him, and without delay, to seek my usual reserved lodgings close by the river.

I journeyed to Bath with three of our servants, one of whom was our trusted William who was to be my dutiful chaperone during my stay. During this time, his Lordship travelled to his fine stud in Leicestershire, which fair county is renowned for breeding the best racing stock in the country. During spring and early summer, all fifteen of his brood mares had foaled successfully and as always, he was keen to look over his future winners, and to see that his prized stallions were receiving the very best attention.

The journey to Bath was long and arduous and, above all, extremely tiring in the overbearing heat. We suffered greatly in the airless coach, such confinement causing poor Polly, my maid, to faint on two occasions though this was, I fear, much due to her ample size; she had never been slight. Even as a young girl of fifteen she was plump, but now nearing her thirty-fifth year, her weight had increased beyond measure. Nevertheless, she had been in our employ for nearly twenty years and a more honest and hardworking servant has yet to be born.

The relentless jolting of the coach, its sweltering interior and the clouds of dust thrown up by its wheels and so entering the open windows, all became unbearable. At nights, we stayed in crowded inns, which gave little relief from the unyielding heat, yet they did afford a modicum of ease to our poor aching bodies.

After three days on the road, our long anticipated arrival at Bath was most welcome. Built of stone with large airy windows, my lodging house overlooked the river and, with stone flags throughout the ground floor, it was a cool oasis.

After two days' rest, I ventured out to the baths for my first session in their wonderful curative waters. The experience was somewhat unpleasant, for the stench of sulphur rising from the waters took one's nose a deal of adjustment. Further, the sweat-laden bodies of many of the bathers intensified the noisome odour. But one must tolerate these inconveniences to ensure the therapeutic waters do their healing.

I received a letter from my husband some two weeks into my stay. It contained a full account of his stock: which mare had produced what foal and its sex, size and colour; the newly-borns that were thriving; and the poor unfortunate ones that were not. As an afterthought, at the foot of the final page, was written.

'Madam, I do hope that your health has improved, and that you are enjoying your leisure time at Bath. On your return to Barnes in August, I shall be at Newmarket and then on to Woodstock.'

I had planned to be in Bath for only a month, but with my husband's racing commitments, I did not return to Barnes until the end of August, which gave me a further two weeks of blissful contentment.

The sultry July heat, so unbearable on our arrival, soon mellowed into bright and sunny warm days that were a joy. My time was spent in the company of good friends whom I had known for many years. After a turn in the waters, we would spend agreeable afternoons strolling the city's thoroughfares and riverbanks and on our return, there would always be an invitation to one lodging or another for dinner. We whiled away the evenings playing at the cards or strolling in our hosts' delightful gardens. We would converse upon the latest gossip to come out of London society, speculating as to who might be the current favourite at Queen Anne's Court.

Once a week, we made for the theatre to watch a play or two or to listen to a grand orchestral recital. On one such occasion, whilst with friends there, I came to feel a little uneasy, for I had noticed a stranger watching me from the opposite galleries. In the half-light, I caught sight of a man, he wearing a coat of crimson velvet. I could not see his face clearly, shadowed as it was in the gloom, but I was in no doubt he was fixed upon me. Feeling unnerved, I left at once, feigning a headache and took coach immediately to my lodgings, in the safe company of William.

The following morning, I dwelt a little on thoughts of the stranger but said naught on the matter, reassuring myself that I must have imagined the whole incident, for surely I had been deceived, swept up in the illusory atmosphere of the theatre. I was thus quite satisfied that the episode should be of no concern.

My time at Bath was idyllic and I felt fully refreshed in body and soul. My servants too benefited a great deal from a turn in the waters, when they were not busy attending to my every need. Above all dear Polly, poor girl, suffered terribly, exhausted by the heat from the moment we had left Barnes. She had eventually braved the waters, after my assurances that she would not sink to the bottom and be drowned by her ample weight, but in the event, it took two attendants to hold her afloat.

All too soon, my stay at Bath was at an end. I was most reluctant to leave, but leave I must, and so was soon journeying home to Barnes, where I was to await the return of my husband from Woodstock.

He arrived on the First of October, some five weeks after me, and seemed pleased to see me looking so well. I could not say the same of him, for it was obvious from his reddened face that he had consumed more than his fair share of strong drink and rich food. He had apparently met with fortuity at the races, with his horses winning outright on three separate occasions, he only spending the prize money at the cards and on drink. Hence, no one but his dubious gambling friends and the landlords of the inns and taverns of Newmarket and Woodstock profited truly from his good fortune.

During October, we were busy overseeing the decoration and furnishings of our new bedchambers at Barnes. Tradesmen and artisans disrupted the usual tranquillity there, with their toing and froing, delivering or fitting all manner of carpets, rugs, curtains, wall hangings, beds and other furniture.

In early November, the disruption came to an end, with the house at last complete for our return in the spring. And so we left and journeyed to Hinchingbrooke, where my husband would take pleasure in the hunt, and I would be kept busy preparing for Christmas and the Twelfth Night festivities there.

᠁

On the day of Twelfth Night, a letter was delivered for my attention. I opened it immediately, being rather curious of its contents, I having not written to anyone of late. It read as follows, *'His Twelfths were legendary'*. That was it. There were no other words on the entire sheet. I supposed it must be a joke of sorts. Though bemused and somewhat surprised by the note, I was for now far too busy with celebratory matters to give it any further thought, and so placed it with my private papers.

The winter had been long and dreary, with the Fenland east wind whistling around every corner. Thankfully, it now abated and on the First of April, the bright sun at last flooded Hinchingbrooke's dark, silent rooms with warmth and light.

I could not resist a stroll with my little dog Joker in our garden, and I watched him run playfully through the grass barking in delight. Presently Polly appeared and, after handing me a note, returned to the house. I sat upon a low stone wall that encircled our orchard and opening the note, instantly recognized its form. Again it was cryptic, the author anonymous as before. This time it read, *'All were fools, but never he'*. As with the first, no other words but these few were written upon the page.

Alarmed, I called to Joker and held him in my arms for comfort, glancing around the desolate garden. I could see nothing but the birds and hear nothing but their song, though I felt sure I was being spied upon. I hurried to my bedchamber, retrieved the earlier note and placed the two side by side. *'His Twelfths were legendary'*. *'All were fools, but never he'*. What did they mean? The more I pondered the words, the more perplexed I became. Who would write such puzzling lines and why had I been singled out to receive them? They made no sense at all. In fact, I believed that someone truly was playing the fool, and that the clown would soon be revealed. Again, I hid the notes and said nothing on the subject to anyone, except that I did later question Polly as to who had brought this second note, but she had simply found it upon the hall floor.

On the Seventh of June, his Lordship and I, together with our servants, travelled to Barnes. The day was warm and sunny, far removed from the dismal winter months spent at Hinchingbrooke. The gardens were in full bloom and the house most pleasing after the recent refurbishments.

After less than two weeks there, my husband announced that he was to travel abroad to Italy on business. He was hopeful of a good return on some trade venture there which he had embarked upon with a Gentleman newly acquainted at Newmarket. I did not enquire as to my husband's foreign investments, for his funds were his own affair, and on the Twentieth of June, mid-summer's eve, he left Barnes for Italy. I had no reliable knowledge as to when he would return, but knew it could be many months as was apparent from the three large trunks loaded onto his coach.

Feeling alone and abandoned, I took it upon myself to spend the summer months visiting friends, some of whom I had not seen for far too long. But before I could embark on my travels, another of those anonymous notes arrived. It read, *'Twenty-six spels buried fourteen days on, it is now thirty'*. If the others were perplexing, this latest note was truly mystifying, and although again somewhat alarmed, I was intrigued and quite captivated by the concealment of the author.

That evening after dining alone, I sat late into the night, long after the servants had all retired to bed. I retrieved the notes from my room, placed them before me on the table and watched the candlelight flicker eerily upon the words. Was their significance malicious, dangerous in fact, or did they denote witchcraft of sorts? Or were they just to frenzy my mind into thinking that I was mad? Whatever their purpose, be it good or evil, I was forced to consider them most seriously now and read the words again and again.

> *'His Twelfths were legendary'.*
> *'All were fools, but never he'.*
> *'Twenty-six spels buried fourteen days on, it is now thirty'.*

My father! My God, they spoke of my dear father! Of a sudden, it made sense, *'His Twelfths were legendary'*; they were, for even though I was very young at the time, I could still recall the house at

Adderbury on Twelfth Night full of guests, laughter and light. Such joyous times for us.

'*All were fools, but never he*'; this note had been delivered on the First of April, All Fools' Day, the day of Rochester's birth.

'*Twenty-six spels buried fourteen days on, it is now thirty*'; next month, on the Twenty-sixth of July, would be the thirtieth anniversary of father's death at High Lodge at Woodstock. Two weeks later his poor emaciated body had been laid to rest in the vault at Spelsbury Church.

Whoever the author was, he had known my father very well and, whether an enemy or friend, had gone to great lengths to seek out his most loyal of daughters. Why? I questioned, after all those years, was this person seeking my attention. I now felt determined to know the truth behind these ambiguous letters, and so began my pursuit of this enigmatic *Riddler*. The visiting of friends must wait awhile, for I now had more pressing matters.

I chose William and my young maidservant Rosie to accompany me on my quest. William was completely dependable, honest and above all discrete; a perfect companion in the arcane circumstance forced upon me. As for Rosie; a dear girl, yet naïve to the point of stupidity and completely illiterate, anything odd disclosed in her presence would mean nothing to her simple mind. The rest of the household were informed that I was to take a short holiday, sightseeing and visiting friends, and so my return should not be expected for several weeks.

With my husband having travelled in our coach and six, bound for Dover, I was left to journey in our more modest of carriages. This had but the one advantage that it would attract less attention at an inn. On the morning of the Seventh of August, my coach and four was driven out of Barnes and onto the open road. Aboard were William, Rosie, two trunks and myself.

Our eventual destination was Wood's End, our fine house at Woodstock. Set on the very edge of the park, it is secluded and tranquil and where both his Lordship and I resided when attending the races each September. This beautifully furnished house stands in ten acres of wooded privacy, with adjoining coach house and stabling. A week before I left Barnes, I had written to inform the resident servants that I would be there on the Eleventh of August, so giving them ample time to prepare for my arrival. Woodstock is conveniently close to High Lodge, and just ten miles from Spelsbury; one of the places alluded to by the *Riddler*. What's more, I felt sure my pursuer had designs to entice me to those secluded settings.

Our first stop was at Banbury for to overnight there, before travelling on to Chipping Norton and the Falcon the following day.

We arrived at the Falcon in good time to secure our rooms for the night. After a late supper served in my room, I felt weary and so retired for the evening. On drawing the hangings at my window that overlooked the crowded, dimly lit courtyard, I became aware of a shadowy figure dallying against a wall. My eyes were drawn to this solitary man who appeared motionless amongst the chaotic hustle and bustle of travellers and the inn's servants scurrying about. I could not perceive his face, as the imperfections in the glass obscured the view, but I knew for certain he was observing my room. I steeled myself and made my way down the stairs to the yard, but once there I found he had absconded into the night.

Arriving at the hamlet of Spelsbury on the Ninth of August as planned, I asked Rosie to stay in the coach, whilst William and I walked the narrow lane leading to the small parish church. The peaceful surroundings of this beautiful little building had not changed since I was a young girl, when my devout grandmother had accompanied my two sisters and me to the church every Sunday without fail. We had been subjected many a time to lengthy sermons, sat upon hard wooden seats until our buttocks were quite numb.

Once inside, I walked across the damp stone floor, my footsteps echoing eerily in the silent building. I came to a halt at the place where deep underground, shrouded in eternal darkness, the dead of the Lee vault lay. Full of sorrow, with my head bowed, my tears fell upon the cold bare floor, I recollecting when, thirty years before to the day, dear father had been carried down into the hidden depths to his everlasting rest. Tragically, before long were laid beside him the bodies of my fine mother and darling brother. This peaceful sanctuary held many a sad memory, yet also evoked happier times with my family at Adderbury.

We left the church, and were glad to feel the warmth of the sun on our faces.

As William closed the ancient oak door behind us, he said, "My Lady, look!"

There upon the door was pinned another note. I recognized the handwriting immediately, and so wrenched it from its anchorage.

The *Riddler* was watching my every move. The stranger in the yard at the Falcon! It *must* be he who is the author of these notes! And now I realized that the stranger there and the man in the shadows at Bath were one and the same, and that he had pursued me for all this time.

I opened the note. It read, *'He was nobody's puppet, for it was he who controlled the strings'*. I knew that whoever this was, he had been in my father's employ. *'He was nobody's puppet,'*; this signified Rochester's free spirit, to be constrained by no one. As for controlling the strings, this was perhaps a reference to the marionette show once held at Adderbury House. My father, hidden in the shadows, had been both the puppeteer and the puppets' voices. The audience had been few in number; just mother, a joiner and his wife, and our servants were present along with my brother, my sister Anne and me. Mallet had been just a baby then, and so asleep in her cot oblivious to all the excitement. And I, at only two years old, had been held in my mother's arms, yet had known something magical was afoot.

The elusive author of the notes was certainly present that

evening. But there were many male servants at Adderbury when I was a child. All but one old retainer, who had retired long before father's death and who had since died himself, were in work there until mother's death. At that time, grandmother had dismissed them all, with Adderbury sadly then unoccupied. The servants knew Rochester well. They were often the butt of his jokes and sometimes his reprimands, but very rarely the victims of his anger. Who could it be? Did he bear a grudge? Did my father, in a fit of delirium, maltreat him? Question after question occupied my thoughts, but no answer emerged. The *Riddler* was resolute, *'but to what end?'* I asked myself. His doggedness was utterly bewildering to me.

Hurrying, I left the building, with William trailing behind. We boarded the coach, where Rosie patiently awaited our return. As the coach rattled its way back along the narrow, uneven lanes to the Falcon, I sat in quiet reflection upon the day, my mind locked in confusion.

After a hearty supper, I retired early to bed, leaving William and Rosie to while away the evening in the company of other servants. I was in dire need of rest but throughout the night, I awoke often, in a state of unease by reason of my disturbing dreams. One of these was in truth a nightmare and caused me much concern. It began where I was alone under a clear moonlit sky, encircled by tall pillars of silent cold stone, their dark menacing shadows piercing dread into my heart. I felt I would be trapped there forever as there was no passage wide enough between the stones to allow my escape. My pulse racing, I ran in breathless panic within that impenetrable circle until dizziness overcame me and I fell to the ground with an abrupt jolt. I awoke in the secure confines of my bed, not daring to close my eyes again for fear that I would be transported at once back to that eerie place.

After a long, lonely night, dawn broke and later that morning I confided in William my menacing dream.

"Perhaps you were dreaming of the Roll Rich Stones, my Lady," William suggested.

He said that the ancient ring of stones was very near, only three miles north of Chipping. William knew of their whereabouts and had actually seen them often as a young boy. Much to my surprise, he said he had been born in the village of Little Roll Rich, close to where they stand. He explained that when he was twelve years of age, his family had then returned to the county where his mother was born, she in desperate need of financial support for herself and her children since his father had died. Her sister and brother-in-law, who had not been blessed with children, and who lived close to Barnes, had kindly welcomed the destitute family into their home.

I now recounted to William that, when I was a young girl at home in Ditchley, my grandmother had told me a strange tale of when father and mother encountered a circle of tall stones, several of which were taller than a man. In turn, they had each proceeded to count them, but could not agree upon their number, for it differed at each attempt. Were they the same stones as in my dream, I wondered? William said that there were many who believed them to be a temple of sorcery, of witchcraft or the lair of the devil himself, and added that many had tried to count their number, but that none had succeeded. However, William believed them quite harmless and that the dark myths were sheer superstitious nonsense. He professed that he, amongst others, was convinced that the circle had merely been used for a simple form of worship and that the stones represented deities sacred to the ancient peoples who had settled in that part of Oxfordshire many hundreds of years before.

Although apprehensive, I told William that I must see them. I felt for once that I might be one step ahead of my pursuer's intentions, my dream forewarning me of where I might catch sight of him.

In the heat of midday, with the sun high above us, William and I precariously negotiated a straight, narrow path overgrown with thorny thickets on either side. After a short time, the path veered abruptly to the right and led to an open space encompassed by a large circle of tall, intimidating stones. Within the ring, the grass appeared stunted, choked by the growth of moss, its young shoots having not strength to flourish, seemingly enslaved by the stones.

There in front of me was the reality of my dream, so I ventured apprehensively through a narrow passage between two of the stones. Once inside the circle, I quickly glanced at each standing stone hoping to catch a glimpse of someone's shadow. But alas, again there was nothing to be seen. Disappointingly, no mysterious note was to be found either, despite my having been quite sure of such a discovery. Strangely, the atmosphere of the Roll Rich ring held no fears for me, for it was one of calm. Never did witchcraft, sorcery or any devilish revelry occur in this odd yet strangely peaceful place.

Back at the Falcon, I sat alone in my room, my thoughts in disarray, pondering the *Riddler's* notes. It was our last evening at the inn, for the following morning, the eleventh, we were to go to Woodstock, far away from the hustle and bustle of the crowded inn and to the peaceful seclusion of Wood's End, our house there.

೭◌৩

Sunlight shimmered through the canopy of mighty oaks that lined the private drive. As we neared the house, John Finstock and his wife Katherine were there to greet us. They had for many years been resident housekeepers at Wood's End, ensuring all was in order in readiness for our visits, and were regarded as old friends rather than as servants. The Finstocks had taken pride in their privileged positions within the household and would tolerate no idleness, indiscretions or laxity in any of the under servants. Such instances of blatant disobedience, of which there were few, met with the full might of John's wrath, at times accompanied by a beating.

John led me to the parlour where a beverage of fresh brewed tea was already to hand to slake my parched throat. The quenching drink was most welcome, following my stifling journey along the dusty roads from Chipping. Katherine in turn accompanied William and Rosie to the servants' quarters in the attic, which although adequate were somewhat spartan compared to those at Hinchingbooke or Barnes.

John enquired after his Lordship, for he seemed puzzled that I was travelling without him. I explained that Edward was abroad on business and was likely to be away for many months. I said that due to his absence, I was taking a short holiday visiting friends, but would first idle my time at Woodstock for a while.

Wood's End afforded ample opportunity for leisure. I would walk aimlessly through its criss-crossing woodland paths in the cool shade under its tall trees, listening to birds singing high up in the branches.

On the morning of the Twentieth, when I had been at Wood's for two delightful weeks, Katherine ran breathless to me in the garden as I sat reading in the arbour, she looking most alarmed.

"My Lady! I have grave news. Young Jack was taken ill during the night in his garret above the coach house. He suffered a sudden fever and violent convulsions, but ere we could summon help, he was dead."

Before dawn broke, Jack's body was with dignity removed from Wood's End and taken to his father's home at Bladon, then the day following to the church, to be buried alongside his dear mother, who herself had suffered a similar, unexpected death some years before.

Jack, a young man of just twenty-five, had been in our employ for five years and had taken over his father's duties at Wood's End when old Jack had become too infirm to continue his work there.

Young Jack was a good, honest man who worked hard. He had been well respected by John and Katherine who, never having been blessed with children, had looked upon him as their own son and were utterly distressed at his loss.

I gave John five shillings for old Jack, who was now an aging man of sixty years, crippled with rheumatism and barely able to stand. He had relied on his only son to provide for him, and this task would now fall to old Jack's daughters Margaret and May. Neither were wealthy women, their husbands but poorly paid labourers and they having the burden of ever-increasing families. Nevertheless, they would give what little they could spare to old Jack and would never see him destitute for the want of food, clothing or wood for his hearth.

Wood's End was quiet on the day of young Jack's burial, with all away at Bladon Church apart from myself, William and Rosie. The weather was bright and sunny, in complete contrast to the sadness of the day.

William and Rosie were busy with extra work for, with the other servants absent, they had generously agreed to carry out some of their duties. In due course, I left them both to their chores and took a walk alone through Woodstock Park. I would not be solitary for long though. The park had been an industry of activity throughout the last five years, with Vanbrugh's workmen labouring in their hundreds on the Marlboroughs' monumental mansion. The land had been a gracious prize given by the Queen to the Duke and Duchess in recognition of John Churchill's military prowess, and in particular of his victory at Blenheim. Five years had now passed since the setting of the foundation stone, but the magnificent structure was still but half complete.

I stood awhile and admired the fine building, then continued my walk to High Lodge, where my father had resided from time to time as Ranger at Woodstock. I had journeyed this path many times before, when at Wood's End for the races, but the green hue of the trees on this warm August day was so very different from the autumnal russets at the time of the late September chase.

High Lodge was a distressing sight with its boarded windows, locked doors and an overgrown wilderness stealing its once beautifully kept garden. The house had not been lived in for many years and was painfully neglected. I was in empathy with this sad edifice, I feeling much the same. Pangs of emotion pierced my heart with memories of that fateful day when dear Rochester was conveyed into the house; so ill, so repentant and so brave. He had suffered his agonies for days on end, 'til at last God had relieved him of his torment and had taken him from us.

Turning for home, I felt sure I heard the distant cracking of twigs upon the ground. I looked about me but could see no one, yet sensed I was being watched. With my pulse racing, I quickened my step down along the secluded paths, and at last reached the safety of Wood's End.

I said nothing of my alarm on the pathway, to either William or Rosie, for I had no real proof that I had been followed. I could have imagined it after all. The dense woodland can often play tricks with your mind and all too quickly invoke undue fear.

By six o'clock that evening, the funeral party had returned to Wood's. John said little of the day, but conveyed old Jack's gratitude for the five shillings I had sent to him. Poor Katherine's eyes were so reddened and swollen, for she had done naught but break her heart all day. The rest of the household set to their chores, with few words being spoken between them.

The evening grew humid, and in the distance thunder rumbled in the heavy skies. Feeling bothersome hot, I retired to my parlour and there reclined upon my daybed close to an open window. The storm quickened its fury and was soon overhead. With it came heavy rain lashing upon the ground, and a welcome cool breeze flowed in through the window.

The exertions of the walk in the heat of that August day had wearied me, but I did not sleep, with my mind still troubled over recent events. I was certain I had not been alone at High Lodge, convinced I had been followed, and I was sure of one thing; he would never relinquish his pursuit until finally we met eye to eye. My unease at the prospect of such a perilous meeting lay heavily upon me.

Body and mind in turmoil, I could not achieve rest, and so ventured to our library next to the parlour. There I chose a book hoping to allay my confused thoughts. Returning, I opened the door to the parlour when a strong gust surged through the window, lifting the silk hangings high into the air. As I followed their descent, my eyes were drawn to something upon the bed. It was another of those intriguing notes. I clutched the book to my breast as my heart raced. 'My God he's here!' He has the nerve of the devil, and a swift devil at that.

I took up the note and, ripping it open nervously, I read it. 'My dear Lady Lizbet...' it began. I was completely and utterly taken aback. LIZBET! None but my closest family had addressed me so. The note continued...

'Please, my Lady, forgive my intrusion at High Lodge. If I had been brave, I would have revealed my identity to you. But I was not, and I despise myself for that. There is no one living upon this earth, other than his dear Lizbet, who truly loved Rochester more than I did. I mean you no harm. You are my Lord's flesh and blood and I admire you above all things.

'I hold in my possession an item of great import and, I suspect, of interest to you. I will be at High Lodge tomorrow at noonday. If you could be so forgiving as to meet me there, I will reveal the item to you. I will be masked, but I wish you no alarm. If you so desire it, I will willingly unmask at your request and reveal my identity.'

I was right; I had been followed in the park. The reference to High Lodge was proof enough.

ॐॶॶ

I woke early next day, ready for my clandestine appointment with the stranger. I asked Rosie to prepare my cool white linen dress and hat, the weather proving particularly hot.

As the hall clock struck half past the eleventh hour on this morning of our rendezvous, I left for High Lodge. I had informed William and Rosie that I was to stroll in the park once again.

I set out at a brisk walk. The sun was high in the clear blue sky, which signalled a hot afternoon ahead. I slowed my pace as I neared the lodge where the old oaks extended welcome shade from the noonday heat. With apprehension, I awaited the *Riddler*.

I was there only a short time before a figure approached, masked as he had forewarned. He halted a short distance away. He was tall and slender. His left hand leaned heavily upon a cane for support. He wore a white linen shirt with markedly dirtied collar and cuffs, and on his right shoulder hung a faded and frayed coat of crimson velvet.

He removed his hat and on bowing spoke gracefully in a gentle voice, "My dear Lady Elizabeth, I am most heartily glad you came."

In his right hand he clasped a leather bag, which he offered without hesitation to place upon the ground, and so be off with no further contact should I wish it. But I did not want this, for I was eager to know who this fellow was.

I begged him to stay and asked to see his face. He bowed his head once more and removed his mask. He was a mature man of some fifty years. Thirty of those years had passed since I had last seen him. His features, much altered by age, were still those of Tom, my father's much loved and trusted servant at Adderbury. Sadly, from the pallor of his skin and his gaunt appearance, I could see that he was desperately consumptive and clearly not long for this earth.

"Tom! Dear Tom!" I exclaimed, smiling, "But why all the riddles and secrecy?"

"I do so apologize for that my Lady, and humbly beg your

forgiveness. But I would not be a true intimate servant of Rochester without having learned a trick or two. I was testing your daring Wilmot spirit, which I hoped would still dwell within you and would not fail you, for your father's never once failed him. As you see before you, I am a man with time against him, and I craved one last Rochester adventure before I lay dead in the cold earth."

The tears in Tom's eyes were proof enough of his devotion. The years had not diminished his love for his master. I had not seen Tom since my mother's demise, when my grandmother had taken charge of the Wilmot orphans to live with her at Ditchley, and had dismissed all the Adderbury servants.

The midday temperature was quite overbearing and Tom grew concerned that the heat would overcome me. He took from his right hand pocket a large key, which apparently had been in his possession ever since my father's death. The key was to the entrance door of High Lodge and Tom begged me to step inside with him to escape the sweltering heat.

A shaft of bright sunlight pierced the gloom as we entered the cool, dank building. The light of the sun revealed years of neglect in the dust and cobwebs that now smothered its once splendid interior. Tom limped slowly ahead and entered a room on the right, but soon returned with the reassuring light of a lanthorn and bade me follow him up the stairs to a first floor room. Slowly, we ascended the creaking, dust-covered stairs. So thick was the dust, our steps left footprints as upon soft snow. As we stepped upon the landing, the boards groaned lamenting with each step we took, akin to an abandoned ship at sea. As we entered the room, my thoughts turned instinctively to that vibrant character whose colourful past still echoed around the pale walls. This haunted room cruelly evoked those last distressing days when, as a young child in the company of my family and Tom, I had witnessed Rochester's decline.

Tom lit candles that he had placed in three handsome silver

sconces; though jaded by time and hanging precariously upon the walls, they still offered a little light within. With my eyes now accustomed to the dimly lit room, I fixed upon the remnants of a bed. Its once grand hangings were ripped, faded and covered in dust, as if in accord with its one time infamous occupant, who too was shrouded in the dust of time, deep in the Spelsbury vault.

Tom invited me politely to sit at a small, round-topped table placed in the centre of the room with a chair on either side. Upon the table was lit a further solitary candle. I refused to sit down until I had helped him be seated in one of the chairs, as it was obvious that the exertion of climbing the stairs had been arduous for him. With a trembling hand, he passed me the bag and bade me open it. Inside was a document, many pages in length, crudely pinned and wrapped in buckram, and with a loose sheet of paper placed therein. I knew not what was written upon that sheet, but could clearly see my father's signature at the foot of the page. I looked at Tom with puzzlement and enquired as to the book's significance.

"It is your father's story, my Lady, in his own hand. Its contents lay bare some shocking, some greatly amusing and at times unforgivable acts. These passages I believe were close to your father's heart and, true or not, it is how he wished the world to view him. But sadly, it is unfinished. I could not go to my grave, my Lady, knowing I held secrets of your father's life that you, and you alone, should learn of from a friend. Such a cruel act to the last daughter of Rochester would have been unthinkable."

Tom said that over the past months, unknown to anyone, he had spent many days and nights in the darkness of High Lodge, with only lit candles and rats for company. He had read the book many times and had agonized over what was to become of it.

I questioned him as to how he came by the book. To my astonishment, it had been in his possession since 1681, when all the Wilmot's possessions had been removed to Ditchley. Tom had found it hidden among the Adderbury attic's sturdy timbers and deceitfully had said naught of it to anyone. I was a little taken aback at this revelation, but it was clear that the love and respect of this servant for his master was beyond measure.

Poor Tom knew that he was dying. He had not the heart to destroy the book, yet was afraid that on his death, if it be found by an unscrupulous sort, it would no doubt be used to pour further scorn on an already tarnished reputation.

"There were many who thought Rochester, even in death, a worthless specimen of human kind and still revile him with a passion," Tom explained.

Tom was aware that Rochester was no angel, yet a man who sincerely loved his wife and family, and whose solemn plea, at the end of his life, was for God's forgiveness for all the ills he had caused.

Later that afternoon, Tom and I left High Lodge to its fate and, for sure, we two were never to meet again. Before our parting Tom pleaded, "It must be concluded, and by you my dear Lady, for there is no other who can do this ultimate kind deed for Rochester."

༺⚹༻

And so in time the book was completed, as dear Tom so desired. I, the most devoted of all Rochester's children, admit to being the author of the two closing chapters, composed with a sad and lamenting heart.

༺⚹༻

At the age of fifty-five, I was by then a widow and no longer a mother, after darling Dicky's tragic death seven years earlier.

So it was that I left England to live in Paris, my exile prompted by an increasing distrust of the continuing Hanoverian reign. As a true Jacobite, I had prayed, aspired and laboured for many years in the hope that King James would one day return as England's true Sovereign.

For Fifty-three years since James's death, I have loyally continued to support his son James Stuart, *The Old Chevalier*, legitimate heir to the English throne, as I had done his father before him.

Now in my eightieth year, though ancient in tooth and limb, I am fortunate indeed, with my mind still as sharp as a razor's edge. Now time is closing on my life, with my own epilogue nearing its end. On that fateful day wherever I be, be it in England or in France, the book will surface and whosoever shall read it, for good or ill, will be certain to proclaim that the illustrious Rochester was, by no shadow of a doubt,

'The Wildest And Most Fantastical Odd Man Alive'

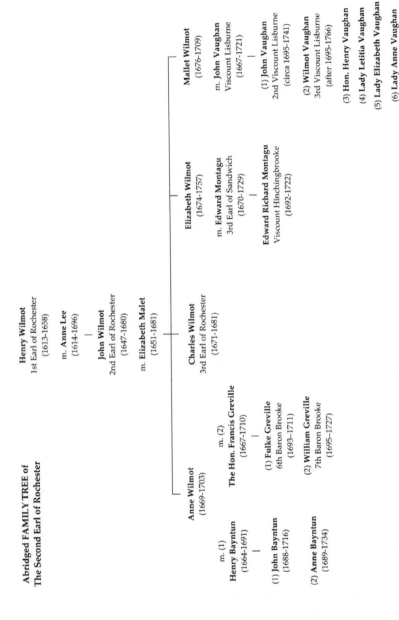

Henry Wilmot
1st Earl of Rochester
(1613-1658)

m. **Anne Lee**
(1614-1696)

John Wilmot
2nd Earl of Rochester
(1647-1680)

m. **Elizabeth Malet**
(1651-1681)

Anne Wilmot
(1669-1703)

m. (1)

Henry Bayntun
(1664-1691)

(1) **John Bayntun**
(1688-1716)

(2) **Anne Bayntun**
(1689-1734)

m. (2)

The Hon. Francis Greville
(1667-1710)

(1) **Fulke Greville**
6th Baron Brooke
(1693-1711)

(2) **William Greville**
7th Baron Brooke
(1695-1727)

Charles Wilmot
3rd Earl of Rochester
(1671-1681)

Elizabeth Wilmot
(1674-1757)

m. **Edward Montagu**
3rd Earl of Sandwich
(1670-1729)

Edward Richard Montagu
Viscount Hinchingbrooke
(1692-1722)

Mallet Wilmot
(1676-1709)

m. **John Vaughan**
Viscount Lisburne
(1667-1721)

(1) **John Vaughan**
2nd Viscount Lisburne
(circa 1695-1741)

(2) **Wilmot Vaughan**
3rd Viscount Lisburne
(after 1695-1766)

(3) **Hon. Henry Vaughan**

(4) **Lady Letitia Vaughan**

(5) **Lady Elizabeth Vaughan**

(6) **Lady Anne Vaughan**

Dramatis Personae:

Wilmot, John, Second Earl of Rochester.

Adam. Assistant tire-man at the Duke's Theatre.

Balfour, Dr. Andrew, M.D. Rochester's companion on the Grand Tour.

Barry, Elizabeth. *Beth.* Actress. Rochester's mistress.

Beale, Bartholomew. Son of Charles and Mary Beale.

Beale, Charles. Husband of Mary Beale.

Beale, Charles. Son of Charles and Mary Beale.

Beale, Mary. Artist.

Bendo, Dr. Alexander. A persona adopted by Rochester.

Bethaven. A persona adopted by Elizabeth Barry.

Betterton, Thomas. Actor. Co-manager of the Duke's Theatre.

Bodicote, Martha. A servant of the Rochesters.

Burnet, Gilbert. Theologian and historian.

Chaffinch, William. *The Royal pimp.*

Charles II. King of England.

Clenston, Emmanuel. *Manny.* Elderly resident of the town of Milton in Dorset.

Clenston, Jemima. *Jem.* Elderly resident of the town of Milton in Dorset.

Clerke, Elizabeth. *Betty.* Illegitimate child of Rochester and Elizabeth Barry.

Constable, Robert, Third Viscount Dunbar. Notorious bully.

Constance. An innkeeper's daughter.

Cromwell, Oliver, Lord Protector. *Old Ironsides.*

Downs. An acquaintance of Rochester.

Edward. A tavern patron in Winchester.

Elm, Suzanne. A joiner's wife.

Elm, William. A joiner.

Etherege, Sir George. Dramatist. One of the *'Merry Gang'*.

Finstock, John. A servant at Wood's End.

Finstock, Katherine. A servant at Wood's End.

Folgate, Lord. Twelfth Night guest.

Giffard, Reverend Francis. Rector. Rochester's early tutor.

Gwyn, Nell. *Nelly*. Actress. Mistress of Charles II.

Hawley, Sir Francis. Grandfather of Elizabeth Malet.

Hellawaits. A persona adopted by Rochester.

Henriette Anne, Duchesse d'Orléans. *Minette*. Sister of Charles II.

Hyde, Edward, Lord Chancellor. A friend of Rochester's mother.

James, Duke of Monmouth. Charles II's bastard son.

James, Duke of York. Later King James II. Brother of Charles II.

Jane. A servant at Enmore.

Kempster, Christopher. Master mason to Sir Christopher Wren.

Killigrew, Thomas. Dramatist. Manager at the King's Theatre.

la Roche, Madame. London dressmaker.

Leafield, Beatrice. A wet-nurse employed by the Wilmots.

Lee, Edward Henry. Son of Frank and Eleanor.

Lee, Eleanor. Wife of Frank Lee.

Lee, Francis. Son of Frank and Eleanor.

Lee, Sir Francis. *Frank*. Rochester's half-brother.

Lee, Sir Francis Henry. *Harry*. Rochester's mother's first husband.

Lee, Sir Henry. *Harry*. Rochester's half-brother.

Louis XIV. *The Sun King*. King of France.

Louise de Kérouaille. *French Louise.* Mistress of Charles II.

Loveall, Dr. Valentine. Physician.

Loveall, Mrs. Wife of Valentine Loveall.

Malet, Elizabeth. Countess of Rochester. Wife of Rochester.

Malet, John III. Elizabeth Malet's father.

Malet, Unton. Elizabeth Malet's mother.

Margaret. Old Jack's daughter.

Martin, John. Headmaster at Burford Grammar School.

May. Old Jack's daughter.

Montagu, Edward Richard, Viscount Hinchingbrooke. *Dicky.* Son of Edward Montague and Lizbet.

Montagu, Edward, Third Earl of Sandwich. Husband of Lizbet.

Morall, Dr. Bartholomew. Physician.

Mountagu, Edward, First Earl of Sandwich. Admiral of Charles II's fleet.

Munnings, Caroline. Wife of Reverend Immanuel Munnings.

Munnings, Reverend Immanuel. *Immy.* Rector of Leiston.

Norton, Will. Tailor to Rochester.

Notgrove, Dinah. Toymaker of Stow.

Notgrove, Draycott. Son of Samuel and Dinah. Toymaker of Stow.

Notgrove, Samuel. Toymaker of Stow.

Notgrove, Willersey. Son of Samuel and Dinah. Toymaker of Stow.

Old Jack. A servant at Wood's End.

Old Shepherd. Retainer at Enmore.

Palmer, Barbara, Lady Castlemaine. Rochester's cousin. A mistress of Charles II.

Parham, Caroline. Mother of Caroline Munnings.

Parham, James. Brother of Caroline Munnings.

Parham, James. Father of Caroline Munnings.

Parham, William. Brother of Caroline Munnings.

Parsons, Dr. Robert. Chaplain.

Pepys, Elizabeth. Wife of Samuel Pepys.

Pepys, Samuel. Clerk of the Acts to the Navy Board.

Petherton, William. A Bridgwater Alderman.

Philippe, Duc d'Orléans. Brother of Louis XIV and husband of Minette.

Pickerel, Benjamin. A servant at Adderbury. Angler.

Polly. A maid of Lizbet.

Popham, Alexander. Father of Elizabeth Popham.

Popham, Elizabeth. Wife of Edward Richard Montagu.

Pullworthy, William. Burford tooth drawer.

Rose, Mr. Gardener to King Charles II.

Rosie. A maid of Lizbet.

Sackville, Charles, Lord Buckhurst. One of the *'Merry Gang'*.

Sarah. The midwife who attended at Rochester's birth.

Savile, Sir Henry. Dear friend of Rochester. One of the *'Merry Gang'*.

Sedley, Sir Charles. One of the *'Merry Gang'*.

Skeleton, Agnes. Wife of Woodcock.

Skeleton, Woodcock. A wise man of Dorset.

Stepping, Nathaniel. London boot maker.

Stuart, Frances. *La Belle Stuart.* Later Duchess of Richmond. Close companion of Elizabeth Malet.

The Riddler. ?

Thomas. A tavern patron in Winchester.

Thoroughgood, John. Clerk of the Works at Barnes Carlton.

Tom. A servant of Rochester.

Villiers, George, Second Duke of Buckingham. A close Friend of Charles II. One of the *'Merry Gang'*.

Warre, Sir John. Second husband of Elizabeth Malet's mother Unton.

William. Rochester's steward at Enmore.

William. A trusted servant of Lizbet.

Wilmot, Anne. Daughter of Rochester and Elizabeth.

Wilmot, Anne, Dowager Countess of Rochester. Rochester's mother.

Wilmot, Charles. Son of Rochester and Elizabeth.

Wilmot, Elizabeth. *Lizbet.* Daughter of Rochester and Elizabeth.

Wilmot, Henry, First Earl of Rochester. Rochester's father. Anne Wilmot's second husband.

Wilmot, Mallet. Daughter of Rochester and Elizabeth.

Wrightwell, Godfrey. Oxford graduate. Rochester's son Charles's tutor.

Wroxton, Lady Hepsibah. Twelfth Night guest.

Young Jack. A servant at Wood's End.

Acknowledgements:

'Of Ink, Wit and Intrigue': This story began for me in 2006 when, allied to a long passion for all things 17th century, I began to focus my research on John Wilmot, Second Earl of Rochester (1647-1680). His unique character fascinated me from the start and his own inventiveness inspired me to mine, and so culminated in this novel.

෧෧

The publication of any book, and *'Of Ink, Wit and Intrigue'* is no exception, owes a great deal to those people involved, after its inception, in helping to bring the work to its eventual fruition and printing. Accordingly, my sincere appreciation goes to J.W. Johnson and to my stalwart proof readers; Janice Dunbar, Aude Valluy-Fitzsimons, and Lita Irbitis, all who gave freely of their invaluable time, not only to the benefit of the manuscript but also to its most grateful author. My thanks are also due to all those helpful people in libraries and other repositories of historic records who have helped me to fulfil my research into Rochester and his life.

෧෧

Lastly, but in no way least, my sincere gratitude must go to my dear husband, Dave. His constant encouragement and painstaking editing of my work have been quite frankly above and beyond the call of duty.

෧෧

The entry of *'Ink, Wit and Intrigue'* into the world of published literature owes a great debt to all these wonderful people.

Citations:

To all gentlemen, ladies, and others...Alexander Bendo

'The Famous Pathologist or the Noble Mountebank' by John Wilmot, 2nd Earl of Rochester. By kind permission of Manuscripts and Special Collections, the University of Nottingham: Reference number MS 98.

Letter from Lord Rochester to Mrs. Barry

Familiar Letters: Vol. II. Containing Thirty Six Letters, By the Right Honourable, John, late Earl of Rochester. Printed from his Original Papers. With Letters and Speeches, by the late Duke of Buckingham, The Honble Henry Savile, Esq; Sir Geo. Etheridge, to several Persons of Honour. And Letters by several Eminent Hands (London: Printed for Sam. Briscoe, at the Corner of Charles-street, in Covent-garden. 1697), p.26.

ॐ◌ॐ

All poems and extracts thereof, here quoted are selected from the many written by John Wilmot, 2nd Earl of Rochester.

JOHN WILMOT
2nd EARL OF ROCHESTER
"so great a man and so great a sinner."

Over a quarter of a century ago, the then vicar of Spelsbury accompanied by church officials, decided to finally settle a rumour current among the local population for centuries, that a certain tomb in the church held riches. They descended into the vault where the coffin rested. The coffin plate was removed and the lid raised. The first thing they saw was a small casket which, when opened, clearly revealed it had contained viscera and which gave off a strong scent of the herbs in which they had been packed more than three centuries before. There was no sign of treasure. Instead the searches found themselves gazing upon the mortal remains of one of the most complex, talented, wayward and controversial figures of the seventeenth century. He was John Wilmot, the second Earl of Rochester, a notorious rake yet a poet so gifted that his lyric and satirical verses are today included in anthologies of the works of the greatest poets in our language.